ROAM

ROAM

A Novel with Music

ALAN LAZAR

ATRIA BOOKS

New York London Toronto Sydney New Delhi

ATRIA BOOKS

A Division of Simon & Schuster, Inc.
1230 Avenue of the Americas
New York, NY 10020

First Atria Books hardcover edition November 2011

ATRIA BOOKS and colophon are trademarks of Simon & Schuster, Inc.

For information about special discounts for bulk purchases, please contact Simon & Schuster Special Sales at 1-866-506-1949 or business@simonandschuster.com.

The Simon & Schuster Speakers Bureau can bring authors to your live event. For more information or to book an event, contact the Simon & Schuster Speakers Bureau at 1-866-248-3049 or visit our website at www.simonspeakers.com.

Designed by Jill Putorti

Manufactured in the United States of America

10 9 8 7 6 5 4 3 2 1

Library of Congress Cataloging-in-Publication Data

Lazar, Alan.
    Roam: a novel with music / Alan Lazar.—1st Atria Books hardcover ed.
        p. cm.
    1. Families—Fiction.   2. Dogs—Fiction.   I. Title.
    PS3612.A972R63 2011
    813'.6—dc22

                                                    2011013151

ISBN 978-1-4516-3290-3
ISBN 978-1-4516-3292-7 (ebook)

For Gustavo and Mia Bella

Listen to a free seven-part piano soundtrack written by the author especially for *Roam!*

Journeys with Thatcher

ATRIA AUTHORS ON YOUR SMARTPHONE

Tag images like the one above are placed throughout *Roam*. Download the free Microsoft Tag app at http://gettag.mobi. Then hold your phone's camera a few inches away from the tag image, and it will automatically play the audio.

List of Songs

ROAM

Part One

The Great Love

1

The first thing Nelson smelled was grass. Rich, beautiful, mysterious grass. It wafted in from the pastures outside Mrs. Anderson's farmhouse, where Nelson and his brothers and sisters lay wriggling, close to their mother. His small nose wrinkled, perplexed by this powerful new stimulus. When he was in his mother's womb, he had whiffed it in the distance as his nose's power expanded exponentially. But when the full power of grass hit him out in the world, it was scary, intoxicating, and deeply mysterious.

The smell had many layers to it. As the years went by, Nelson would learn to discern the meaning of those multiple deep scents. They held information about the day—which creatures had walked nearby and left their mark, how much dew there had been that morning, and hints of the distant meadows where that dew had come from. They held information about the rain two days earlier and about the ants and other bugs that lived in the grass. But also, deep from within the soil in which it grew, the grass held sometimes murky hints about summers past, and winters from long ago, about the creatures that had lived and died in the New Hampshire county where Nelson was born. It held the history of all the roots and bones that had lain in that rich soil for centuries.

Nelson was one of a litter of six mutts. In fact, he was not meant to be a mutt. Mrs. Anderson had bred pedigree beagles and poodles for many years. Her puppies sold for thousands of dollars each and were shipped to locations all across America. Nelson's mother, Lola, a gentle apricot miniature poodle, had given birth to several litters of puppies before. Nelson's father, King, a beagle much photographed as a perfect specimen at the annual county fair, was not meant to gain access to Lola's compound when she was in heat two months earlier. He had successfully impregnated Nougat, another beagle, several times, and Mrs. Anderson adored him. But she had planned for Lola to breed with her normal mate, Kennedy, a dark brown poodle with a warm heart. She had no idea that King had been bewitched by Lola's rich bouquet as it wafted from her kennel the previous spring. Noticing the beginnings of a small hole under the wooden fence surrounding Lola's kennel, King dug furiously when Mrs. Anderson was not around, and lovemaking with Lola followed. Mrs. Anderson suspected nothing until Lola's pups came out one day looking unlike anything she had seen. She had a moment of anger when she realized what King had done. She also had a moment of regret when she realized that the thousands of dollars she knew she would make from a pedigree poodle litter was not to be. But when she held Nelson's older sister in the palm of her hand and felt the little dog's heart beating, her own heart swiftly melted, and she knew she would raise these puppies for the first two months of their lives with all the love she normally gave to her pedigree pups.

Mrs. Anderson was accustomed to seeing two or three pups in a poodle litter. Lola gave birth to six this time. Perhaps it was King's unrelenting lovemaking to Lola that had caused this anomaly. The fragrance of Lola in heat was so utterly compelling that each time he thought their lovemaking was coming to an end King somehow felt another burst of energy inside his beagle heart.

The six puppies that emerged from her small frame surprised Lola. She was sad when number four lay there, unmoving, after he emerged. After she ate the small bag of afterbirth that had protected him in the womb, she licked him again and again, trying to bring him back to life. Mrs. Anderson watched, praying for some movement, but after half an hour, and not a sign of life, she gently pulled the small pup away from Lola and wrapped him in a white towel. Later that night she would burn his remains and scatter them in the pastures outside her farmhouse. She would look up at the crescent moon and pray for the little dog that had never known the world beyond his mother's womb.

Lola felt an intangible sadness come over her as she saw her pup disappear from sight. But she could not be sad for long. The convulsions in her stomach started again, and soon enough, another beautiful puppy emerged into the world. Nelson was largely light brown, or apricot, with splashes of white, particularly over his face. A dark brown circle surrounded the one eye, and a white circle surrounded the other. From an early age this gave all the impression that he was "wide-eyed" and fascinated by the world. But at the time of his birth, his eyes were firmly closed, as they would be for the first week of his life.

His nose twitched excitedly as the smell of grass filled his world for the first time. He felt his mother lick him, and her scent, too, filled his senses, rich and comforting. Mrs. Anderson entered the room again, noticed the new puppy and patted him ever so gently on his small head. And so, he whiffed a human being for the first time, and that smell, although complex, was also warm and good.

This was a lot to happen to such a young soul in the first minutes of his life, and Nelson was suddenly struck by an overwhelming hunger. His mother saw the quivers in his small body, and those of her other pups. She pushed and pushed and her final puppy, Nelson's little sister, emerged into the world, wriggling and sniffing. Gently, Mrs. Anderson placed each of the puppies near Lola's six nipples, and they wriggled inward toward their first meal.

The first week of Nelson's life passed in a blur. As the days went by, his nose explored with greater and greater skill the scents around him. Then hunger would strike again. Sometimes Lola would be sleeping when he crawled toward her, desperate for sustenance. He did not know of course how exhausted she was from feeding her five surviving puppies. Secretly, Mrs. Anderson was very concerned. Lola was a small dog by any standard. Once, many years before, another poodle owned by Mrs. Anderson, Lola's grandmother, had developed a severe calcium deficiency from feeding a large litter, and had died on the way to the emergency veterinary clinic in the small town of Nelson, New Hampshire, nearby. Mrs. Anderson had fed the remaining pups, including Lola's gorgeous mother, a pearly white poodle, with a bottle every four hours.

Often Nelson would wake up to Lola licking his stomach. He loved this, and he liked the smell of the warm liquid that seemed to flow from his own body after she did this. Its smell would never last for too long. He would whiff Mrs. Anderson close by and feel her hands on his body, and then most of the smell of his excrement would be gone. Nelson soon noticed that all of his brothers and sisters had a similar liquid that would come out of their bodies. While it smelled very similar to his own, his little nose soon identified very specific scents in theirs that allowed him to identify them. Sometimes, when he suckled on his mother's nipples, he would notice a very similar but much more intense odor coming from her. It was pungent and strong and earthy. Sometimes Mrs. Anderson would take Lola outside for an hour or two, and Nelson would quietly cry until this reassuring smell was close by again.

Smell would always be the great and overwhelming presence that defined Nelson's perception of the world. But about a week after he was born, his little eyes drifted slowly open, and the comforting gray blur of Mrs. Anderson's face looked down on him. Nelson was the first of the litter to look into the world, and with the special coloring he had around his eyes, Mrs. Anderson could only smile when she saw the wide-eyed puppy looking up at her. Her own eyes were slowly losing their ability to see, and the strong glasses the eye doctor had prescribed for her the summer before were probably going to need to be replaced soon. Many pups had passed through this small room at the back of her farmhouse where she looked after Lola's and Nougat's litters for many years after her own son had left to live in Oregon. Most puppies were cute and cuddly, and she adored them all. But there was something quite special about the way Nelson looked up at her that morning. Mrs. Anderson knew the eyesight of dogs was limited compared to that of humans. They did see more than just black and white, but they were color-blind when it came to reds and greens. She knew that dogs lacked the depth of field of human vision, although movement of any sort excited them. But Mrs. Anderson could swear she saw a special curiosity and openness to the world in Nelson's wide eyes that morning. Many years later she still thought about him.

Soon, all of Lola's five children had opened their eyes. She braced herself for what she sensed was to come. Their little legs would grow stronger, and they would develop rapidly, all the while hungering for more and more of her milk. Whereas at birth there was little hair on their soft bodies, it was just a few weeks before light and semicurly fur would clothe them. Lola had memories of the long sleep she had had in the months after her previous litters had left her, but she also remembered the sadness of those days.

By the time Nelson and his brothers and sisters were one month old, they were a rambunctious bunch. His family fascinated Nelson. They were all playful to an extreme, obsessed with tripping each other and tugging at each other's now-full fur. But some of his siblings were quieter than the others, happy sometimes to just lie with their mother or each other, quietly wriggling while their scents intertwined. Others never gave up their pursuit of proving they were the most agile, the fastest, the ones who kept control of the ball of red wool Mrs. Anderson had thrown into the small pen they shared with their mother.

Nelson's curiosity soon emerged as the trait that defined him. Mrs. Anderson noticed him constantly trying to find a way out of their small pen, and indeed one day he did. She entered the room, almost stepping on the tiny pup that was waiting by the door, smelling the new odors that glided in through the small gap between the door and the floor. Chiding him quietly, she picked him up and put him back with his family. It was just moments, though, before the wide-eyed puppy returned to the small opening he had found at the back of the pen and found his way out once again. She blocked it up with a pair of old socks. More and more, the smells that entered the room fed little Nelson's curiosity. He whiffed sweet and meaty odors coming from a clangy place elsewhere in the house, aromas that made him so hungry even his mother's milk did not entirely satisfy him.

Mrs. Anderson took to picking up Nelson every night and holding him in her large worn hands, stroking him quietly while she listened to music. Nelson loved this, and would drift off to sleep in a state of bliss. He would awake and lick her fingers in the same loving way his mother would lick his stomach, and she seemed to like this. He was not aware that he was the only puppy for which she reserved this special honor. Sometimes Mrs. Anderson held Nelson close to her face. By then his eyes were seeing a great degree of detail, and he observed her blue eyes looking directly at him. Sometimes he would lick her face, and a few times he tasted the salt of little tears. Later in his life he would come to understand the fuller meaning of this salty liquid that human beings sometimes emitted, but for now he just enjoyed its taste.

One morning, when Nelson was five weeks old, Mrs. Anderson put him and his siblings into a small box. Lola watched earnestly, but she did not stop Mrs. Anderson, with whom she had a deep bond of trust. Mrs. Anderson opened the door to their small pen and walked out of the room, carrying the box of pups. Lola walked close behind her.

Mrs. Anderson's house was a little dark, but that of course did not limit the symphony of smells that Nelson inhaled as they passed through to the garden. There were the remnants of those kitchen smells, which he sometimes whiffed in the pen. There was the smell of meat, and fried eggs, and melted butter. There was the round, smooth aroma of pancakes cooked a couple of days before, which lingered in the corners of Mrs. Anderson's living room. As they walked past the kitchen itself, the scent of green apples entered Nelson's nose for the first time, and it was scintillating in a very different sort of way.

As they exited into Mrs. Anderson's garden, Nelson's head almost exploded from what entered his nose. First there was grass, endless amounts of it, and smelling it close up was profoundly more intense than its more distant scent. Mrs. Anderson placed each of the pups down on her front lawn and let them wander. Nelson's small, wet nose touched grass for the first time, and it was like an electric current ran through his body. The puppies scattered over the lawn, as each was drawn by multiple separate strands and substrands of odor. Occasionally, if one pup got too close to the fence that separated the garden from the pasture where horses and cows milled around, Mrs. Anderson would pick it up and return it to a position closer to her house. Lola, too, kept a watchful eye on her children, barking loudly if they went too far. The five fluffy puppies were scarcely aware of their two mothers, though. They burrowed their noses as deep as they could into the soil, lost in something close to ecstasy.

Finally when Nelson looked up, he saw the beds of flowers flanking the garden. He gingerly approached them, unsure of what they were. But when their scents drifted down toward him, he knew that these strange objects could not be harmful to him. There were red roses and yellow roses, agapanthus and daffodils, lilies and African violets. As he sniffed them, he slowed down, entranced, closed his eyes, and let the sun shine down on him. Many years later when Nelson found himself in broken city streets surrounded by concrete, he would still distantly remember this garden, and his first encounter with flowers, and it would revive him almost magically, at least for a short time.

Mrs. Anderson disappeared for a few minutes, and when she returned, another dog, about the same size as Lola, was with her. Nelson did not know he was meeting his father, King, the beagle, a dog with an emphatic gait. Nelson sensed the strength and nobility of the larger dog. Lola stayed close to her babies when King arrived, eying him and growling. King himself did not seem terribly interested in Nelson or his siblings that morning, sniffing them briefly, then running off barking at a nearby squirrel. Neither parent seemed to have any recollection of their passionate lovemaking just a few months before. Mrs. Anderson sighed as King ignored his puppies, but she also knew inside that she should have known better than to hope he would take to them.

This was also the day that Mrs. Anderson first fed the pups something other than their mother's milk. Mrs. Anderson was keeping a close eye on Lola, and her exhaustion from the constant feeding of her pups was easily visible. She had previously preferred to wait until six weeks before giving puppies solid food, but she decided to try giving them some bread and cow's milk for the first time, so that hopefully Lola would get a chance to rest a little.

Nelson and his siblings did not know what to do with the

small bowls of warm milk and old bread broken in pieces that she put down in front of them. Nelson jumped right into the middle of one bowl with a big splash. It felt good. Mrs. Anderson fished him out and cleaned him, and then holding him in her hands tried to teach him how to lick the milk from the bowl. In the days to come, Mrs. Anderson would cut up small pieces of apples and carrots, and she chopped up a boiled egg into pieces one day for the puppy's enjoyment.

Late one night Nelson was awakened by a new sound. It was Mrs. Anderson's voice. But whereas he was accustomed to it being calm and serene, this time it was high pitched and loud even though it was elsewhere in the house, and somehow it scared the dog. He did not understand what was causing her to behave like this, and when she entered the room half an hour later, he could smell something new on her, the sediment of intense anger that had just passed. This was the first time in his short life he had encountered the smell of anger, and he did not like it at all. He never would like it. It was not something he ever smelled on dogs, and he learned it was one of the things that distinguished dogs from human beings. Nelson himself would experience many, many emotions in his lifetime, but anger was never one of them.

Mrs. Anderson looked down at Nelson, noticed him watching her, and picked him up. She stroked him on his little head. When she put him close to her face, he quickly licked at her tears, and she smiled limply. Nelson enjoyed the saltiness of her tears, but this time he was also happy that the scent of her happiness was returning. She put him down and exited from the room, but was back just a moment later with a small plate. When she picked up Nelson and put him on her lap again he quickly recognized that the food on the plate emitted the same meaty scent he had smelled several times during the past weeks. It was probably the most wonderful smell he'd ever encountered. The young dog gulped down the small pieces of sausage she had brought for him and she giggled as he licked the plate, yearning for more.

Lola awoke from the smell of the sausage and lazily opened her eyes. It was one of her favorite dishes, and normally she would have politely barked to remind Mrs. Anderson to give her some. But this time she just went back to sleep. She knew that some time soon her puppies would no longer surround her, and once again it would be her, Mrs. Anderson, King, Kennedy, and Nougat that would walk the woods together. She knew she would return to sleeping at the foot of Mrs. Anderson's bed at night, and the memories of her puppies would soon fade. So, that night, she let little Nelson eat all of the treat.

Mrs. Anderson was in fact considering keeping little Nelson. It was always difficult letting the puppies go, but she had to remind herself that she needed the supplemental income from the litter, and this time it would be much less than usual. Luckily, some of the pet shops around the country where her pedigree pups were normally sold had reluctantly agreed to take her beagle-poodle mixes. The pet shop owners knew that the pups she normally provided were not only beautiful examples of the breed, but displayed the sort of temperaments that dog owners loved. They were playful but obedient, cheeky but loving. One joked he would call Lola and King's offspring either "beadles" or "poogles." Of course, she would receive only a fraction of the payment she normally received for her pups. To sell Nelson for only 150 dollars seemed silly; it was so little in the grander scheme of things. But she had a gate that needed fixing, and she needed to buy some more hens, and her pension hardly covered the bills.

Mrs. Anderson regularly cleaned the puppies with a damp towel. This had become a twice-daily occurrence with their poop becoming thicker with each solid meal they ate. One morning, however, Nelson sensed they were in for something new when she carried them all through to the laundry room at the back of her house. The smell there was comforting and dry, and it reminded Nelson of lying in Mrs. Anderson's bed with her that one night.

She left the puppies writhing together in the small crate, and prepared a small tub of gentle, warm soapy water. One by one, she bathed them. Nelson instantly loved the sensation. Mrs. Anderson gently rubbed his entire body, which was like being licked all over by his mother. Soon, he felt fresh and alive and the lavender smell of the soap lulled him into a contented bliss. When she had thoroughly cleaned the pup, she rinsed him in another small tub. Then using a thick towel, she rubbed him dry. Holding his head carefully between her hands, she used small but sharp scissors to trim his fluffy hair. Nelson writhed a little, and Mrs. Anderson narrowly averted poking him in the eye once as she trimmed the little hairs around his eyes. At the end of it all she lifted him up close and kissed him several times. Nelson licked her face and tasted salty water around her eyes.

That night, Mrs. Anderson would bring in a wide selection of the pups' favorite foods. There was milk and bread, but also little pieces of cheese, eggs, apples, and sausage. One by one, she fed Lola's litter of puppies. Exhausted, Lola ate a few morsels herself.

As Nelson snuggled up next to his mother to sleep, he could smell his brothers and sisters all around him, clean as a whistle. He could hear their little bodies rising and falling with each breath, and the occasional tiny rumble of their full stomachs. The lights were off, but he could smell Mrs. Anderson sitting in her chair nearby. This was the best day of Nelson's life so far. The happiness he felt as he drifted off to sleep that night was soft and enveloping. He dreamed of fields of grass covered in sausages, where he played endlessly with his brothers and sisters.

But when Nelson woke up the next day, his life would become very different.

The Smell of Grass

What does it feel like to be a puppy mysteriously bewitched by "The Smell of Grass"? Scan here to listen, or go to www.youtube.com/watch?v=aelhnPp2w9M.

2

When the dog awoke, he was experiencing a strange new sensation. He and his four siblings were in a crate in the back of Mrs. Anderson's pickup truck. As the vehicle motored along the bumpy country roads, the puppies swayed back and forth, and sometimes were thrown into one another. Even when Mrs. Anderson tried to drive smoothly, it felt to Nelson like the innards of his stomach were shifting around inside of him, and he felt queasy. He and his siblings cried softly and mournfully, but no one came to reassure them. They could still smell their mother on each other's fur, but Lola was nowhere to be seen.

Eventually the car came to a stop, and Mrs. Anderson's face appeared above them. She stroked the puppies on their small heads and they licked her hands hungrily, reassured. One by one she picked them up and fed them milk from a small bottle. The plastic had a rather horrible taste to it, but nonetheless the milk smelled and tasted good. After she'd put them down again, Nelson drifted off to sleep as the car moved forward. Occasionally he would find himself half-awake with strange new smells wafting in from the window. Sometimes he would whiff stronger versions of scents he remembered being distant at the farm. All around him there was still grass, and this reassured him.

After some two hours, Nelson awoke to new and pungent odors. Although his siblings still slept, his eyes were wide open, and he sat alert and somewhat fearful. He could sniff Mrs. Anderson was still close by, and knew he must stay close to her somehow.

Nelson knew the smell of smoke from the fires Mrs. Anderson would sometimes burn at night. This was the closest comparison the young dog could make to the new smells that wafted through the truck. But they were tinged with odors that seemed unnatural to him. There were noises, too, sharp and high in frequency, and the sounds of people out on the streets speaking with a sharpness that he was not used to. The sound of Mrs. Anderson's pickup truck had not bothered him much, but now he noticed the roaring of other cars and vehicles everywhere around him, and it became overwhelming. Nelson whimpered. Quickly, he felt Mrs. Anderson's hand stroking his little head, and he quieted down. Where was his mother, Lola, he wondered? Why was she not with them?

Suddenly the car engine was turned off, and the jerky back and forth movement of the last few hours ceased. Nelson rested easy for a few moments. His siblings were all straining their heads, trying to see beyond the four walls of the crate.

Nelson whiffed Mrs. Anderson putting on lipstick. Then there was the sudden explosion of scent from her perfume. She leaned over and spoke to the pups and Nelson sensed sadness in her voice. He felt like something big was about to happen as she picked up each pup, stroked it and kissed it. She lingered longer with Nelson than any of the others.

One by one, Mrs. Anderson transferred the puppies into small traveling crates at the back of the pickup truck. As Nelson was moved from the crate he shared with his siblings, he caught glimpses of the new world around him. A huge concrete building stood in front of him, and hundreds of cars and people were everywhere. A few people nearby looked at him with smiles on their faces, and nodded at Mrs. Anderson.

Nelson was placed in a small traveling crate with his younger sister. As they looked out, he saw Mrs. Anderson place his other whimpering siblings into traveling crates nearby. One by one, Mrs. Anderson fed the puppies water and small pieces of sausage. Then she picked up the three crates and walked into the large train station in Concord, New Hampshire.

Nelson was scared. The station was noisy and full of people moving about at high speeds. There was a cacophony of smells, and he struggled to interpret them. When Nelson's traveling crate was placed on a large scale and weighed he glanced at Mrs. Anderson and smelled her thick sadness. She came right up to the door of the crate, and Nelson licked her face for a final time. Then she was gone.

Nelson and his sister lay close to one another. They burrowed deep into one another's fur, where their mother and siblings' scents lingered. Nelson's little sister cried mournfully, and Nelson gently nibbled on her ear to try and cheer her up.

A couple of hours passed like this. The fear subsided after a while, and Nelson soon wanted to venture outside his little crate and explore some of the interesting new odors around him. He scratched the door of his cage but soon realized he was stuck in there. He hated that feeling, and started whimpering loudly. After a few moments, a man came up and stuck his finger through the door of Nelson's travel crate. The two little dogs smelled and licked the finger. A friendly face with a blue cap looked inside and smiled at them. Nelson smelled some of the warm and comforting scents that Mrs. Anderson had emitted, and immediately he felt better.

A short time later, the friendly man picked up the crates with the puppies and carried them through the station. Nelson was a little apprehensive when he saw trains for the first time. Were these animals? Or houses? The smells that emanated from them were many and varied.

The nice man placed Nelson and his sister down in a carriage of one of the trains, and tickled their faces again. Then he disappeared. The door of the carriage slammed shut, and they were left in near darkness. Nelson could sniff other animals in the carriage. He thought there might be some other dogs, and perhaps rabbits and chickens. He could no longer smell his other siblings anywhere close. He and his little sister lay silent and fearful, and they were getting hungry, too.

The train suddenly moved with a jolt, and Nelson and his sister were shoved into a corner of the crate. They yelped, and Nelson smelled fear in the other animals in the carriage. The chickens started making a loud ruckus. But as the train motored along, its smooth motion soon settled the animals down. When the fear had left Nelson, and he smelled his sister was calmer, too, he allowed himself to enjoy the new scents entering the carriage from outside. The city odors had been overwhelmed by country ones once again, and Nelson imbibed the grassy pastures and forests outside with great pleasure. It was rather strange experiencing smelling from a train. While certain scents were constant, there was also a continual bombardment of new ones, some of which rapidly disappeared. Nelson tried to hang on to them, particularly the interesting ones, but they were gone in a flash. The little dog's interest was piqued.

Nelson and his sister's train journey was not very long. After just an hour or so, the train slowly started slowing down. The sounds and smells of the city returned, and Nelson whiffed water, lots of it.

When the train finally came to a stop, and the carriage door was opened, Nelson inhaled Boston South station.

3

Over twenty years the neighborhood pet store owned by Emil Holmes in the South End of Boston had built a reputation for only selling pedigree puppies. That meant breeders needed to supply paperwork from the American Kennel Club to prove the lineage of their dogs, and copies of this paperwork would be provided to buyers to justify the sometimes high prices Emil charged for his puppies.

Emil had become a pet-store owner not through any careful decision, but because his father had died when he was twenty-three years old and had passed on the store to him. Emil had not seen his father since he was five years old, and so the small estate he inherited was not expected. His only memories of his father involved drunken yelling and the crash of broken plates in the kitchen as young Emil shivered in his bed. His father had never laid hands on the boy, but his mother was not spared from the occasional fisticuffs. Eventually, she summoned the courage to be rid of her belligerent husband, but his presence still reverberated in Emil's mind many years later.

Emil had an acumen for numbers, and started a business selling second-hand musical equipment after he finished high school. For a time he did quite well and married his high-school sweetheart, Evelina, before his twenty-first birthday. But as many first-time businesses do, it eventually failed, and Evelina left shortly afterward, breaking Emil's heart. For a while, he bounced around from job to job, nursing the wounds of his losses. At first it seemed like a bad omen when news of his father's estate reached him. But he soon realized that buying and selling puppies could be quite profitable. He loved the business aspect of his new pet store, and was determined to make his second attempt in business a success. With that, he hoped, perhaps a new wife and family might follow. Emil would relentlessly focus on the bottom line with his second business. Within a few years he could figure out with a great accuracy the value of a litter, based on the breed, and often the breeder. Certain breeders provided him with excellent puppies, whose buyers were happy and told their friends about Emil's little pet store. Gradually Emil edged up his prices, and he was soon making large profits on the dogs he sold.

However, he hated much of the other work involved in maintaining the store. He did not have a particular liking for dogs, and he grew tired of their smell, which came to permeate his life. Sometimes in his apartment at night, he imagined he was whiffing puppy shit, though he knew this was impossible. But puppy shit was the smell he lived with during the day, and he knew he would live with it for the rest of his life, or as long as he owned the business. As the years went by, and any meaningful romance eluded him, he came to blame the smell of puppy shit for making him unattractive to women. The money he made helped him get over his negative feelings about his work, but if the money were not there, he would not have anything to do with puppies. He saw people fawning over his puppies day in and out, and he could not understand it. A dog was an animal, nothing more. For God's sake, the Chinese ate them like chickens, he sometimes thought to himself.

It was with great irritation that Emil received Mrs. Anderson's request to sell two mutt puppies. He didn't like her suggestion that he could sell them as novelty "beadles" or "poogles." A mutt was a mutt. A mutt was a useless animal worth much, much less than one of his pedigreed dogs. The cost of feeding a mutt, and cleaning a mutt, and wiping the shit out of their cage every day, was probably more than the money he would receive for selling the mutt. He was also worried that selling mutts in his store would affect his carefully preserved reputation.

But Mrs. Anderson was one of his best breeders. He knew that King always produced beautiful beagles, and Lola always produced mild-mannered and lovable poodles, the type those women he thought of as "rich bitches" from Cambridge loved. He knew Mrs. Anderson was just an old kook living out on a farm by herself, but he didn't want to piss her off and lose a good breeder who always accepted his first price offer. So, he agreed to take the two mutt puppies she wanted to sell him. He was relieved she had found a buyer for the other three in the litter, a pet store in Connecticut.

When he saw the two puppies, though, he regretted his decision. As was often the case with mutt litters, the two puppies looked quite different from each other. The smaller one, the girl, was reasonably cute, but the boy had strange coloring, particularly over his eyes. He looked like a cartoon dog. Their fur was weird, too; neither smooth like a beagle's, nor fluffy like a poodle's. It branched out in random directions. He thought he could maybe even it out by shaving them prior to their sale.

Emil thought the worst thing of all about the mutt puppies was their tails. People who came to buy a pedigree puppy liked it when their tails were cut off. It was standard practice. All of his breeders delivered their puppies in this very sellable state, and Mrs. Anderson normally did as well. She obviously hadn't bothered to cut off these mutts' tails, maybe because she, too, wasn't interested in anything not pedigreed, he reckoned.

Mrs. Anderson normally did remove the tails of puppies when they were two or three days old but she never enjoyed this. Some said young puppies didn't feel this, but she knew they did. They always cried mournfully after she held them firmly and cut off their tails with a sharp knife. Her heart was always breaking by the time she applied disinfectant and bandaged up the small remaining piece of tail. But she knew within a day the puppies would be back to normal, and she knew as well she had to do this in order to ensure a decent market price for her litters.

But something inside her had resisted removing the tails of Nelson and his family. If these puppies were mutts, she thought to herself, there was no particular reason to remove their tails. She tried very hard to envisage what these pups would look like later in their life, and she thought perhaps they would benefit from what her grandmother used to call "the fifth leg of a dog." She had claimed a tail would balance a dog as he or she ambled along.

But Emil was convinced in order to sell these puppies he would need to remove their tails. He had never done it, and he would need to schedule an appointment with the vet as soon as possible. That would eat further into his profits on these damn dogs. He had one small viewing cage free at the bottom of his puppy storage wall, he remembered. He'd put the two runts in there for now, but if they didn't sell by the time he got in his new batch of Pomeranians, they'd have to go.

The pet store was clean and bright and well kept. Emil's customers were generally well off and he had realized early on that they liked to come to a place with a degree of class. There were rows of dog and cat paraphernalia for sale, and the puppies were all placed in small viewing cages or cubicles that lined the high wall of one side of the store. The puppy wall was built of white sheet metal, and each cubicle was brightly lit. Water dripped in from a central system, and the puppies sucked it out of a tube, as they needed it. Pellets of puppy food were placed in a small bowl at each side of the cubicle. On the other side of the puppy wall, in Emil's backroom, there were separate doors to each cubicle.

The front of the puppy wall was covered in glass. This was to prevent potential buyers from sticking their fingers through and letting the puppies lick them and nip them. Emil worried that some "rich bitch" would probably sue him or something similar if one of the pups nipped her too hard. So, a customer had to request a pup be placed in a nearby playpen for her, and she could spend a little time playing with the puppy there.

The small white metal cage Nelson and his sister found themselves in was strangely devoid of smells. There was the smell of the water, but it was different from the water at the farm. Nelson could discern strange chemicals in the pet-shop water, and he tried to resist drinking it as much as he could.

There was a distant scent of other puppies, but the glass and the sheet metal seemed to cut out most of the odors that entered the small chamber. Nelson and his sister comforted one another by snuggling deep into each other's fur. His sister's scent was strong, and in her fur he could still whiff his mother, Lola, and Mrs. Anderson. He inhaled deeply, although little did he know that over a couple of days those smells would disappear forever.

There was another strange odor in the cubicle, the small pellets of food that were left in a little bowl in one corner. Nelson recognized it as dog food. Mrs. Anderson had fed them limited quantities of it, along with the milk and bread, and other delicious snacks she would bring them from her kitchen. But these pellets tasted and smelled quite horrible. For a while Nelson could not bring himself to touch them, but eventually his hunger became so overwhelming that he chewed on them, forcing them down.

There was little sound in the small cubicle. Nelson's little sister cried, and the water would drip ever so slowly, but he could not hear much else. Out in the store, he could make out human beings milling around slowly. Often he would see their feet, as they looked at puppies in the puppy wall above him. Few made it down to the level of him and his sister. Sometimes he would see them grinning and smiling as they looked at them, but much of the time they would glance quickly and then disappear.

Nelson grew to look forward to his nights at the pet store. At around five o'clock every day, Emil would begin to close up, and an older man with black skin would arrive at the store. Without much ceremony, Emil would leave the store, and the man would begin to sweep the floors and shine the windows.

After that, he would open up each of the puppy's cages one by one. When Nelson heard him starting to do this in the distance, the dog soon became excited, as he knew soon it would be his and his sister's turn. The door to their cage would open, and Vernon McKinney's large, warm hands would take the two puppies out of their cage. He would stroke them for a moment, just like Mrs. Anderson had done. Soon, he took to kissing Nelson on his head, and the dog would lick his face. Vernon tasted different than Mrs. Anderson, but Nelson liked the taste. The man seemed to like Nelson licking him, too.

Then, Vernon would place the two puppies in the small playpen next to the puppy wall. Inside the pen were many toys to play with—small stuffed animals, balls, and squeaky toys. Nelson liked these, and he would soon excitedly play around with them and his sister. But even more interesting, he could smell that lots of other dogs had been in this pen. He would check out every inch of the little pen for new scents, and they would all be cataloged in his still enlarging brain.

Every few days, Vernon would bathe the puppies. Nelson loved this—just being in water left him feeling infinitely happier. He just didn't particularly like the final stage; Vernon would hold Nelson in his big hands as he gave the animal an extra drying with a hairdryer. But he would all too soon return the puppies to their odorless and clinical living space. Vernon would have cleaned out the puppies' excrement and filled up their bowl of pellets, and replaced some of the straw that they lay on during the day, if it was soiled. The reek of chemicals sometimes made Nelson want to retch. But he whiffed Vernon

on his fur, and that smelled good. If he focused on the scent of
the man and his sister, he would drift off to sleep. He would
dream of grass and sausages.

After three days in the pet shop, one of the young women who
peered into Nelson and his sister's cage disappeared and came
back a few moments later with Emil. Shortly after, Emil lifted
Nelson out of his cubicle, and he felt scared. He heard his sister
crying as the door to their cubicle was closed. Emil carried the
little dog to the playpen and put him down on the floor. The
woman he'd seen looking at him came in, too, and sat down. He
stared up at her, not sure what to do. Nearby, Emil was watching
him carefully. This scared him. The young woman came closer
and picked Nelson up. She stroked his little head, examining
him quizzically. Nelson licked her fingers a couple of times. She
smiled, then stroked him some more.

But after a few moments, she put the dog down and disappeared
from the pen without another look at him. Nelson stood there all
alone for about ten minutes. Then Emil entered, and picked him up
a little roughly, hurting his small ribs. He could hear Emil talking
angrily to him, and he sniffed the air. He knew Emil was not to be
trusted, and his anger made Nelson feel very uneasy. He would do
everything he could to avoid him. Soon Nelson was shoved back in
his cubicle, where he lay shivering next to his little sister.

Over the next week, Nelson and his sister were taken out of their
cubicle several times, and placed in the small pen where potential
buyers played with them. Nelson came to dread these moments. It

was not the customers he dreaded. Often their smell was comforting, and he longed to spend hours playing with them. In fact, he learned that Emil was less angry toward him if he played as much as possible with the humans in the playpen. The more he played, the more they smiled, and the more he could smell their happiness.

But as each potential buyer decided against taking Nelson home, Emil treated the puppy with greater disdain. Nelson was just over two months old, and was still not much bigger than a human fist. He was strong for his age, but even a little extra force in Emil's squeeze when he would return Nelson to his cubicle could be quite painful. Once, Emil shoved him carelessly up against the wall of the cubicle, and Nelson whimpered from the pain. It hurt for two or three days. Nelson once tried licking Emil's hand in an attempt to befriend him, but Emil hated this and yelled at the small dog. Nelson shivered for an hour afterward.

When the cubicle door opened, and Emil's hand reached in, he could smell the fear on his little sister as well. If Emil reached for her, Nelson felt temporary relief, but then fear for his sister. He would wait anxiously while she was gone, and when the door opened and she was returned to the cubicle, he would always feel relieved. Her little heart was always beating fast when she came back, and he would lick her and bite her gently on the ear to reassure her.

One morning, early, the door opened unexpectedly. Nelson had not yet noticed any customers in the store. Emil took both Nelson and his little sister out of their cubicle, squeezing them tightly in his hands. He put them both in a small traveling crate, of the type they had been transported in in the train, and locked the door. He swore at them as he looked at them in the cage. Then Emil threw the crate into the back of his old pickup truck. Nelson and his sister were scared as the truck roared to life, and then bumped along. The crate was thrown back and forth in the rear, and Nelson and his little sister yelped. Nelson smelled they were out in the city again. There was lots of noise, mainly cars, and toxic odors everywhere.

Shortly afterward, the pickup truck came to a stop, and Emil pulled them out of the back of the truck. The vet's waiting room had a similar clinical smell to their cubicle back at the pet store. Nelson sniffed Emil's impatience, as he waited with the two puppies in the crate on his lap. A young man nearby, holding a large Labrador on a leash, looked at the two puppies in the cage and grinned. He started chatting to Emil, but Nelson heard Emil's gruff response, and the conversation ended. Nelson could smell several other dogs in the waiting room, and he could smell humans, too. With Emil close by, it was difficult to remember that most humans emitted a warm and comforting scent, but nonetheless Nelson did whiff this coming from some of the other humans in the waiting room.

After some time, a tall man with curly hair in a white suit came into the room and called Emil in. Inside the examination room, the vet took Nelson and his sister out of their traveling cage and held them in his warm hands, patting them on their heads. Nelson instantly liked the vet. There was something about his smell and the feel of his hands, soft but firm, on Nelson's body that relaxed the dog. Emil and the vet talked, and soon the conversation got mildly heated. At one point, Emil gently yanked Nelson's little tail. Soon, Emil swore and left the room, shaking his head.

So it was that a kind Boston vet declined Emil's request to cut off Nelson's and his sister's tails. The pups were way too old for this to happen, the vet knew. He would not inflict that sort of pain on an animal. As if to thank the vet, Nelson and his sister looked up at him and wagged the tails they might have lost. The vet could only smile.

The vet held Nelson in his hands and took out a shiny syringe. Nelson didn't like the smell of the liquid inside it, but he trusted the vet. There was a short jab of pain on his rump as he was inoculated three times. The spot where he had received the injections was painful for several days, but Nelson sensed they were for his own good. The vet inoculated Nelson's little sister too, and Nelson chewed gently on her ear as she whimpered.

The next night when Vernon arrived, he took Nelson and his sister from their cubicle prior to any of the other pups. He had known about Emil's plans to have their tails removed, and he was relieved to see Nelson wagging with full force. That night he had brought some leftover pieces of steak from a barbecue his family had enjoyed that weekend, and Nelson and his sister gulped it down. Emil would be angry if he found out about this, but Vernon couldn't resist bringing the extra food.

Normally pups sold within a week at Emil's store, but it had been almost three weeks since Nelson and his sister had arrived, and no one had bought them. Vernon did not quite understand this. As each day went by, he thought the two puppies were becoming cuter and cuter. Their fur was growing out a little, and their little tails wagging melted his heart every day. He supposed that the clientele who frequented Emil's store were probably quite snobbish, and only wanted puppies that came with a pedigree certificate.

Vernon was a curious person who, despite his lack of a college education, spent his spare time on weekends reading about all sorts of unusual subjects that interested him. He consumed material on Galapagos turtles, and hot springs in Iceland, and Chinese history. So, he thought the curiousness he saw in Nelson's every look made him a rather fascinating young dog. Of course it was not truly his eyes that fulfilled Nelson's curiosity. It was smells that drove him. But Vernon was not wrong in seeing a little of himself in the dog.

Vernon knew Emil was financially driven, and there was a small part of him that was concerned at what Emil might do with these puppies if no one bought them soon. Emil paid his salary check perfectly on time every month, and had only yelled at him once in the eight years he had worked in the pet store. Vernon was a very conscientious worker, so there was never much reason for Emil to be angry with him. But he knew Emil did not like dogs. Sometimes Vernon was scared by the look in Emil's eyes when he glared at Nelson and his sister.

So, it was with some anxiety that Vernon arrived at the pet store one night, and quickly noticed that Nelson's little sister was no longer in the cubicle with him. He looked at Nelson, sitting there all by himself, a mournful look on his face. Vernon lifted him out, and he could sense the sadness in the little puppy. Normally, when he lifted him out of the cubicle, he was a bundle of joy. His tail would wag and he would lick Vernon's hands and his face, and bite him gently. Tonight, though, he lay there listless, hardly moving. He ignored the piece of beef jerky that Vernon produced from his bag.

For one horrible moment, Vernon thought that Emil had done something unspeakable with the little female puppy. But when he looked on the front of the puppy cubicle, there was a SOLD notice under the FEMALE BEADLE sign.

He spent about half an hour holding Nelson in his hands, patting him and trying to bring him back to life. The dog licked Vernon's hands quietly a few times, but remained sad. The small dog never got to say good-bye to his sister. The cubicle door had opened, and as usual he felt the apprehension at smelling Emil's hand. His sister was pulled out of the cubicle, and the door slammed shut. He waited anxiously for her return. But hours passed, and there was no sign of her. By the time Vernon arrived that night, a deep sadness had fallen upon him.

He could still smell his sister on his fur. But try as he might, he could not smell Lola, his mother, or Mrs. Anderson anymore. He could still vividly remember their fragrances, but his nose could no longer locate them anywhere close by. Somewhere inside he knew his sister's scent would also slowly disappear from his world.

Vernon comforted Nelson that night, enough that he could sleep. The little dog drifted off into pungent dreams, filled with Emil's odor. Perhaps Nelson sensed that Emil was lying awake in his bed, mentally examining his inventory of puppies, and noting that there would be no space for Nelson anymore when the four new Chihuahuas arrived the following day. The puppy would need to be deleted from the inventory.

4

Katey Entwhistle had enjoyed her two-week honeymoon in Italy, though there had not been much time for relaxing. Don was a relentless sightseer. He also had a voracious appetite for lovemaking, and so they had returned to America quite tired. But tired as they were, she was happier than she had ever been.

They had scoured Rome at night, and eaten endless delicious meals. They had toured Tuscany and Umbria in an overpowered little Fiat, and imbibed the striking green countryside and uplifting Renaissance art. Finally, they had spent a few days down in Positano, exploring the steep mountainous scenery and sparkling waters. Both of them were sunburned and glowing. Katey was feeling guilty she had not played her beloved piano for a full two weeks, longer than any time since when she was a little girl. But she knew as well that that could wait. Life would return to normal on their return, except that she was now with a husband she loved dearly.

*   *   *

The Alitalia flight to Boston was long and uneventful. At Don's suggestion, they had decided to stop there for a few days before driving back to Albany in a rental car. His mother was too ill to attend their wedding in New York, and although she had minimal understanding of what had been happening, he felt she would appreciate a visit from them.

Every day they were in Boston, they would spend a few hours visiting her in the retirement home. Her room, like the rest of the place, had that smell of old people everywhere—a mixture of cheap deodorizers, starch, uneaten boiled food, and faint urine. It was not necessarily unpleasant, but it made you know exactly where you were.

Katey could see that Don's mother, Estelle, had once been quite a beautiful woman, and a vivacious one, too. They received fragments of her storytelling, and Katey only wished she could piece together or predict the entire story Estelle was telling before she would suddenly look into space, confused. After just a moment or two she would start talking again, but about a completely different subject. Don got impatient after a while, and would often suggest leaving before Katey thought it was time. She tried to make the most of her acquaintance with Don's mother, whom she had not known before she got ill. At times Estelle thought Katey was her sister, the daughter she had never had, Don's old girlfriend, or once, her cleaning lady. As many times as Don repeated that Katey was now Don's beautiful wife, Estelle could never remember it. She did enjoy the tasty truffle cheese Katey had slipped into her baggage for her, back in Italy. So, Katey took to bringing her food every day, which she always enjoyed.

*   *   *

Katey felt a strange feeling of being cheated when she returned from Italy, and she could see Don felt the same. Life was meant to be like it was on their honeymoon—walking and looking at beautiful places, enjoying delicious meals together, and making love until the early hours of each morning. Katey had basked in Don's warm smile, passion for history, and lively sense of humor. She wished that life could always remain like it was in Italy. They tried to extend their honeymoon with romantic dinners at Boston restaurants and walks around the Common. But the famous Swan Boats on the small lagoon felt a little cheap compared to the boats in which they'd explored the coves off the Italian coast.

One afternoon, after visiting Don's mother, they wandered slowly around the streets of Boston, arm in arm, giggling and laughing as newlyweds do. They munched on a pretzel, and looked inside the antique shops. They had pretty much everything they needed in their small house in Albany, and their wedding gifts would fill in the gaps. But they were still looking for that small memento of their honeymoon that they could keep to always remember it. This was more Katey's idea than Don's. He had taken well over six hundred photographs with his fancy camera, and these would be more memories than they needed, he said. A few times on their Italian trip, Katey had found a small statue, or piece of porcelain, and they had bought a few of them. But somehow nothing they found seemed like quite the right memento. Katey was superstitious and kept on hoping they would find that special thing. This was a tradition of her parents—to always bring home something from a trip that sort of encapsulated the meaning of the trip.

Many years earlier, when Katey was nine years old, her mother had come into her room one day and sadly told her that her father, a soldier, would not be returning home. He had lost his life in a country far away. For years after, Katey had found solace in a toy crocodile her parents had bought when they vacationed in Florida one year. When she squeezed the toy it sang an Elvis song. Her grandmother had always chided her father for his lack of taste, but after she lost him, Katey was very grateful for the tasteless toy crocodile.

It was Don who suggested they enter the small pet shop they walked past on one of the side streets. Don's mother had kept lovebirds and a parrot when he was a child, and he always liked to watch birds when he had a chance. They weren't inside for long when they realized the store didn't keep birds, and Don wanted to leave. But by then, Katey was checking out the large puppy wall at one side of the store. While she hadn't thought much about dogs since being an adult, she had loved dogs when she was a kid. She could see there was a very good selection of puppies in this store. There were Pomeranians, and terriers, and pugs, and poodles, and Chihuahuas. There was a large Great Dane puppy in one of the bigger cubicles, and a black Lab. Katey could have spent hours there, but she could sense Don's impatience, and so they headed toward the door.

Nelson huddled in the small traveling crate Emil had thrown him in an hour before. The small puppy had time to smell everything in the small store as he waited on the counter next to the cash register. But whereas under normal circumstances this would have been a feast of scents, Nelson's overwhelming emotion as he waited in the small crate was fear. Emil wandered round the store, unpacking boxes and doing other chores. Occasionally he would smile warmly at a new customer who wandered the store, and Nelson could smell his happiness as he sold a small Chihuahua to an elderly lady. But most of the time, Nelson could only smell anger, particularly when Emil stared at him and cursed loudly.

He hardly noticed when the young woman and man entered the store a few moments before. He was watching Emil closely, and only saw from the corner of his eye that the young woman was looking at all the puppies in the puppy wall. Nelson was surprised when a few moments later she was sticking her fingers through the entrance to the small travel crate in which he was sitting, and smiling at him.

Katey noticed the small puppy sitting forlornly in the cage just as she and Don were about to leave the store. He was small and quite fluffy, with mixed coloring—patches of white and tan and brown. His eyes were noticeable, as if someone had colored around them—a brown patch on his left side, and a white patch on the right side. His tail was also noticeable, and about half the size of the rest of his body, with multicolored fur. But she was struck by the puppy's sadness, and she reached into his little cage to try and cheer him up. The little dog ignored her at first, but soon was licking her excitedly and staring at her with his big brown eyes.

Katey had not thought of owning a puppy for many years. It had not ever been possible all those years she lived in apartments. She knew others kept small dogs inside apartments, walking them twice a day, but she knew if she were to have a dog it needed a yard to play in. She knew that much about dogs from her childhood. But when she and Don moved into their house a few months earlier, the thought of a dog had not even entered her head, perhaps because they were so busy unpacking boxes and learning the ins and outs of living together.

But when she played with this small puppy in the pet pen at Emil's store that day, the desire to take him home with her was quickly overwhelming. The little dog licked her face excitedly, and jumped around near the animal toys, beckoning to her to play with him. When she picked him up, he snuggled naturally into her, and sniffed her. She glanced at her husband inquiringly as he smiled back at her. Nelson felt instantly comforted by the young woman's warm fragrance, her gentleness, and her kind dark-brown eyes. As she looked down at him, her welcoming smile framed by her smooth pearly skin and gently curled black hair, Nelson's entire body softened.

After she picked him up and took him back to the counter, he expected her to hand him back to Emil, just as so many customers before had handed him back after playing with him for a few minutes. But she didn't. A conversation took place. Emil was polite and friendly to the young woman. The young woman spoke gently, in a tone that Nelson found quite calming. The man she was with also joined the conversation. Nelson could smell much of the woman on the man, and much of the man on the woman, and they seemed quite connected to each other. Nelson observed a strong scent on both of them he had never encountered before that was intense, and sparkling, and quite compelling. Later, he would learn that this was the scent of human desire.

Nelson's body tensed when the woman gently placed him

back in the traveling crate and closed the door firmly shut. He huddled near the entrance of the crate, trying to lick her fingers, and whimpering quietly. He looked up at Emil, who looked down at him for a moment, and the young dog shuddered. But it was not Emil that carried him from the store that day, as he had felt in his bones it would be. It was Katey.

Nelson did not know that day that Katey was the Great Love of his life.

5

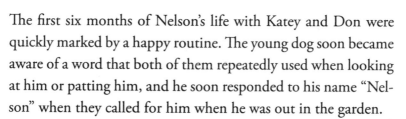

The first six months of Nelson's life with Katey and Don were quickly marked by a happy routine. The young dog soon became aware of a word that both of them repeatedly used when looking at him or patting him, and he soon responded to his name "Nelson" when they called for him when he was out in the garden.

There had been some debate on their car journey from Boston to Albany as to what the young pup should be called. He was a difficult dog to name, as he had such specific features and demeanor. After some hours of trying out many of the usual suspects, Katey was browsing through the paperwork Emil had given them after their purchase and noticed that the puppy was born in Nelson, New Hampshire. Somehow the name *Nelson* seemed to be just perfect for the puppy. Don liked it because it reminded him of Lord Nelson, the British navy admiral, whom he admired greatly and taught with great passion to his classes at the university. Katey thought the name had a good ring to it, and Nelson Mandela had always been a man she admired greatly. Nelson himself neither liked nor disliked the name, but it did make him feel happy that there was this special word for him, and soon the sound of Katey calling him made his heart leap.

The house in Albany was rather small, with two bedrooms, one of them tiny. The bathroom and kitchen were old, and the roof needed some work. But it was freshly painted, and Katey had taken care to decorate it thoughtfully. It was bright and cheerful. More important to Nelson, it smelled good. It smelled good the moment he walked up to the front door with Katey and Don and sniffed as they French-kissed each other to celebrate their arrival home.

The house was in a leafy suburb, and Nelson loved the freshness of the air, and the melodic aromas that drifted in on the constant breezes. Inside, the home was warm and cozy. Once again Nelson smelled the scent of laundry. The bags of lavender Katey had left in carefully chosen places rounded out a likeable smellscape.

Outside was a garden. It was not large like Mrs. Anderson's, perhaps a couple of hundred square feet. But over time, Nelson would develop a close relationship with that garden. Growing rapidly by the time he found a home with Katey and Don, the young dog's nose was growing, too. He came to know every inch of that garden in extraordinary detail. Though he would never be able to express it, in his own head he soon carried a story larger than a Bible. It was not a human story, connected in an intelligible narrative. The story in Nelson's head was a story defined merely by a myriad of connected smells. He unearthed this story simply by exploring the grass in Katey's garden. It was a story of creatures great and small that had lived on these lands for millennia. It was a story about the water that fell from the skies and made the grass and flowers grow. It was a beautiful, and sometimes sad, story that Nelson dreamed of every night and added to every day.

Katey and Don had planted several beds of pretty flowers—impatiens and marigolds and daisies and roses. When the roses were blooming they were irresistible to the young dog. But his favorite of all was the beautiful white tuberoses that Katey had planted a few months earlier. Their scent was pretty during the day, but Nelson particularly loved inhaling them at night, when their true, mystical fragrance emerged. Often Katey and Nelson would go out to the garden after dinner and smell the tuberoses together. She would hold him, scratching his head with her long fingers, as he loved, and they would both sniff the rich scent of the flowers. They left him dizzy. Katey had loved the sculpted white flowers since her Indian roommate at college had often brought them home to their dorm room.

As Nelson grew, the energy exploded uncontrollably out of him. He ate little in his first days with Katey and Don, but soon, as he realized Emil was just a bad memory, his appetite became voracious. He chowed down the two bowls of dog food Katey presented to him daily, and guzzled every other human snack she or Don threw his way. Katey loved to try out different human foods on him, avoiding grapes and chocolate as the books had told her. Nelson willingly ate everything else, absorbing its scent first, and then gobbling it down.

The first meal was in the morning, after Katey and Don ate their breakfast. Shortly afterward, Don would leave the house for the day, and although Nelson was vaguely concerned he might not return, he was soon distracted by Katey. She would feed him his breakfast, taking a few minutes to scratch the top of his head, and wrestle him with one of his toys. She would clean up the plates from the kitchen, and he would sit nearby as she did her morning exercises, and then showered. Then for four hours, she would practice the piano. Nelson loved this part of the day. He would lie under the Steinway grand piano Katey had inherited from her grandmother, which was squeezed into one corner of Katey and Don's living room. Katey would move her hands gracefully up and down, and sometimes soft, sometimes loud sounds would come from the piano. Nelson found the classical music very calming. While his ears could not interpret the sounds of music as precisely as human ears could, he could hear the broad variations of pitch and rhythm, and found them pleasing much of the time. In fact, he could hear many high frequencies and harmonics from the piano that no human could.

Even better to him, though, was the smell of the piano. Katey's scent was everywhere, but the piano too emitted more distant but alluring perfumes. Eventually, Nelson could discern thirty, perhaps forty different types of wood that had been used in constructing the piano. Some were young woods, some were very old. In each was a story, a story of the life of a tree, its growth, its times of plenty, its times of need. Sometimes Nelson discerned smaller stories about animals that had lived in the tree, earthbound or birds. Together, all of these stories were fascinating to the young dog. He never comprehended them in words, or in a linear fashion. They were stories told in the fleeting, dynamic, quicksilver language of smell.

Each day when Katey had finished practicing her classical pieces, she would tap her feet vigorously on the floor, and begin to play one of her favorite pop songs, "Here Comes the Sun," by the Beatles. When she was a toddler, her father had sung along to the LP while he cuddled her on his lap. The song's cheerful harmonies were the perfect release from the strict devotion her classical training required. Nelson soon became accustomed to this daily ritual. During her practice, he knew not to disturb her. But when her feet began to tap, the rhythm would pulse through his body, and he would jump up on the piano stool, excitedly licking her while she sang to him in quite a carefree, joyful voice. He grew to recognize and love the song deeply, because he knew what came afterward. When the song was done, Katey would grab his leash, and they would go out on their daily walk, his very favorite part of the day with her.

For half an hour, sometimes more, they would wander through the suburb around their house. Nelson found it difficult not to strain on his leash, but he soon learned to stay as close to Katey's side as possible. His walk was a daily visit to an opera of smells. There was never enough time to absorb all of them, never enough time to catalog them all in his expanding brain.

As Nelson grew, and his nose's power expanded, powerful new urges took hold of him sometimes on his daily walks. There were more distant scents that fascinated him, fragrances that entered his nostrils and then disappeared after just a moment—smells from distant forests and mountains and cities. He swiftly came to recognize the scents of certain humans and dogs and other animals that were constant in the suburb. But in the air he often sniffed multiple other humans and animals out in the world. What was out there? Was the universe endless like his nose was suggesting? At times, he strained on his leash desperate to find some answers. Then Katey would pull him back, and her fragrance would overtake him again, and he would forget all about his desires to smell the world out there. They would return home. As she took off his leash, she would pick him up, and he would lick her face to thank her for his daily adventure.

In the afternoons, Katey would leave him out in the garden. Sometimes he would smell her inside the house, but sometimes he would hear the click of the front door and the beep of her car door opening, and she would leave the house for a few hours. This came to concern him greatly. He would busy himself nosing in the garden, and playing with his toys. But he would wait anxiously for her to return. When he heard the beep of her locking her car on her return, his bodily reaction was uncontrollable. His tail would wag from joy, and his steadily loudening bark would roar from his throat. Soon she would be outside to greet him, and he would welcome her home with every fiber of his being. He was proud he had kept their land safe while she was away.

In the late afternoon she would feed him dinner, and soon afterward Don would come home. Katey's focus shifted to her husband when he returned every day, but Nelson did not mind so much. Don did not give him much attention, but when he did he was generally friendly. Sometimes, Nelson smelled some irritation and once or twice the first scents of anger when Don wanted Katey to himself. When he sniffed this, Nelson would quietly leave the room or sit in a corner, careful to leave Don alone.

Nelson was not allowed to sit near the dinner table while Katey and Don ate their dinner. The door would be closed to the small laundry area at the back of the house, and he would wait anxiously by that door, as the aromas and sounds of their evening meal wafted in. Katey and Don would chat as one of them prepared food. In the early days of their marriage, Nelson could smell the happiness in the air as they chitchatted about the events of their day. Don liked to cook, and Nelson would hear him chopping and cutting meat, chicken, fish, and vegetables, and then sautéing or grilling. The small dog's mouth would water sometimes, and hope for scraps. Most of the time he would receive a few after the couple had finished eating. Katey would let him into the kitchen, and tantalize him by holding bits of chicken skin or leftover pasta up in the air. Soon, Nelson learned that to receive these treats, he should not jump up to get them, but rather sit down. Then Katey would hand them to him. These were like dessert to him, after his dinner of kibble and dog food.

Sometimes they would let the dog lie with them as they watched television for a while. On some nights, Don would excitedly take in a sports game, actively shouting and yelling at the TV set in a way that Nelson found a little startling at times. He would lie on Katey's lap as she read a book. At times she would cuddle up to Don as they watched a movie or TV show. Nelson would lie at their feet, and soon learned that this type of cuddling between Katey and Don often led to them making love.

Making love was something that happened almost every night upstairs in their bedroom during the first months of Katey and Don's marriage. From the very first night Nelson arrived in Albany he had slept in the bed with them. He sensed some apprehension from Don when Katey brought him into the bedroom, but they had eventually compromised on having a small, soft kennel with a zipper front door for Nelson in the bedroom, which he could sleep in if they wanted their privacy. Effectively, he slept most nights on the bed with them.

After Katey let him into the bedroom each night, Nelson's first order of business was to search for a large and ugly toy rat that Katey had bought for Nelson at the supermarket, on a mischievous whim one day. It swiftly became his favorite toy, probably because it somehow resisted destruction as others of his toys had not. On locating the toy rat, Nelson would run up to Katey with it and insist on some playtime. Katey would wrestle the rat away from Nelson and then throw it across the room for him to catch it. Eventually he would retreat into a corner chewing on it while Katey and Don got ready for bed. Nelson became remarkably stubborn about his nightly ritual. Katey sometimes reflected on how important the routines of family were to the small animal. It seemed like so many other human concerns, like ambition and drive and ego, were simply irrelevant to dogs.

Soon Katey, Don, and Nelson would retreat to their large queen-size bed. Nelson knew when they were about to make love, as strong scents emerged from both of them when it was about to happen. Nelson was never sure what to make of their lovemaking. He would move to the other side of the bed when it started, and sometimes stare at them to try and figure out what they were up to. Don made some loud noises, and sometimes Katey did too. Sometimes, they would make love for quite a long time, and more smells would emerge from their bodies. Eventually the scents would reach a climax and then subside. Sometime after that they would fall asleep.

During their lovemaking, Nelson would spend time working on his rat. When he knew their lovemaking was finished he would find his place to sleep during the night. Katey liked to hug Don and fall asleep in that position, but he liked his own space when he was sleeping, and before long their bodies would separate. At first, Nelson would gravitate to whatever the most comfortable spot seemed to be, and often that was a hairy area of Don's body, his legs or chest. But Don disliked sleeping with the dog right next to him. He would throw him off, or push him away, not hurtfully but in a way that took Nelson aback. Katey, on the other hand, loved Nelson sleeping right next to her. He would wriggle himself into a little ball just next to her stomach, and gently drift off to sleep. The closeness of her scent was calming and gentle. He would stay close to her like that the whole night. Sometimes Katey would have a bad dream. After so many years, she would still sometimes wake up with a start, with some fractured memory of her dead father lingering. Sometimes there was the belch of machine guns or aggressive voices in a foreign tongue that she could not understand. As the months went by, it was Nelson's little snores after such dreams that calmed her more than anything. She would kiss the small dog on his head as his body quietly rose and fell. Soon, she would fall back into sleep, where calmer dreams awaited her.

So, little Nelson's life became intricately connected with Katey. Yes, Don was a member of their family, too, but Nelson's days and nights were so defined by Katey and her life that she became the overarching figure in his world. The complexity of her scent became the defining feature of the air he breathed. From deep within the small dog's heart, a love for her grew. It did not happen overnight, but over several months. It was a Great Love. It was not about the food that she fed him, although he was grateful to her for that. It was a Great Love because she made his whole universe a beautiful place, a place that made him deeply happy. The young dog did not yet know deep loss, which he would one day experience in terrible ways, but even for the few hours a day Katey would leave, he would feel her absence acutely. So, his love grew. With that love, other emotions grew in his canine heart. He felt the need to protect her, the need to show his love to her as much as he could. He felt the need to praise her, the need to share all he had with her. He knew he would defend her with all his strength from anything that might ever threaten her.

Nelson sensed, too, that Katey loved him. It was there in the way she touched him and scratched him on his head. It was there in the way she spoke to him often, when she had finished practicing her piano, or cleaning the house, or cooking. He did not understand what she was saying apart from odd words here or there, but he knew it was him that was being spoken to, and he loved that.

A lesser love was the one Nelson developed for bones. Sometimes Don would bring them home for him. The dog would lie out in the garden chewing them. As his teeth, growing stronger each day, bit into the bone, smells would begin to emanate, stories of the animal this had been and its history. Bones carried almost as many stories as grass did. But when Nelson had done some work on the bone, he would like to dig a small hole in the garden and bury it. Katey might need it at some point. What if she ran out of food? He would build up his own special supply, so that she would always be able to eat and never go hungry.

Sometimes after he buried a bone, Nelson would bark. As a

small pup, his yaps had been nothing more than cute. But the young dog's bark was becoming quite notable. It had the intensity of a poodle's and the deep, bassy throatiness of a beagle's. Katey smiled to herself when she heard him barking out in the garden. He would never bark more than two or three times in a row, except when the mailman was coming. She knew what that meant; *I, Nelson, the great protector of Katey Entwhistle, hereby declares himself here, tall and proud, defender of this house and garden and family.*

One morning, instead of practicing the piano, Katey took out Nelson's leash. He was excited as he usually was when he heard the jingle of the leash, but was also confused. Normally, this only happened later in the day. Katey was reassuring, however, and so Nelson trusted her.

When they had left the house, Nelson pulled on the leash to go in the normal direction they would travel on their daily walk, but instead Katey picked him up and put him on the front seat of her car. She entered from the other side and turned on the engine. Nelson was confused. He had been with her long enough that he did not fear anything she did, but he was very used to their daily routine, and its predictability gave him great pleasure. As if she was sensing his apprehension, Katey opened the passenger door window ever so slightly, and scents poured in from outside the car. This distracted Nelson, and he was preoccupied with them for the rest of their trip to the vet, about fifteen minutes away.

Nelson still had quite a strong memory of his time at the vet with Emil months before. The sterile smells brought Emil back to his memory, and the dog's heart beat fast for a moment or two. But Katey's warm scent was still all around him, and she was stroking his head and patting him, speaking to him as she did. He was sure everything would be fine.

But there was an extra tinge of sadness in her eyes as Katey kissed Nelson good-bye and handed him to the vet. As he entered the operating room with the vet, he didn't think about the vet's smell except that it was not threatening. He was thinking about Katey. Nelson whimpered for her. Where had she gone?

He quieted down soon, slightly fearful as the vet and two nurses crowded around him and looked down at him. Nelson sniffed the liquid dripping out of the large syringe the vet held, but before he had time to try and figure out what it was, the vet had injected him with the needle, and Nelson was fast asleep.

6

Katey did not want to get Nelson fixed. She adored the little dog, and nurtured ideas about him siring children one day. But both Don and her vet had encouraged her to do it. She had got into email conversations with some animal rights activists she had found on message boards on the Web, and while some were a little too strident for her liking, calling breeders "murderers" and the like, the more approachable ones had a persuasive argument. If hundreds of thousands of dogs were being put down in pounds across the United States every year, where was the morality in allowing your dog to breed? Yes, you might find a home for those pups, but somewhere that meant other dogs in pounds would not find a home and would be put down.

So, Katey made up her mind this was the right thing to do. Nonetheless, her heart skipped a beat when she handed Nelson to the vet one morning, knowing he would be going through some pain he didn't understand, and that he would come back unable to breed. He was quite dopey when she picked him up a couple of hours later. Feeling a little guilty about what she had put the dog through, Katey purchased a pricy new brown leather collar for him, with thick metal studs. She also purchased a new engraved silver name tag for him, with her name and phone number, to replace his small plastic one. However, the dog seemed unaware of these material gifts. He spent the rest of the day seemingly in quiet pain from the operation.

Nelson had only vague recollections of waking up from his operation. He was injected another couple of times, and was taken back and forth from machine to machine, all of which beeped loudly. That night as he lay with Katey, having received a special hamburger dinner, he was not specifically aware of the operation he had just undergone, beyond a dull ache by his rear. He whimpered, and Katey lay scratching his head for about an hour, just the way he liked it. Don kissed her and told her not to worry, Nelson would be fine in a day or two.

And he was. The energy returned, and soon the dull aching was gone. Katey thought she noticed a slight change in his behavior, as if a certain edge was gone from him. He was a little less rowdy, a little less boisterous. Don thought it made his personality even better.

As Nelson whiffed the garden air the morning after his operation, the smells from the outside world were as strong as ever. Only curiosity filled his nose that morning, not the knowledge that he could no longer reproduce. If Katey had not fixed him, perhaps many of his children would eventually have wandered the world, some lucky enough to find a home with humans, and others only to have their lives extinguished in a gray pound somewhere. But this was not to be. Nelson was to be the last of his line. Never in his life would the dog reflect on this, and wonder what his purpose in the world was, if it was not to have children. Katey was the only one to consider this question.

Far more distressing than his operation to the young dog was the trip Katey took the following week. She would be gone for six days, and Nelson was aware of every single minute she was away. Don would leave him outside in the garden during the days, and would return in the early evening. Some of the time he would take Nelson for his daily walk, but sometimes Don seemed a little bored and distracted on these outings, and more often than not, he would just hang out in front of the TV drinking beer and eating pizza with Nelson close by. The pizza was definitely something Nelson grew to look forward to. Sometimes Don gave it to him cold in the mornings. It was just as good as when it was warm. Sometimes Don threw him a full piece, and Nelson enjoyed it like a bone, chewing on it until it disappeared.

Katey missed Nelson more than she expected as she did her small concert tour. Her playing was well received in four different cities, and she felt a great sense of satisfaction. Her agent was reporting many more bookings in the year to come. She was excited about her burgeoning career, but also a little apprehensive. Part of her didn't want to spend too much time away from Don. Or, if she admitted it to herself, too much time away from Nelson. She was surprised at herself, that in the midst of performing in front of thousands of people, meeting exciting musicians and conductors from all around the globe, and dining out with her colleagues at pricy restaurants, she often longed to just be at home with her husband and her dog.

When she finally arrived home, Nelson welcomed her for more than twenty minutes. His tail beat the air furiously, he jumped up and down, he barked with joy. When she picked him up, he licked her face furiously, and his nose inhaled her scent in short, rapid blasts. She hugged and kissed the small dog. He would follow her around all day, not letting her out of his sight. His joy could not be contained.

The Great Love

Scan here to feel the warm embrace of "The Great Love," or go to www.youtube.com/watch?v=_WPdZIOulqw.

7

Nelson was fully grown by the time he was about one year old. But he was still as boisterous as a puppy, and chewing everything he could lay his paws on. By the time he was two years old, he had attained a sense of adulthood about him. His tail stood tall and proud, like a Roman army's banner announcing his presence. He ran around the garden with great gusto. And in his eyes, Katey imagined she saw a certain wisdom. Perhaps it was just the colored rings around them, but they seemed to look at her with such deep knowledge.

Soon after his second birthday, Katey and Don and Nelson's life began to change quite rapidly. Suddenly, Don was at home all the time. At first it seemed to Nelson as if it was going to be an endless weekend, but he soon sensed that Don was not happy to be at home so much. The young dog did not know the events that had led to his unfair dismissal from the university, but he observed the anger and frustration that oozed from Don's pores. Don had loved being a professor, and had delivered his history classes with humor, detail, and vigor. When deep layoffs at the university followed state budget cuts, Don had watched in quiet dismay as other professors kept their jobs due to seniority and tenure, even though they had long ago lost the passion and caring that Don had for the subject matter and students. After losing his position, for some hours each day he would sit at the computer, searching for new openings with a sense of urgency. He also tried to fill up his time by keeping up to date on his reading in the field, and by writing some academic papers. But as the months went by, the possibility of finding a new job in academia seemed more remote, and he began spending time just watching TV or wandering around the house aimlessly. When Nelson whiffed a beer bottle opening, he would tread carefully. Sometimes, there would be an argument later that day. He did not understand what Katey and Don were talking about; he did not understand Don's quiet sense of failure was growing as Katey's career was blooming. But the dog did sense the agitation and tension growing in their tones. Sometimes they did more than talk. Don would begin to yell at Katey, and once or twice she yelled back at him. This made Nelson very uncomfortable. He huddled in a corner and watched carefully, whiffing the thick air.

At times he tried to comfort Don by licking him, or playing with him out in the garden. Sometimes Don was responsive, and Nelson was happy to see a smile on his face, and smell the dissipation of his negativity. But sometimes Don just pushed Nelson away with a gruff word. Katey needed comfort, too, and Nelson gave it to her freely. Their time together as she did her daily piano practice was not like it used to be. More often than not, it would be interrupted by Don entering the room, and some sort of negative conversation occurring. When he walked away, she would continue practicing, but Nelson could smell her thoughts were elsewhere, and not with the music. On several occasions, she skipped her daily ritual of singing "Here Comes the Sun" to Nelson. The dog would look at her with mournful eyes, aware something had changed.

If lovemaking happened between Don and Katey more than twice a week now that was a lot. It was not marked by the same explosion of scents Nelson had noticed before. They were muted, and they would finish quickly. Before, they would fall asleep rapidly. But these days, Nelson noticed that both of them would lie awake sometimes for a long time before he sensed they were sleeping. He would always wait for both of them to sleep before he did. He wanted to make sure that they were both all right.

Katey encouraged Don to take Nelson on his daily walk several times, thinking it might clear his head in the same way it did hers. But whereas Katey let him stop and sniff the trees and other dogs that crossed their path, Don always seemed in a hurry to get home. He would keep Nelson on a tight leash.

Nelson felt slightly fearful, for the first time in a long time, when Katey kissed Don good-bye one day, carrying a large suitcase. When she carried that suitcase, he knew she would be gone for quite a few days. She did always seem to return, but although he knew this, he always feared that one day she might not. This was not what was preoccupying Nelson, though. It was a strange odor he was picking up on Don. It was not anything he had smelled before. It left him feeling unsettled and worried.

That night, soon after a pizza dinner in front of the television, Don showered and sprayed on some cologne. Nelson was only used to smelling that cologne in the mornings. A little while later, the front door bell rang. As he always did, Nelson ran to the front door, barking, eager to protect the family from any intruders. He made it to the door in advance of Don, and he wagged his tail when Don arrived to show him the good deed he was performing.

Don opened the door, and there was a woman standing there. She was about the same age as Katey, in her late twenties. Nelson instantly smelled her perfume, and whiffed her strident nail polish. His heart thumped. Who was this woman? Where was Katey? And so he barked, loudly. The woman laughed, as did Don nervously. He knelt down trying to pat the small dog, but that only made Nelson bark louder. As the woman came closer and her unknown odor mingled with the air in the house, which always contained good portions of Katey's fragrance, Nelson felt deep in his bones something was wrong. His barking became manic.

Don yelled at the dog to stop. Nelson resisted, as his feeling of something being wrong was so strong, but eventually he relented when Don came close and looked at him with a vaguely threatening glance. Don picked him up and took him to the laundry room, closing the door as he left. Nelson waited anxiously by that door all night. In the background he heard Don and the woman giggling and laughing. He barked again when they came into the kitchen, and Nelson heard a bottle of wine being opened. After that, he heard them go upstairs.

This was the first time Nelson had slept alone by himself in the laundry room, and he hated it. It was cold, even in the basket with pillows that Katey had left for him to lie in when she was doing the laundry. When Don entered in the morning to let Nelson out, he found a well-placed piece of dog turd right in the middle of the room. He chided the shivering Nelson, but as the dog eyed him suspiciously, Don didn't have the guts to say anything more.

The following night, things seemed to return to their normal routine. Nelson was allowed upstairs, and Don let him sleep on the bed with him. Normally, this would have made for a happy dog, but Nelson did not sleep much at all. The woman from the night before had left her scent all over the bed. It was strong, and with pungent tones that engulfed most of Katey's warm and comforting fragrance. Nelson could also whiff the after-tones of the smell Don emitted when he was passionately making love to Katey. This new, ugly scentscape in the bedroom disturbed the dog. He was used to things a certain way, and he did not want them to change.

The woman came to the house several times while Katey was away. As Nelson learned to recognize her, with her freckles and her short hair, he stopped barking at her as much. Don, perhaps feeling guilty at how cold Nelson had been in the laundry room, allowed him to sleep upstairs in the bedroom, but left Nelson in his zipper kennel. Nelson lay there fuming as Don and the red-haired woman had sex for hours on end. The odors offended him. He wished Katey would come home.

When finally she returned after a week, she thought she noticed something restrained about Nelson, as if he was a little depressed. He gave her the usual hero's welcome, but as he followed her about for the rest of the day he was listless and clingy. Katey asked Don if he thought something was wrong with Nelson, but he just mumbled something in response.

Katey and Don's lovemaking that night was flat. They talked afterward. Nelson could smell the quiet tension in the air. A sort of normality returned in the following two weeks, and Nelson's happy air returned soon. The events with the woman were quickly forgotten. Once or twice he thought he could smell her on Don when he came back to the house after a few hours away. But the important thing was that Katey was at home.

Don and Katey did not fight much, but they did not talk much either. They faithfully followed their daily routines. Katey was practicing her piano for longer every day. As Nelson lay under the Steinway, he could pick up a certain distant anxiety in the air as she played. Nelson wished he could make it go away, so he gave her all the love he could find in himself. As his love for Katey grew, slowly Don became someone in the small dog's brain who was to be tolerated, but not fully respected as a member of the family. He did not show affection toward him much, and he generally tried to avoid him. As a certain coldness settled into Katey and Don's relationship, she spent more time with Nelson. A few times, she would sit outside with Nelson at night, for several hours. They would still sniff the tuberoses together, but Nelson could sense her thoughts were elsewhere. She would sit quietly in a deck chair looking up at the stars, scratching Nelson's head in her lap. In the distance, Nelson could hear Don watching sports on TV.

Sooner than expected, Katey once again packed her bags and left on tour. Nelson stood mournfully at the front door, as she and Don hugged each other good-bye, neither with much intensity.

She hugged Nelson good-bye, but after she had left, Nelson felt bereft. That afternoon Don spent a good few hours playing with the dog in the garden. This was unusual, but Nelson went along with it. Hopefully it meant things were going to get better. Don threw a ball for Nelson, and wrestled him in the grass. The sun was warm, and Nelson's playful pleasure was intense. That night Nelson lay happily at his feet as Don watched TV. He patted and cuddled the animal, and although Nelson missed Katey, things felt better with Don.

Later that evening, the doorbell rang. Nelson leaped up and ran to the door barking. He felt Don slowly follow behind him. Under the door Nelson could smell the other woman. He barked with all he had in him. Don paused by the front door. Then he opened it just a little, picking up Nelson and holding him in his arms. He told him to stop barking, and the dog listened to him reluctantly. As the door opened, the full reek of the woman's perfume entered the house.

Don kept the door open just a little with the latch chain still on, and he and the woman talked for some time. Once or twice Nelson felt her moving toward the entrance as if she wanted to enter. But Don did not allow it. At times the tone of their conversation became quite heated, but ended on a quieter note. Don closed the door, and she left.

He seemed distracted as they resumed their place in front of the television. Nelson tried to reassure him by licking his face, but Don pushed him away. Don was watching a sports game, but did not get involved in it like he normally did. He just sat there quietly, sighing occasionally, and sipping a beer. Nelson drifted off to sleep. He dreamed he was out in their garden, and the flowers had all started to stink of the woman's perfume.

When Nelson awoke a few hours later, Don was on the phone. He talked in low tones. The odor of desire hung in the air.

Nelson slept in the laundry room again that night. At times, he could hear the muffled sounds of Don and the woman making love upstairs. He scratched on the door, desperate to get to the bedroom and stop them. Katey needed to be protected. But the door was firmly closed.

The next morning Nelson barked at Don when he entered. Don returned to the kitchen and came back with a bone. When Nelson kept on barking, Don yelled at him to stop. The dog obeyed only because he smelled anger in Don's pores, and it scared him.

Nelson was relieved to see Katey later that day. He knew now she needed to be protected from Don. He stayed close by her side, and occasionally barked when Don was nearby. Don chuckled nervously, but Katey was surprised. She spent an hour alone with Nelson out in the garden, playing with him and stroking his head to try and figure out what was wrong with him. She feared her frequent trips away might somehow be impacting the dog. She considered taking him with her, but with the tightness of a touring schedule, it was not truly practical. She wished she could simply ask Nelson what was wrong, but of course he merely looked up at her puzzled when she tried.

That night Katey went upstairs before Don. He wanted to watch a late show on TV, and she didn't argue. She was tired anyhow from her trip. She let Nelson in, and carried him to the bedroom. She put him down near the bed, and went to the mirror to brush her hair, something that always relaxed her before she went to sleep.

Nelson jumped up on the bed. He could smell the other woman everywhere. It was like she was in the room right then and there. Nelson inhaled, hating the odor but wanting to get to the bottom of it. She was there somewhere in the unmade sheets and blankets. He dug in with his nose, pushing toward the source of the intense smell.

Katey suddenly heard Nelson barking loudly. She called to him to stop, but he wouldn't. He barked intensely, and she ran to the bed, fearful there was an intruder or the like. He stood in the midst of the sheets and blankets barking, and she hopped on the bed to calm him down. That was when she saw a silver piece of women's underwear that was not her own.

8

Nelson smelled Katey's intense emotions for weeks afterward. He did not understand the details of why she was feeling them. He did not grasp what it felt like to have the fragile vase of a marriage shattered. He did not understand the particularly human emotion of feeling betrayed. But he understood deeply that these feelings were painful and horrible, and had shaken the heart of his Great Love. So, the young dog did all he could to uplift her, and remind her that the world could still be a happy place. Katey took to lying in the grass with Nelson for hours when the sun was shining. She did not want to play, but Nelson enticed her, and jumped all over her body. When she cried, he licked away the tears. When Don and her father intermingled in strange nightmares, Nelson would be there when Katey's body convulsed awake with jagged emotions. He would snuggle deep into her, and gradually the shadows of the night around her would seem less oppressive.

There were several huge confrontations between Katey and

Don. On the immediate discovery of the other woman's under-wear in their bed, Katey waited half an hour, thinking deeply, before she quietly confronted her husband. He responded by sobbing, and this led Katey to yell at him with an intensity Nelson had never seen. The dog was not scared. It was a very focused anger, directed at her husband, and he knew she would never physically hurt either of them.

Don did not leave the house. For weeks, he slept on the couch in the living room. Often, Don spoke to Katey softly, crying some, but she found it difficult to let him get very close. Sometimes he was angry, too.

After a week or so, Don took to doing all the household chores. He would clean the house, and cook, not saying much to Katey, but constantly doing small favors for her. She ignored him, but slowly Nelson sensed some of her anger subside. Slowly, the odor of the other woman in the house dissipated, and Nelson felt the beginning of a certain return to a normal routine.

After a month, Don began sleeping upstairs with them again. He and Katey did not touch one another or speak. She lay with her back to him. Nelson could smell both of them awake. At least there was silence.

Katey took Nelson for his daily walks. They took their time. Often Katey let Nelson linger for as long as he wanted on a particular tree or bed of flowers. He would sniff other dogs with great interest. His yearning to smell and understand the whole universe only grew, and he constantly strained on his leash. Sometimes Katey took him to a neighborhood park and let him run free on the vast expanses of green grass. When he started getting too far away from her, she would call him, and he would come running back, jumping all over her. He would return home from his walks tired but exhilarated. His spirits were only dampened by Katey's quiet sadness.

One night, Don reached over and began stroking Katey's back gently with his finger. Nelson growled at him, but Katey pulled the dog close to her, and calmed him down. She did not respond to Don, but let him continue. He did this for an hour, eventually stopping only when he heard Katey's deep breathing and quiet snores. Nelson slept peacefully that evening.

In the nights to come, Katey and Don began making love again. It was very quiet and without much movement. Nelson smelled some pleasure, but it was far from the couple that had returned from their Italian honeymoon a few years earlier.

On a summer morning one July, Nelson was out in the garden when he heard a huge row going on inside. Katey and Don screamed at each other. Nelson listened quietly. The stench of intense anger floated through the kitchen window. That was all Nelson could observe, not the content of their discussion, Don's feelings that Katey was not sympathetic enough when yet another of his job applications, one that had seemed to have a chance, was rejected at the last minute. That night Nelson was relieved to see them hug, as Katey packed her suitcase and headed out through the front door to her waiting taxi.

The night was uneventful. Don fell asleep in front of the TV. Nelson was at his feet. Don was in a bad mood the following morning. Nelson watched him as he showered and shaved and got dressed. He was not sure, but it seemed like Don put on more cologne than usual. Nelson barked at him. Don turned around and lost it at the small animal. He put him out in the

garden, where Nelson whimpered quietly. A few moments later
Don brought out a small bowl of food for the dog, and put it
down, glaring at the dog.

Don walked out into the yard an hour later. There was a
cocky and slightly angry air about him and Nelson could sense
something was wrong. He barked at Don, loudly and unapolo-
getically. He ignored the bone that Don threw him, and continued barking. Don yelled and swore at the dog, but Nelson
felt compelled by something inside of him, and he continued
barking loudly.

Don walked away in resignation, slamming the side gate behind him. He ran to his car, and turned on the radio loud. Then
he drove off to see his girlfriend.

The side gate to the garden had a complicated latch on it. If
you closed the gate carefully, a small metal slider would lock it
shut. When Don slammed it that day, the gate did not close properly. It looked closed, but the latch was not properly shut, and it
was in fact about an inch open. Normally, he and Katey would
double check the gate before they left, but he did not that day. A
few hours later, a light breeze pushed it open another foot or so.

Nelson lay quietly in the yard after Don left. He was very
worried about Katey. He wished she would come home. As the
day wore on, he sniffed around the garden some, as he normally
did. Often during the day, he would make several visits to the
front of the house to check if anyone was coming. Around mid-
day he would make frequent patrols to see if the mailman was
nearby. Today, his trip to the front of the yard had an explicit
purpose—was Katey nearby? Was she coming home?

The young dog was confused at first when he saw the gate
open. Normally it only opened when Katey was taking him for

a walk. He stood there for a few minutes, smelling intensely. He smelled the familiar smellscape of their home, and Katey and Don. But the breeze was bringing in faint smells from far up the river that winded through Albany. Nelson had whiffed these scents for a year now. He looked out the gate with his wide eyes, and for a fateful moment, the young dog's powerful curiosity took over. He forgot all about Katey, and Don, and his life here at the home in Albany. He wanted to know what those distant scents were. He wanted to smell the whole universe he knew was out there. The urge was strong and overwhelming. For that moment, it was as strong and overwhelming as his feelings for his Great Love.

Nelson walked out the open gate, and began to roam.

9

The small dog raced up the middle of the boulevard. On either side of him cars roared by at high speed, their horns blaring in his ears. He panted, his heart beating. On the sidewalk, kids from the neighborhood high school laughed at him. Some adult humans on the sidewalk called to him as there were gaps in the traffic, but he would only answer Katey's call. He inhaled deep gulps of the cold afternoon air, searching for her scent. She was nowhere around.

Nelson's afternoon had started joyfully as he exited Katey and Don's house and wandered freely along the roads he had previously walked on a leash. It was a strange sensation. When he desired to explore a scent trail in greater detail, or an enticing odor pulled him in an unexpected direction, he did not need to pull on his leash, sometimes to have his desire satisfied and sometimes to have it ignored. The young dog's heart soared. He devoured the scentscape, marking his own scent everywhere, and following his nose with total freedom for the first time. He did not even think of Katey in his first hour away from the house.

As the smells of the outside universe pulled him in all directions, he was unaware that he was slowly moving away from the quiet, leafy suburb that was his home. The yards became a little smaller, the houses a little more rundown, and the pollution levels in the air slowly rose. Katey had never walked him on anything more than a quiet suburban street. The boulevard that aimed toward the heart of the city had four lanes of traffic, and the cars whizzed by at speeds Nelson had not seen in his speed-bumped suburban street. But there were smells on the other side of the boulevard that drew him. He had to know what they were. There were dogs and humans and plants and grass that lived there. He was beckoned by stories he had never dreamed of. He was scared of the cars, but he would run over the big street quickly when there were no cars around, and make it to the other side where his nose could rejoice. That was the plan anyway. Nelson was not quite aware of how he became trapped in the middle of the boulevard, dodging the cars on either side. The smells that had pulled him were faint now. There were only the fumes of a hundred cars, and the stench was repulsive and the noise was overwhelming.

For a moment the traffic eased. Nelson sat frozen in the middle of the road, panting. Before he had time to react, he was grabbed and picked up by a smelly man with a long beard who ran to the sidewalk, holding him. The man sat down with Nelson, gripping him tightly in a way the dog did not enjoy. He looked directly into the dog's eyes and spoke to him in an edgy manner. His long hair stunk, his clothes were unwashed, his body odor reeked of something that resembled the beer Don used to drink in front of the television at night, but stronger. Nelson writhed, but the man held him tighter. Nearby was a pile of something that stunk like garbage to Nelson. The man reached inside and found a stinking chicken leg bone with flies buzzing around it, and pushed it in Nelson's face. The dog turned away. The man pushed it into his mouth. The dog barked and the man started yelling. Three children walked nearby, and shouted at the man. He yelled back at them. As they argued, his grip on Nelson loosened for a second, and Nelson writhed free, managing to pull his head out of the studded leather collar Katey had bought him just a few weeks before. The homeless man was left holding just the collar and its shiny name tag. He sold the collar for a dollar the following day.

Nelson ran for his life. A leafy suburban road of the sort he knew well beckoned in the opposite direction. He scampered up there. When the reek of the homeless man was completely gone, Nelson curled up under a shady tree, and closed his eyes, panting. Where was Katey?

When he woke up an hour later, there were flickers of familiar smells to him. He was close to home. He knew it. There was the scent of other dogs he had smelled on the grass before. The grass was similar to the street on which his home was. His nose searched the air, and blotted out all the alluring scents that had pulled him out the gate to the house just a few hours before.

The small dog walked slowly up the street in a direction the smells seemed to say would lead him home. It was a breezy day, however. The scents in the air continually shifted. They were not reliable, but Nelson could not see any visual markers that would take him home. For hours he wandered like this. Sometimes people on the street would try and come up to him. Some seemed friendly, but he could not trust them after that smelly man. When they got too close he would scamper away, growling at them.

He was getting tired, and he was getting hungry. It was almost time for his daily dinner. It was perhaps eight hours since Don had given him breakfast. There was a hole in his stomach, and it was beginning to hurt. His mouth was dry and he panted uncontrollably. His heart sunk when he realized he had walked up the same street an hour before. Still, the smells seemed familiar. He must be close to home.

He had not smelled Katey once that afternoon. It was the scent he yearned for more than anything. As his nose filtered the complex union of smells that filled every breath, it was her deep fragrance that he was looking for with all his heart. But it was nowhere to be found. The sun disappeared from the sky, anxious winds stirred in the trees around him, and night came.

Then, after hours, out of nowhere, he heard her voice. It began distantly at first. She was calling for him. At first the voice was so distant he thought it was maybe just his imagination. But then it got slowly louder. It was Katey. It was unmistakable. Even from a distance he could hear the desperation in her voice. He wanted to leap into her arms. He wanted to kiss her and comfort her and let her know that everything was okay.

The voice calling got closer and closer. Nelson barked as loud as he could. He looked all around trying to find her. He took deep gulps of the air, his nose frenetic, trying to locate her scent. He was convinced she was close by. With all the energy he had left, Nelson sprinted toward where he imagined the voice was coming from. Katey's calling him grew louder and louder. Nelson barked again with all the force he had.

Then, silence for a moment. Nelson stopped, his heart beating. She must be close. Any moment now, he would see her, and then he would go home and eat his dinner. Her voice started calling again soon after that. It was so close, so close. For a moment, her fragrance filled his nose. He breathed it in deep, joy exploding. He ran down an alleyway toward the smell as fast as he could.

Inexplicably, the voice slowly disappeared again. It faded into the night air in a matter of seconds. The scent was gone, along with the distant sound of her car disappearing into the night.

The small dog was panicked now. He barked and barked. A woman came out of a nearby house, and yelled at him to shoo. His tail between his legs, the young dog ran away.

The night fell and Nelson sat panting under a tall tree. As a cold breeze chilled his bones, he felt for the first time what it was like to be lost.

10

When Katey arrived home that afternoon and saw the open gate, she panicked. She rushed into the yard, hoping to find Nelson still there. But he was nowhere to be seen. She called Don, but got his voicemail. She left a loud message. She ran through their neighborhood looking for Nelson, calling for him, hoping to see him running toward her as he always did, with his tail wagging furiously in the air. She asked a few neighbors if they had seen the dog, but no one had. It was a terrible, hollow feeling not knowing where Nelson was. Surely, she would find him. People found lost dogs all the time. She knew already it must have been Don that had carelessly left the gate open, but she quashed the wave of anger she felt rise up inside her. She knew it would not help her find Nelson.

After an hour she returned to the house and checked the yard again, but Nelson was still not there. She ran for her car and tried to systematically widen her search from the immediate neighborhood. Once, her phone rang with a number she did not recognize, and she hoped it was a neighbor calling, with Nelson safe and sound. It was a wrong number. She was also vaguely aware that Don had still not called her back.

The hours went by. The sun disappeared as cold breezes enveloped the new night. Katey had not taken a sweater with her, and she was shivering from the cold. But she did not even register the feeling. She kept on calling for Nelson, driving up and down streets several times looking for him before moving on to another.

Finally, just after nine o'clock she heard a distinctive bark pierce the night, rising and falling in volume intermittently. She was certain it was Nelson. That was the bark that welcomed her home from her concert tours. She stopped the car for a moment, shouting for him, trying to place where the bark was coming from. He must be close by. Trying to remain calm, she scanned the dark streets around her, edging her car slowly forward, hoping Nelson would emerge from one of the alleys or yards. She could hear him barking again and again, somewhere close by, as if he knew she was near.

But both sound and scent traveled with great deception on air that was not still. Just as the sound of Katey calling for Nelson disappeared from his ears, his barks disappeared from hers. She did not give up for many hours, faithfully driving the same streets again and again searching for him. But Nelson was soon asleep under a tall tree in a thicket of tall trees, and he no longer heard her calls for him. Finally, at four the following morning, Katey drove home. The house was in darkness, and there was no sign of her husband. She pushed that fact into some future she would have to face when she had found Nelson.

As she slumped onto the couch of her living room, exhausted, she wondered if the dog had eaten or drunken anything. If he was outside, he must be freezing with cold. For a long moment, she wondered if a car had run him over. She would search again for Nelson first thing in the morning.

Part Two

Roam

11

||||||||||||||||||||||||||||||||||||||||||||||||||||||||||||||||||||||||||||||||||||||||||||||||||||||||||||||||||||||||||||||||||||||||||||||||||||||||||||||||||||||

Nelson slept fitfully. He woke up shivering several times, but even the cool night did not keep him from falling asleep again soon. The events of the day had exhausted the small animal. He had walked and run for hours, and he had been bombarded by a hundred stimuli he had never felt before.

He dreamed of his Great Love. He lay with her in her bed. He lay under her piano. He played with her in her garden where the flowers were sausages and the grass was made of string cheese. Before he bolted awake the following morning, he was dreaming of Don. Covered in the stench of his mistress, he was biting Katey all over her body. Nelson could smell the blood. He jumped at Don, trying to stop him. The dream was violent, intense. Nelson woke up with his heart pumping.

Nelson inhaled the scent of the suburb. He could still smell some of the familiarity of home, but most of it was new and quite unknown to him. He whiffed unknown dogs and humans and squirrels all around him. Katey was nowhere around. The small dog sat quietly for a couple of minutes. He whimpered, but no one came. In the distance a big dog barked. Nelson kept quiet.

Hunger hit him. It welled up from inside of him like nothing he had ever felt in his young life. He had not eaten for a day, longer than he had ever gone without food, and when the hunger came, it was intense and all consuming. He had woken with an overwhelming desire to find Katey, but that was soon replaced by a much more immediate need. He had to eat.

Nelson observed the air. Normally his brain categorized and analyzed smells according to a variety of factors, his curiosity paramount. Today, his intense smelling was all about finding food. He sniffed and sniffed, trying to find some scent that could lead him toward a satisfaction of his hunger.

Nelson had playfully chased both birds and squirrels many times in his short life. He did not know that these playful urges were in fact the adolescent behavior of wolves, who were educated by their parents in the art of killing for food. Nelson had never captured a bird or a squirrel, and had never seriously considered them as food. As he searched the air that morning for a meal, a small swallow hopped around on the ground nearby him, singing. Without thinking, Nelson pounced in the direction of the bird. But there had been no one helping him before when he played at hunting, no elder wolf guiding him, and so he did not know the precise movements required to successfully kill an animal smaller than himself. The bird escaped, disappearing off into the sky. Nelson watched it fly away. Its smell was similar to the many other birds he had smelled before, but this was the first time that its scent became something potentially edible. It was a strange feeling for the dog.

As a pair of mating squirrels scurried around the nearby grassy sidewalk, similar strange feelings erupted in Nelson's brain. His front paws firmly on the ground, and his rear end raised, Nelson stared at the two squirrels as they courted one another. As they were still for a moment grooming one another, Nelson leaped forward clumsily, attempting to pin them to the ground. One ran away immediately. Nelson managed to land his paw on the other, but it wriggled free of him within seconds. Both disappeared up into a tree, where they continued their flirtation. And so, Nelson was unable to taste the raw flesh that for the first time smelled appealing to his palate. Had Nelson lived his entire life in a human household, he would never have even considered live animals as food, happy to remain perpetually adolescent in his canine hunting skills, with a tasty diet afforded him by his human patrons.

In a nearby house, a man cooked himself bacon and eggs for breakfast. The aromas drifted out his kitchen window, and Nelson sat quietly, his mouth watering. He whimpered again and again, and didn't stop. Eventually, the man eating his breakfast heard the young dog outside, and looked out. But Nelson was scared and ran away.

As Nelson walked slowly along unknown streets searching for food, he occasionally found water in puddles by the side of the road and would lap it up. After some hours, desperate for food, he was drawn into the back alley of a row of houses. Before this day, the smell of trash was not one he associated with food. But as he whiffed the odors coming from the trashcans lining the alleyway, he could discern among the foul overall smell hints of the foods he loved, the scraps from Katey and Don's table. There was the smell of raw eggs, and meat scraps, and other leftovers. He ran toward one of the trashcans and inhaled deeply. There was food inside it. He could smell it. He knew his hunger would soon be satisfied, and then he could search for Katey again.

But Nelson was a small dog. He jumped up but could not get to the top of trashcan. He tried unsuccessfully to topple it over, but soon had to give up. Ravenous, he ran from trashcan to trashcan. Finally toward the end of an alley, he found three over-flowing trashcans and a large black garbage bag standing next to one of them. Nelson bit into the bag, tearing it to pieces. He could smell his breakfast waiting for him. He rummaged among the empty bottles and candy wrappers, and other debris. Finally, he found what he was looking for. He ate some week-old kung pao chicken and stale bread, and chewed on some hard cheese. Soon he was full. Nearby, another house had left out a broken up old sofa to be collected as a heavy trash item. Nelson jumped on the sofa and slept again in the warm sunlight.

The next morning the large trash collection truck moved slowly up the alleyway emptying the trash cans into its large stomach. Nelson was scared of the loud large truck, and he disappeared under some bushes before it reached the couch where he had spent the night. He heard the workers on the truck cursing as they saw the mess he had left. Bit by bit, they dragged the trash from the black garbage bag into the back of the truck, and then emptied the remaining trash cans.

Nelson smelled the foul stench of the garbage collection truck. Filled with trash, it emitted powerful odors. He had en-joyed his meal the day before, and he could sense in that truck plenty more meals. For a moment he almost darted out and jumped into the back of the truck, but the workers scared him somewhat. In the young dog's brain, however, trash and food were becoming synonymous.

In the weeks to come, trash became the smell for which the young dog searched constantly. In the moments when he had finished a meal, before he drifted off into a worried sleep, he would think of Katey. He would sniff the air hoping for her arrival. But his longing for Katey was always quickly overwhelmed by a search for trash. Sometimes, he would find his meal with ease. Sometimes he would go for a full day, even more, without eating. Sometimes the meals were tasty, leftovers from a dinner the night before. Nelson would devour roast chicken, or the remains of hamburgers, or cold pizza that reminded him of Don. But sometimes, there was little worthwhile to eat in a pile of trash. Several times Nelson got violently ill from a meal, especially leftovers that had been in someone's fridge for way too long. Nelson learned to avoid chocolate. Twice he licked a Hershey wrapper and threw up an hour later. Once, Nelson finished a half-eaten bunch of grapes and retched uncontrollably. He would never eat a grape again, even though their smell was enticing.

As the young dog followed the scent of trash, he covered miles and miles daily. Soon, there was no scent that he could identify even vaguely as home. Home was gone, something that existed only in his dreams at night. He would sleep under bushes or trees, or sometimes on a dirty old cushion or piece of clothing someone had left out by their trashcans. He would try and snuggle in as deep as he could to keep warm, rolling himself into a tight ball, and trying to imagine it was Katey's warm body he was moving into.

Ever since his experience on the boulevard, Nelson had learned to avoid cars as much as possible, and he made his path on sidewalks and back alleys and deserted streets as much as he could.

After ten days away from Katey's house, Nelson was on the far edge of Albany in run-down neighborhoods, where he could often sniff aggression and fear in the air. The smell of garbage trucks was constant, becoming more and more concentrated. He became slowly aware that he was getting closer and closer to a place where there were huge piles of garbage, trash as far as the eye could see, a place of endless food. Nelson felt himself propelled to it. The small dog with the wide eyes and noble heart spent hours each day trying to find that. And soon he found himself standing at the entrance to the city garbage dump. It was much as he imagined it. Miles and miles of trash surrounded him. The stench was overwhelming, but in that stench, Nelson's keen sense of smell could already discern much edible. His heart was beating fast.

At one side of the garbage dump, huge generators processed the trash, turning it into the material trucks would cart off to the landfill. They hummed all night. Nelson slept his first night at the dump close to them, as they were warm. He slept peacefully, his bones warmer than they had been for weeks.

In two weeks, Nelson had traveled thirty miles from his home. He did not reflect on the fact that many dogs, particularly big ones who needed a lot of food, died only two or three days away from their owner's home, due to heat exhaustion, or lack of food and water. He did not know this. All he knew was he desperately wanted to find his Great Love and, until then, he needed to eat.

12

Nelson soon settled into a routine at the garbage dump. He had loved his day-to-day at Katey and Don's house. There was something hardwired in his brain that searched for routine, no matter his circumstances. It somehow made him feel like he was part of a family, even though he was all alone now.

He soon learned to forage for meals in the trash dump either in the early morning or early evening. During the day, there were workers all around, and trucks driving in to dump their trash. A few times, an aggressive worker came after Nelson trying to chase him away with a rake, and he barely escaped. After that he learned to be secretive and careful when he sneaked into the dump.

He was never hungry. But he learned to be cautious in searching through the piles of rubbish. Several times he scratched himself on old razors. Once he pricked his foot on a syringe he did not see hiding under a pile of carrot scrapings. His foot hurt for days, and he was unable to sleep. He licked it, trying to suck away the pain, biting at the wound. Finally, the pain dulled.

There were several other dogs that lived at the dump. When Nelson first came into contact with them, he approached them playfully, hoping for some companionship. But without exception, they growled at him, warning him to keep his distance. As he whiffed the air, imbibing their smells, most of what he sensed was fear and pain. He did not know yet what the odor of death and disease were, but these too were the smells that emanated from these dogs' bodies, and he did not like it.

There were rats, too, everywhere. They scurried around him as he searched the garbage dump for food. He did not like the creatures and their dank smell, which in his mind made them very different than the toy rat he had loved playing with. A few times they tried to bite him, and he responded aggressively, chasing them away.

During the nights, Nelson slept near the warmth of the trash-compacting machinery. There were dark shadows there where he felt safe. He could smell other dogs nearby, but they left him alone if he left them alone. Every morning when he woke up, he would be overwhelmed by sadness when he realized he was not in Katey's warm bed, about to bound out into a green yard. There were few plants in this neighborhood, just a couple of gray bushes and world-weary trees. Nelson sniffed them regularly, nostalgic for the scents of nature. There was little in this neighborhood that smelled good to Nelson. There were traffic fumes everywhere, and smoky stenches from the factories that dotted the industrial areas nearby. Occasionally on a windy day, Nelson would catch a whiff of the river, or forests or mountains way in the distance. It would revive him and fill him with energy. That night he would have joyful dreams. But these moments were not frequent.

During the days Nelson would do all he could to avoid trouble.

That meant staying away from garbage trucks and workers. Some humans seemed to live in the area, but they smelled like the man who had saved him from the traffic and stolen his collar. Their pores oozed alcohol and other substances. Nelson often whiffed the scent of loneliness and sadness on these homeless people, and he would think of comforting them. But in just his few weeks away from home, Nelson was learning to protect himself from danger, and he avoided human contact. None of the humans he encountered here had that warm and welcoming fragrance that Mrs. Anderson, Vernon, the vet, or the Great Love, had emanated.

Sometimes when the young dog had eaten his fill, he would wander the garbage dump from pure curiosity. It was interesting what human beings put in their trash. Sometimes he would spend hours delving into the odor of old clothes or ragged towels. Human scents were so complicated and he yearned to understand them. Sometimes he would find some children's broken old dolls or stuffed animals, and he would carry them with him to his resting place at night. There he would play by himself, shaking them, and imagining Katey was with him. Once another big dog growled at him loudly, and Nelson dropped a broken toy rat, scampering away. The big dog stole it, and chewed on it. Something in Nelson told him to always do what these big dogs wanted. He would find another toy for himself the following day.

One night, Nelson noticed a new dog had begun sleeping nearby. His scent was strong, and he seemed aggressive. Nelson lay half-awake for most of the night. It was not only the fear that kept him awake. A loud and aggressive barker, the new visitor did not stop for most of the night. It was a piercing sound, and when Nelson drifted awake the following dawn, having slept little, he felt tired and irritable. He wandered into the dump slowly, and stood on a dead rat. He pushed the animal away and looked for breakfast.

That night, the loud barking dog was at it again. But this time, after an hour of the noise, a fat man came out of one of the buildings running the compacting machinery. Sometimes Nelson had smelled the night workers as they exited or entered the building, but had glimpsed them only once or twice. It was the first time he had seen one of them close up. The large man came outside yelling and carrying a newspaper. He also carried a flashlight. Nelson watched as he yelled at the large barking dog, a black beast who growled back at him. As the large man smacked him hard on the nose, the big dog whimpered and disappeared into the shadows. The man retreated inside.

But the following night, the big dog barked loudly again. This time, the man came outside with one of his friends. They came close to Nelson, who was exhausted from two nights of little sleep, but it was the big dog they were after. He barked loudly and snarled as they got close. This time, as the man hit the dog with the newspaper he did not retreat, but instead jumped toward the humans, trying to attack the fat man. Nelson smelled the fresh blood fly through the air. He did not know what the quick flash of silver was that came from the man's friend's pocket, but he shivered as shots rang out into the air, and the explosion reverberated around him. The big dog ran for his life. Nelson was frozen for a few moments. As the wounded large man yelled, his friend looked all around with a flashlight. Nelson saw three or four dogs caught in the light, and the gun went off several more times. Nelson heard the high-pitched squeal of one of the other dogs as a bullet hit him and he fell lifeless to the ground.

Nelson ran off into the dark streets. He heard two more shots in the distance. Nearby he could smell some other dogs as they ran from the trash dump. There was more snarling and yelping. Nelson's adrenaline pumped, and he disappeared into the night.

Wide-eyed, Nelson walked slowly along the cracked pavement, not sure where to go. It was a desolate concrete landscape, with only an occasional streetlight. There were few smells that seemed welcoming. Homeless people crouched in cardboard boxes, snoring or sobbing or speaking in ways that disturbed Nelson. The smell of drugs was everywhere. Rats and smoke and trash filled out the barrage of bad odors.

From a few blocks away, Nelson sniffed the meaty scent of hamburgers and onions on a grill. He was not hungry, but this was the only scent that seemed to signify some safety in this midnight roam. Nelson's pace picked up and he half walked, half ran toward the late-night diner. As he got close, he saw a row of twenty, thirty trucks parked nearby in huge parking places. The scent of goods ready for transportation also floated into his consciousness—fresh vegetables and new clothes and raw meat, all packaged in big wooden crates and plastic. The smells seemed the opposite of trash. They were the scents of things ready for human consumption, long before their debris would be thrown away and discarded for dumping in a landfill somewhere.

The small diner at the truck stop was open until very late, and the reason was obvious. Even at 2:00 AM, several truckers had drifted in, having just arrived from a long trip out west, or fancying a snack after a final night of drinking and partying before they hit the road the following day with new cargo.

*   *   *

Thatcher Stevens exited the diner carrying a cheese-and-egg hamburger in a brown bag. He had just eaten another one. The burgers were particularly good at this small diner, and he made a
point of eating one, or more, whenever he was in Albany. The
extra one would be good for breakfast tomorrow. He would warm
it up in the small microwave that rattled at the back of his cab.

He was on the way to his truck when he saw the small pooch
shivering under the huge wheels of another truck. Thatcher had
always enjoyed the company of dogs since he was a kid and three
black Labs were his playmates at his grandmother's house on weekends. He had never owned one, but sometimes thought about it.
The idea never lasted long because he himself did not have a steady
home beyond the small house in upstate New York his parents had
left him, and he only stayed there for three or four weeks a year.

Thatcher whistled at the small dog, but he just backed off into
the shadows. Thatcher shrugged and carried on toward his truck.
He climbed into the large cab and lay down on the slim bed where
he slept most nights. There were late night reruns of old cop shows
on his tiny TV set, and normally these would put him right to sleep.

For reasons he himself could not quite discern, Thatcher did
not fall asleep that night as he normally did. That dog remained
on his mind. Something about its eyes, and the way it looked up
at him, kept coming back to him. Eventually he hopped down
from his cab with a flashlight and walked around the trucks
looking for the little pooch.

Nelson had not moved in the last hour. The aroma from the
diner was comforting, but he was not hungry, so he did not
get too close. He would just sit there quietly, which somehow
calmed him down. When the tall man with the ponytail and
goatee came back the second time and beckoned to him, his

natural instinct was to back away. None of the humans he had encountered in the past weeks had been welcoming to him.

But then the man began to quietly sing to him, while holding out his hand. His warm and raspy voice floated in the night air, and it calmed Nelson just as Katey's playing always had. The voice was not full of the anger or frustration or madness of every other human he had encountered in the past month. As the man got within a foot of the dog, Nelson edged forward and sniffed his hand. It had a round, warm smell, similar to Vernon's. Nelson licked him. He tasted salty and sweaty and rather good. The man responded with a pat and a smile, as his singing continued and Nelson licked him again. It was weeks since he had had any real contact with a human being, and he had forgotten how good, and how natural, it could feel.

Thatcher loved listening to Willie Nelson songs late at night when he needed to relax, so he had seen no reason why a dog should not respond in the same way to his singing. After a couple of minutes playing with the small dog, Thatcher tried to pick him up so he could take him back to his truck with him. At that the dog jumped away and growled quietly at him. Thatcher paused, then put out his hand again and began to sing some Willie once more. Cautiously, the dog licked him again. Then slowly Thatcher stood up and walked in small steps back to his truck, watching the dog all the time. The dog followed him ever so cautiously. When he was back at his cab, Thatcher hopped up and got the still warm hamburger he was saving for breakfast. He broke off a piece of it and hopped down. The dog stood a couple of feet away from him. Thatcher beckoned to him, holding a small piece of burger.

Nelson sniffed the air. The burger smelled good, and fresh. Fresh food was so different from the leftovers he'd been consuming at the garbage dump. He was not very hungry, but still he lunged forward and gulped down the piece of burger. In a couple of minutes, half of it was gone. When Thatcher tried to pick him up again, Nelson let him this time. Up in the cab of Thatcher's truck, Nelson consumed the rest of the burger, Thatcher stroking him and chuckling as he enjoyed it. The strong odor of the little dog tingled in Thatcher's nostrils, but he felt too tired to wash the animal so late at night. He opened the windows of his truck wide, and Nelson could have easily escaped if he'd wished. But as Thatcher collapsed into a loudly snoring mass, the young dog curled up at his feet and slept himself. It was warm in the cab, and the air smelled good, if a little stale from cigar smoke. It was the closest thing Nelson had smelled to Katey's home in a month, and so he stayed, falling into a deep sleep.

When he woke up the following morning, the truck was roaring through the countryside. The dog was bewildered at first by the loud growl of the truck as it rocketed along the asphalt. Nelson slid around the rear seat as the truck slowed and swerved on a tight bend. But the windows were down, and the smell of grass flooded into Nelson's heart. In the driver's seat, Thatcher was joyfully singing along to a country music station. Nelson's body relaxed, and he felt his tail starting to twitch. Soon it was wagging uncontrollably.

Journeys with Thatcher

Scan here to feel the wind through your hair, on the road again in "Journeys with Thatcher," or go to
www.youtube.com/watch?v=JdHgflc-AEs.

13

Thatcher Stevens was a lonely man, though he was not particularly aware of this affliction. When he thought about his life, he thought it was good. There was no wife or children to tie him down. His money was his own, to do with as he wished. His job was interesting. He was always traveling to new places, seeing more of the great natural splendor of his country, America. He knew others yearned to travel as he did. Growing up, he watched constant arguments between his mother and father. His mother desperately wanted to travel, but her mate was a homebody. This was not the central pivot of their failed marriage, but he knew it had contributed. When he set off on his career as a trucker twelve years earlier, he soon realized what his mother had been missing. Traveling to new places was an adrenaline rush. New scenery, new people, and new food were all things to be enjoyed.

So, he did not think he had much to complain about. His life certainly had moments of real happiness. When he was setting off on a new route, with a new cargo, to a place he had never been before, he would crank up the radio loud and sing along. This was his alter ego, he thought. As a boy he had nurtured fantasies of becoming a singer, and although they had never come to fruition, he still believed himself to be talented. In such moments, with the road ahead of him, he felt such excitement, and sense of anticipation of things to come. Often, this would last for weeks as he passed through America's grand mountain ranges and forests and along its immense rivers and lakes.

If the loneliness that was deep within him surfaced, it was only at times when the endless driving became tedious. Much of the United States was flat, and with the world as it was these days, much of it began to resemble so many other parts of the huge land, what with its chain stores, strip malls, and cookie-cutter housing developments. As the road extended endlessly into nowhere, a feeling of pointlessness would creep up on Thatcher. His sadness was always mild, as he was not a man prone to extremes, except when he had drunk a lot or had been involved in other forms of substance abuse.

A similar sadness would drift over Thatcher as he came to the end of a trip and headed back to his little house in Sullivan County in upstate New York. It was a beautiful part of the world, but Thatcher spent most of his time inside when he was there. He had never changed his parents' gloomy old furniture and drapes, and they themselves had not changed them for many years before they died. Thatcher would lie on his bed and watch TV, and drink some beer, and warm up one of the frozen Hungry Man dinners in his refrigerator. He would look around at the walls, and remind himself to pick up some new pictures next time he was on the road, although he never did. He would urge himself to fix the leaking faucet and maybe buy some new colorful drapes, but all of these things seemed to drift off into a future to do list that never quite became reality. The night before he was due to leave again, a sense of relief would overwhelm him. The next day, on the road, the roar of his truck's engine and the quicksilver flash of new scenery that would paper the day, would also paper over the loneliness that was beginning to eke into his existence.

Thatcher was an attractive man. Roadside food had left him somewhat chubby at thirty-eight years old, but his large frame disguised his paunch quite well. His blond-brown hair hung in a ponytail, and his goatee framed a friendly face with piercing blue eyes. Several times on his early trucking trips he had encountered women for whom he had fallen quite deeply. But he had soon learned it was virtually impossible to maintain any sort of real relationship with someone when one traveled as much as he did. An early love, Ivy, had lasted some eight months, but in reality he had only spent about sixteen days with her during that time, and although she had also fallen hard for Thatcher, she had eventually chosen to leave him for another young man who lived and worked in her hometown in Wisconsin.

Other of Thatcher's flames had turned into long relationships of sorts. In his small book of phone numbers, there were ten or fifteen women scattered round the country that he would call when he was in town. They would get together for a dinner of chicken and ribs or whatever else was the local specialty, and then they would have sex at the woman's house, or at a motel, or most of the time in the cab of Thatcher's truck. For some reason women liked having sex up there. It turned them on. Thatcher liked it there too. When he slept at their houses on occasion it would always be a little difficult to leave a warm bed in a warm house late at night, especially when it was cold outside.

Thatcher talked of settling down one day, but as the years went by, he realized this was becoming a slimmer and slimmer possibility. He would need to carry on working until he was sixty-five years old, and he didn't know how to do much else besides drive a truck. He knew no woman would marry him when most of his life was spent driving, away from home. So, he contented himself with the four or five nights of intimacy he had monthly with his regular flings, or one-night stands, on the road.

As Nelson awoke to Thatcher's singing that summer morning, he was being transported rapidly away from Albany and Katey. After rejoicing in the overwhelming grassy scent entering the cab from outside, he sniffed the small sleeping area of Thatcher's cab where he had slept the night before. The couch itself had the smell of old, worn leather, and the blankets had not been washed for some time. The scent of Thatcher was everywhere. There was also the smell of fresh cigars from a box of Cubans stowed away under the couch, and the vague stench of smoked ones permeated the blankets and upholstery poking through the cracks in the leather.

Nelson whiffed the remains of the previous night's burger, as well as chocolate chip cookies and Pringles and trail mix. The smell of the fresh laundry that Thatcher had washed in a coin laundromat a couple of days before reminded him of home. It made him want to stay with Thatcher, as if it would somehow return him to Katey. A few bottles of cheap cologne were also stashed away nearby, and a few bars of soap, bottles of shampoo. These were scents Nelson associated with home, and they calmed the young dog.

In front of him Thatcher beat his hands on the steering wheel and sang along to the country music station. Nelson could smell the happiness in the air, and it smelled good. He hopped into the front seat next to Thatcher. Thatcher looked happy to see the small dog, and patted him as he drove. Nelson licked his fingers and wagged his tail, looking up at him.

The landscape rushing past invaded the cabin of the truck. Thatcher drove fast, and the smells of new trees and plants flew into Nelson's nose. After the stench of smoke and trash he had become used to the last month, Nelson felt like the whole interior of his being was being scrubbed clean and fresh. The fear of the past few nights swiftly vanished, and the young dog felt alive again.

A couple of hours later they pulled up at a truck refueling station. Thatcher picked up Nelson, who went with him easily this time. He also grabbed a bar of soap and a towel, and Nelson soon found himself in the open showers nearby. Thatcher scrubbed him thoroughly and vigorously. It was a little rougher than his cleaning sessions with Katey had been, but the dog enjoyed it. Once Nelson had been cleaned, Thatcher showered himself, and the dog waited at his feet. Thatcher dried himself off with the towel first, then rubbed Nelson almost dry. Katey had blow-dried him, as opposed to just a straight towel drying, but he preferred the fresher feeling he had now. He shook himself in characteristic fashion and wagged his big fluffy tail up at Thatcher, who chuckled.

Thatcher never bought a leash for Nelson. He would carry him around, or let Nelson walk behind him. He kept a watchful eye on the dog and whistled or called him if he strayed more than a few feet away. He recognized in the dog the same incurable curiosity that was also his defining trait. He knew curiosity was something that led to the most wonderful things in life, but was also something that could be a trap.

After their shower, Thatcher went for lunch. The official rules of most of the dining establishments he frequented were that no pets were allowed. But he was well liked in most of the places he ate, even if the waitresses who knew him by name only saw him once or twice a year. The sparkle in his blue eyes was quite memorable. So they were happy to let him bring his small dog inside. Nelson sat quietly on the seat next to Thatcher in his booth as he perused the menu. He surreptitiously fed Nelson little pieces of steak and fries, and even some of the apple pie with cream he had for dessert, which Nelson devoured. In the time that Nelson spent with Thatcher, he would become quite accustomed to eating human food, and after that would never seriously consider packaged dog food as a viable alternative. His digestive tract was designed for human scraps, and as the dog became set in his ways in adulthood, he avoided dog food. It became normal for him to eat a small portion of every meal that Thatcher ate.

Sometimes in their travels across the United States, Thatcher would rent a small motel room for the night. Nelson became accustomed to the smell of these places, which were always the same no matter which town or state they were in. There would be the lingering odor of old cigarette fumes, and towels and sheets washed with a little too much bleach. Often, in the older motels, the carpets had a sort of damp smell. Sometimes there were strange noises at night while Thatcher slept, and Nelson took it upon himself to guard Thatcher, growling and barking if any of the other residents of the motel appeared to threaten him in any way. Thatcher was a sound sleeper and loud snorer, and he did not often wake when Nelson barked at the sound of strangers making love next door or raucous behavior from some humans who had imbibed a few too many drinks. Nelson would lick Thatcher's face to wake him in the morning, and Thatcher would lumber outside in his boxer shorts with the dog and let him pee. This was Nelson's reward for a job well done.

Sometimes Thatcher would leave Nelson in the motel room for a couple of hours by himself. Nelson felt a little fearful when first put into this position. But the small dog was learning to stand up to the emotion of fear. Instead of hiding, scared, he would stand proudly next to the bed, waiting for Thatcher to return while guarding their temporary home. Once, a cleaning lady entered the room, then hurriedly left as Nelson barked loudly at her, refusing her access. Incidents like this reinforced the dog's growing belief that he was strong and powerful despite his size.

Thatcher would return by himself sometimes, his breath reeking of alcohol. This left Nelson nervous, as it provoked the faint memory of the homeless man who had stolen his collar. But Thatcher generally fell straight to sleep when under the influence, only to snore a little louder than usual. Once, Thatcher fell asleep after a brief fling with a tall woman he'd picked up at a bar, and she quietly edged her way toward his pair of jeans, searching for his wallet. But Nelson was not sleeping, and he barked loudly. When Thatcher awoke to find the woman standing guiltily over his pants, he knew Nelson had just saved him the hundreds of dollars in his wallet. The woman hightailed it out of the room, and Thatcher rewarded the dog with his own plate of bacon at breakfast.

More often than not, Thatcher would sleep in the cab of his truck. Nelson grew to love it there. He liked the fact it was a small space, compared to the motel rooms they sometimes used.

Nelson liked being in a small confined area that he felt he could protect well. It made him feel very safe and secure. At first, the dog slept at Thatcher's feet, but on one cold night he snuggled right up next to his broad chest, and slept like a young puppy despite Thatcher's insistent snores. This became his favored resting place. Thatcher would sometimes wake at night to see Nelson on his chest fast asleep and would grin to himself.

As Thatcher would sometimes leave Nelson alone in a motel room, he would sometimes leave him alone at night for a few hours in the cab of his truck. He would open one of the windows ever so slightly, and scents of the surrounding neighborhood would keep the dog entertained until his return. Nelson was soon used to women coming back with Thatcher, and they would make clumsy love in the small space in the truck. The whole cab would sometimes shake back and forth, as Thatcher was quite a passionate person. Each time Nelson felt he had found a place to relax and fall asleep, he would be dislodged again by the sweaty human bodies on top of him. Sometimes he would even bark to let Thatcher and his lover know they were disturbing him, but they would merely giggle and carry on with their business. The women would make up for their disturbing his sleep by playing with Nelson after they'd finished. He enjoyed the attention, as well as the occasional beef jerky or peanuts they would produce from their handbags.

In the time that Nelson spent with Thatcher they would crisscross America at least ten times. They would follow Highway 20 all the way past Chicago, across the flat plains of Iowa, through the mountains of Montana, finally delivering a cargo in Oregon. Following Highway 2 from Seattle, they would cut back across the United States close to the Canadian border, back into Montana, across the Great Plains, where Nelson learned the unmistakable scent of buffalo, and into the woods of Minnesota, with its manifold animal and plant scents. On Highway 50, they would cross the Mississippi, eventually climbing the steep Rockies, where Nelson whiffed eagles, and hawks, and ancient Native American dwellings. They would rumble across the Sierra Nevada, where the clear intense smells of the desert would enchant the young dog's nose. They would amble across the country in the far south, close to the Mexican border, where Nelson would smell oil and cattle in Texas. Finally this would give way to the Cajun scents of the Mississippi Delta. They would head up the backbone of the Appalachians, and Nelson would spend a weekend in Sullivan County, at Thatcher's parents' house. Nelson longed to study the woods and rivers he whiffed in the distance, but Thatcher just wanted to stay inside.

The young dog's curiosity was not satiated by his endless smell discoveries out on the road. As the stories each of the state's odors left him to contemplate grew, he wanted more and more. Back in Albany, he had imagined the world was a fascinating place. Now, he knew it was fascinating, and his desire for more was only lessened in the moments he remembered his Great Love, and knew nothing could ever replace her. He daydreamed of magnificent white tuberoses that emitted the fragrance of Katey at night.

One night, in North Carolina, a state Thatcher loved with its combination of beautiful coastline and pleasing mountain ranges, a woman came to visit him. He had not seen her for more than a year, and he was looking forward to it. Their sex was always exciting and something that made him happy. But more than that, the previous time he'd seen her she'd made strange allusions to something she needed to tell him, although she'd clammed up when he pushed her, mumbling something about next time. Thatcher was puzzled, and a small part of him was secretly hoping she might want something more serious together, although he couldn't even conceive what that might mean for his life. He took extra care in shaving that day, and applied some of the expensive cologne he only used for very special occasions. Nelson watched him as he clipped his fingernails, and knew he was anticipating an interesting evening.

The woman knocked on the door at around 6:00 PM. Nelson barked and stood guard next to the entrance. Thatcher, who was lying on the bed of the motel room watching *Animal Planet*, jumped up and checked his hair a final time. He motioned to Nelson to calm down. Then, he opened the door.

The woman standing there was pretty, with brown hair. Nelson did not smell the scent he knew of a night out on the town—perfume, lipstick, and hair spray. She had a pleasant smell, but the strongest scent coming from her was of her freshly washed jeans and T-shirt. Thatcher was about to hug her, but stopped when he saw the four-year-old boy standing next to her.

The boy was excited the moment he saw Nelson, and ran inside and started playing with him. Thatcher liked to carry a small doggy toy and ball around with him for Nelson, and there was also a large T-bone from dinner the night before. The boy, full of energy, played a game of tug with Nelson and his small rope toy. Nelson loved the energy of small children when they played, and he did not fully notice the conversation going on between

Thatcher and the woman. Nelson had been prepared for a night alone in the motel room, and instead he got an hour of playing with a young boy. This boy was in fact Thatcher Stevens' son.

Thatcher called in an order to a nearby pizza parlor and soon two large pizzas arrived at the door. They all shared, Thatcher allowing his son to give Nelson small pieces. There was some more talking, this time with the boy. At one point, Thatcher gestured to him to come to him, and they hugged briefly. Nelson could sniff the emotion on Thatcher's skin, but the boy was much more concerned with getting back to playing with Nelson, and it was a brief hug.

A couple of hours later, Nelson noticed the boy begin to tire, and the woman and the boy left the room soon after that. Everyone hugged good-bye. That night, Nelson did not sleep much mainly because Thatcher did not sleep at all, tossing and turning. Nelson was so used to his constant loud snoring, he felt uneasy when it was absent.

In the morning, there was a series of rushed phone calls. Nelson was not used to spending daytime in a motel room. Generally, they would check into one at night, if they were not sleeping in the truck, and leave early, often before the sun had even risen. The night after Thatcher met his son for the first time, they spent most of the day in the room, watching movies and eating leftover pizza. Nelson sensed the anxiety on Thatcher's skin. Around four in the afternoon, the woman and the boy returned. Most of their time there on that day was similar to the day before. Nelson liked his new playmate. But after they had eaten some Chinese dinner, Thatcher and the woman's conversation rapidly escalated into shouting. Nelson was transported back to Katey and Don's fights many months before. He had not often smelled anger on

Thatcher, and it was a smell that left the dog feeling queasy in the base of his stomach. As their yelling did not stop, the boy retreated into a corner of the room, and soon he was crying. Nelson walked up to him and licked him to try and make him feel better. The boy picked him up, but continued crying. After a few moments both Thatcher and the woman stopped their yelling. The woman came over and comforted the boy, but he just sobbed more. Thatcher also tried, but both the woman and the boy pushed him away. The woman and the boy left soon after that.

That night, Thatcher also cried. Nelson lay next to him quietly, not knowing what to make of this unexpected behavior. Finally, he slept, but Nelson lay awake sensing some change was coming. He snuggled deep into Thatcher's chest, and Thatcher quietly stroked the dog as he passed through uneasy dreams.

Thatcher was more subdued over the next few weeks as he and Nelson scoured America in his grand truck. Nelson often caught him with a small tear in his eye. He did not often sing along to the radio as he had before with great gusto. Before there had been a woman or sometimes two, every week, sharing Thatcher's bed with him and Nelson. Now, it was just the two of them.

Nelson also noticed an anger boiling in Thatcher. It was not visible most of the time, but occasionally when a driver pulled in front of Thatcher's truck a little too fast, or a food order at a restaurant took a little too long to come, the anger would surface. Thatcher would curse and bristle in a way Nelson had hardly seen before.

They would see the mother of Thatcher's child and his son twice more. It seemed Thatcher had gone out of his way to return to North Carolina en route, driving up to fifteen hours a day sometimes, so that he was tired and irritable for long periods of time, lost in his own world. The next meeting with the boy was not marked by any of the arguing that had happened before. There was a controlled silence between Thatcher and the woman, marked only by brief confrontation when the pile of bills she handed him was not to his liking. Nelson could sense powerful emotions when Thatcher hugged his son, and watched as he tried to converse with the boy. For an hour or two they would throw a football around in the parking lot of the motel. Nelson was part of the action, and he enjoyed it.

Nelson was confused by the differing emotions that characterized Thatcher in these days. His love for the boy was readily apparent, but still this strange new anger surfaced at other times. As the loneliness that had been only background noise in Thatcher's life surfaced with intensity after the discovery of his son, the joy Thatcher had felt as a constant traveler diminished. He felt like a ghost as he endlessly passed through the highways and byways of the huge country. Each time he saw the boy, confusing and unruly emotions about his own childhood he had suppressed for so long came hurtling to the surface. Nelson was a blessing, Thatcher felt. God had sent him this little dog just in time. God had known his son was soon going to enter into his life, and God had sent Nelson to help him. At nights, he would stroke the little dog for hours, and hold him close. He tried to call his son now as often as he could, and it was Nelson whom he held as he tried to communicate with the child who had come into his life.

But Thatcher was realizing that it would be very difficult to change his life to fully incorporate the boy. Suddenly, he wanted everything he thought he hated. He wanted a settled life with a family. He did not want to travel constantly. But it was difficult to change his life. How would he earn a living doing something other than trucking? And while he loved the little boy, he realized he did not love the boy's mother. She had been a good sex partner for quite a few nights, but when it came down to it, he could not imagine their relationship being anything more than that. So, there he was, almost forty, with a certain life that he had created. He was suddenly realizing it was not quite what he wanted, but he had no choice but to accept it for what it was. There might be small changes he could make, but there was no overarching new life he could go and trade in like some used car. He felt frustrated at his inability to be a good father to his young son, and somehow felt his own parents were to blame, even though he absolutely knew this to be irrational and unfair to them.

One night, Thatcher pulled up the truck in a small town in Montana called Kalispell. He had woken up in a bad mood that day. Nelson sat quietly in the back of the truck sleeping on the blankets, not venturing much into the front seat. He sensed Thatcher wanted to be left alone.

When they pulled into the parking lot of the truck stop, Nelson smelled fir trees outside. Thatcher parked the truck. He picked up the dog and took him outside. Nelson sniffed around the thick grass and did his business. He liked these small country towns. The truck stops in the bigger cities always smelled of smoke and the industrial areas Nelson had first encountered around the garbage dump. There was plenty of nature in the small towns, and that made the small dog's heart lift.

Back in the truck, Thatcher broke a couple of Pringles into small pieces and left them as a snack for Nelson. He didn't say much of a good-bye, leaving the window ever so slightly down.

Night came, and Nelson lay quietly, sometimes dozing but alert, guarding the truck as he waited for Thatcher to return from dinner or wherever else he had gone. Nelson had been through this many times. He felt quite safe in the cab of the truck, and as much as he waited for Thatcher's return, he thought he would be fine.

Late that night, he heard the sound of drunken revelers nearby, and this left him wide awake. The young dog did not know what time was, and he did not know that it was 3:00 AM, way past Thatcher's normal time of return. All Nelson felt was a nagging unease. When the very first few rays of the dawn's sunlight poked into the cab of the truck, Nelson knew something was wrong. Thatcher had never left him alone like this all night.

As the dawn turned into day and the cab heated up, Nelson began to bark, loudly. He hated doing it, but he finally peed on the front seat of the cab out of desperation. Once again, the terrible hunger that had first hit him when he got lost in Albany, hit him again. He rummaged in Thatcher's stuff and found a bag of pretzels that satisfied him. He was thirsty, though, and it got painfully hot in the truck. Nelson lay quietly in the shade under the steering wheel trying to conserve energy.

The day turned into night. Nelson was relieved as the temperature cooled. He ate the remaining pretzels, and pooped on the front seat near the place where he had peed.

*   *   *

Nelson was concerned about Thatcher. He wished he were with him. Without Nelson guarding him, bad things would happen to him, Nelson knew. In fact, Thatcher's anger had finally boiled over in a small country bar in Montana. A surly waiter had ignored Thatcher's repeated requests for service, and a fight had erupted. Thatcher was a friendly man, not easily provoked. But he had already had four beers when he stood up and grabbed the waiter by his shirt, after he had called Thatcher an out-of-towner and a lowlife. The waiter swiped at Thatcher, who ducked. Thatcher responded with a hard punch to the man's stomach, and he crumpled to the floor. Two of the locals were friends of the waiter, and they jumped into the fray. Thatcher was a strong man, but it was difficult to take on three other men at once. They punched and kicked him to the ground, relentlessly.

One never knew who was carrying guns and who wasn't in a small country bar like this one. Thatcher never did carry a gun. His father had loved guns when he was a kid, and once or twice Thatcher had seen him threaten his mother with one. So, he had promised himself as a teenager he would never carry one. But as Thatcher looked up at the men battering him, the blood from his nose flowing down his face, he saw the flash of steel as one of the men reached into his jeans, and Thatcher lunged for the man's gun to protect himself. As the men collided, the weapon went off, a bullet flying into Thatcher's shin. The other customers who had been cheering on the fight, now acted swiftly to intervene and separate the parties.

As Thatcher lay in the hospital, his leg throbbing with pain, his face and body bruised purple from hard punches, he tried to tell the police officer to look after his dog when he went to move Thatcher's truck to the police station. But the police officer was in his late fifties and suffering from problems of his own. As he climbed up onto Thatcher's truck, he was thinking about his cholesterol levels and his wayward son, and he expended no effort in chasing the small dog that darted out of the truck and disappeared into the woods, as he opened the door. He reckoned he might try and find him after he moved the truck to the police station two hundred yards away. But when he had to spend half an hour cleaning up Nelson's piss and shit, and his wife was calling to let him know his dinner of mac and cheese was getting cold, the cop decided he would tell Thatcher that the dog had escaped, and he couldn't find him even though he tried.

Thatcher sobbed uncontrollably when the nurse at the hospital conveyed to him that his dog had escaped his truck and could not be found. He implored the nurse to help, but she was unsympathetic, a cousin of one of the men Thatcher had fought with. The Vicodin and the antibiotics carried him away into a long, dark sleep. He dreamed he was trapped in a deep pit in a thick forest. Nelson stood at the top of the pit barking loudly, Thatcher's only hope that someone might find him.

14

Like Thatcher, the small dog dreamed. His life had been short, very short, if one compared it to the age of some of the other creatures with whom he shared the planet, but already his brain had detailed and spectacular memories hidden in its labyrinths, memories composed of a complex network of smells. When Nelson dreamed, the many smells, sweet and pungent, that he had encountered in his short life combined in new and unusual forms and linked to the deep emotions, hopes and fears, love and sadness, the young dog had felt in his time on earth.

As Nelson lay dreaming, his nose twitched as he navigated a complex path from the sweet-scented flowers and grass of Mrs. Anderson's farm to the warm hands of Vernon in the pet shop. He dreamed of the multiple woody layers of the piano of the Great Love. Most of his dreams were in the language of smell, but in this dream he could also hear the very highest frequencies of her piano, the heavenly notes that humans heard only echoes of. The fragrance of the wood and the sounds of the piano were beautiful, but in his dream they were constantly invaded by dark and fearful odors and clanging from the endless trashcans and piles of human refuse that Nelson had been forced to explore. Although he was looking for her everywhere in the dream, the Great Love herself was nowhere to be seen.

The scent of Thatcher was still all over the dog and his fur. The man was powerful and present in the dog's psyche, and he expected to see him as the dog entered the semiconscious moments between sleep and waking up. Like Katey had once been, Thatcher had become the center of Nelson's daily life. The dog yearned for a routine based on place, based on a home, but in his long travels with Thatcher he had learned that one did not need a geographical home to feel rooted. Thatcher had come to root him, as much as Nelson had come to root Thatcher.

When Nelson awoke that morning, though, Thatcher was nowhere to be seen. The dog lay under tall pine trees on the edge of a forest of pine trees that stretched for miles. His nose inhaled the cool morning air. It was not unpleasant. Trees and grass could never be unpleasant. From deep in the forest there also wafted the scents of other animals—small rodents, birds, and other animals Nelson could not quite identify. There were smells that were similar to the smell of dog, but were somehow more intense, wilder. The hairs on Nelson's back rose and fell ever so slightly as the distant scents of wolf and coyote prickled the nerve endings in his voluminous nose.

But any fear he had subsided rapidly. He could smell the familiar odors of human settlement nearby. There was the tantalizing whiff of burgers on grills and fresh French fries. There was freshly mowed grass, and cars, and rain on tar, and wood, hewn and treated and sealed as humans knew how to do. When humans used wood in their dwelling and on their fires, it had a distinctive and different smell from natural wood, from trees, which were growing, alive, creatures too in Nelson's smell inventory. He liked the smell of trees, but to him human wood meant safe houses, and most of all, lying under the piano of his Great Love.

The dog rose to his feet. The town was close by. When he had escaped from Thatcher's truck the previous day, he was bewildered and had run without much thought, finally resting under the tree on the edge of the forest for the night. Now he wandered slowly back toward the center of town. He inhaled, searching for Thatcher. For a moment he thought he could smell him, and indeed Thatcher was just a few hundred feet away in a hospital bed, fast asleep. But the two were not destined to connect again.

Nelson was hungry again. This did not provoke the same terror and desperation in the young dog that it once had. From his more than a year out in the world, he knew that food would always come to him somehow. Hunger created a dull and empty pain in his stomach, but the dog inhaled the sweet air of the small Montana country town, Kalispell, and knew his hunger would be short-lived.

The smell of burger and fries he had inhaled earlier came from a small lodge built of redwood where truckers stayed and ate in a large restaurant, which served not only burgers, but steaks, fried chicken, burritos, and pancakes. The restaurant's trash was disposed in a large trash container outside, which was emptied every three days, and was generally overflowing by the time the trash man arrived. Nelson was drawn to the restaurant not only by the smell of its food, but also by the smell of truckers. Of course, Thatcher's smell was unique, but it also exhibited characteristics of a generic trucker scent, a combination of the particular sweat that came from spending long hours in a confined truck cab surrounded by air-conditioning, cheap motel soap, and a diet of endless comfort food from restaurants just like the one Nelson found in this small town. Nelson was still expecting to find Thatcher just as he did every morning, and so the smell of truckers everywhere was reassuring to the small dog.

There was a hole at the bottom of the old trash container in which the restaurant placed its trash. Rats and other small creatures used it frequently. Already adept with trash from his months at the trash heap in Albany, Nelson pulled out his breakfast from the large container. He enjoyed some hash browns stained with fried eggs, and the fat off a rib eye steak that an obese trucker had reluctantly carved off. The cooking was good, and Nelson enjoyed the food, which had been quite easy to find. As he ate, the cook herself was in fact watching him. A large lady born in Mexico, Marta Herrera smiled to herself when she saw the dog gulping down the remains of her food. Elsewhere in the town, a stray dog near the trash would have provoked an aggressive response, but Marta came from Ciudad Juárez, where stray dogs were common, and it was understood they could steal from humans the scraps left for trash. In fact, Marta was always puzzled by her American husband's insistence on buying dog food for their German shepherd, and his refusal to give him scraps from their table. Her husband was militant about this, claiming that scraps were bad for a dog and would make him sick. Marta had hated the pain and suffering of many of the stray dogs she saw in Mexico as a child. But she knew that human scraps were fine food for a dog. Her grandfather had told her how dogs had evolved from wolves eating scraps around human campfires many millennia before, and there was no reason not to continue this tradition.

So Marta let the dog eat as much as he needed when he hung around the restaurant. Whenever she saw one of her staff trying to shoo him away, she would gently chide them, and it became accepted that Nelson could eat from the restaurant's trash whenever he so desired. Sometimes in the morning, she would spare him some extra special scraps, like a half-eaten fillet or a piece of cheesecake, and feed it to Nelson personally. She even had thoughts of taking the dog home sometimes, but her husband would hear none of it. Marta loved the curiosity on Nelson's face, and the way his tail flapped up in the air like an elephant fanning a maharaja, and she imagined he would clean up good. But her husband only wanted a purebred on his property, and a big dog at that.

Nelson did not ever make a conscious decision to stay in the small town. It was a combination of events that led to his time there. It was the overall sweet smell of the air. It was Marta's cooking. It was a desire to find Thatcher, which gradually faded, but by the time Thatcher was a distant memory, Nelson had acclimatized to Kalispell.

But more than anything, what kept Nelson in Kalispell was a female.

15

Lucy had not roamed like Nelson had. Yes, she too was a stray, but she had never left Montana. A mutt who combined so many breeds it was impossible to isolate her genealogy just by looking at her, Lucy was one of a litter of four, born on the streets of Helena, Montana. Her father was a mutt, and her mother was a mutt. Her father was dead before she was born, run over by a truck. Her mother gave birth in the small, dark confines of an air-conditioning duct carved into one of Helena's old buildings. She was exhausted after childbirth, but still found the strength to rummage in the trashcans nearby so that she could produce milk to feed her voracious pups.

It was not enough milk, though, for all the pups to survive, and two died. One night a man and his daughter heard the cries of the remaining puppies as they whimpered for more food. Their mother was away searching for enough to quell her own hunger. The man's daughter begged her father to let them take the puppies home. Reluctantly, he agreed. Lucy's sister died two days later.

But Lucy survived. Her new owner, Caitlin, named her after the Beatles song. She was a sandy-colored dog, small, with short legs and piercing eyes. Her tail was fluffy and expressive, not unlike Nelson's. She soon forgot about her mother and her sister, and Caitlin became her Great Love.

Six months later, Caitlin's renegade mother finally won her custody appeal, and Caitlin flew to California to live with her. Caitlin loved Lucy, and desperately wanted to take the small dog with her. But her mother was allergic to dogs and cats, and regarded herself as the queen of her home. Caitlin cried for a week. Her father kept Lucy, but he had never particularly liked dogs, and he did it only to try and lure Caitlin back for frequent visits.

Lucy did not give up on Caitlin, though. She soon realized she needed to escape from Caitlin's father's house and search for her. Lucy was a skilled digger, and surreptitiously began work on a hole under the fence that would set her free. Each day, while Caitlin's father was at work, Lucy dug. Caitlin's father was surprised to see the dog was gone when he came home one day, and soon discovered the hole under the fence where she had escaped. His daughter cried for days when he told her Lucy had escaped. But deep inside, he was quite relieved that the dog was gone, and did not expend much effort looking for her in the days that followed.

Like Nelson's journey, Lucy's journey to Kalispell had been complicated and at times, she had been scared and lost. The odds of a stray dog surviving for very long were not good. But Lucy was a very resourceful dog, with a feisty disposition and a happy heart. So she survived. Her initial intention of finding Caitlin was soon dulled by the need to survive.

*   *   *

Nelson was not generally awakened by smell in the same way a human might be awakened by a loud noise. But one morning, a month or so after his arrival in Kalispell, he bolted awake when a powerful and intoxicating perfume invaded his consciousness.

Nelson had taken to sleeping near the heating vent outlets of the truckers' lodge where he ate his breakfast every morning. Winter was coming, but the blast of hot air through the outlets kept him warm on most nights. He could sense it was slowly getting colder, but the small dog did not piece together that a harsh winter was coming. It would have scared him greatly if he knew.

Nelson was dreaming about Thatcher and Katey. He slept next to them in a house he did not know, one built of strange wood. Nelson could smell rats in the rafters and under the floors. But his unsettling dream was interrupted by Lucy's smell. It was no average smell. When Nelson sat up wide-awake, a light rain was falling, although sunshine still peeped through the grayish clouds above. Although rain generally cleaned the air of most odors, the scent that had landed in Nelson's nostrils seemed somehow to become even more powerful, enhanced by the droplets of rain. Nelson knew it was the smell of another dog. But it was the smell of something much more. It was filled with life, and some essential universal odor that was totally compelling. It beckoned to him; no, it grabbed him and told him to find its source.

Lucy was wandering around the nearby parking lot, looking for food. She had wandered into town early that morning. She was exhausted but could not sleep on her empty stomach. Whenever she was in heat, her hunger accelerated dramatically, and it became difficult to find enough food to satiate her endless appetite.

She had been drawn to Kalispell by the aromas of human food that wafted up the interstate. Human food was always good if you could find it. When she found a town where she could spend some time without distraction, she would always take advantage. Once she had been picked up by dogcatchers and put in a depressing gray pound she hated. She could inhale the stench of death in the background. Sometimes, other dogs nearby would be scooped up reluctantly by the volunteers working at the pound, and taken off to some place not far away, where their familiar doggy smells would be turned into something Lucy found deeply discomforting. There would be the whiff of flames and smoke, and only the slightest remainder of the dog's odor would hang in the air. Lucy felt determined to escape that fate, and fear bristled on the hairs on her back.

Small dogs had a better chance of getting out of the pound, of slipping between the legs of the humans who caged them and dashing away, and Lucy had successfully made it out.

From her experiences, Lucy had developed a keen sense of when her chances of surviving in a town without being picked up by dogcatchers were worth the risk of staying there. In some towns, the humans actively pursued any dog without a collar and a leash. Lucy could sense many of the humans were well meaning, but she did not want to return to the pound. In other towns, the humans left a stray dog largely alone, only occasionally giving it a morsel of food, which Lucy always appreciated.

When she wandered into Kalispell that day she was not immediately sure whether it would be a welcoming town for a dog like her. But that was not what was on her mind anyway. Food was her concern, and so it was no coincidence really that Lucy was drawn to the truckers' lodge where Nelson was sleeping. The delicious scents of Marta's cooking hung in rain-specked air.

Lucy was taken aback when Nelson approached her, running, from behind, and began aggressively nuzzling her, trying to mount her. Nelson, too, was taken aback by his own actions. He was a virgin still, and had not been prepared for the act of sex by knowledge passed on by his parents or his peers, like humans were. Lucy's scent simply set alight his senses, and his body reacted. Inasmuch as a smell could be a saturated magnificent color, Lucy's fragrance was a rainbow that invaded his heart and mind. He simply had to connect and be one with this other small dog that had walked into his life with such sensory gusto.

Lucy would have none of it. She snarled at him and looked him in the eyes, her own nose bristling to interpret what this other dog wanted. Nelson's odor did not overtake her as her own was overtaking him. But she found his scent strangely sweet, and somehow noble. So, she stopped snarling and merely growled quietly at him. Yet he bounded right back up at her, licking her face and biting her gently under the neck.

She was hungry and wanted to eat, so she ran from him as fast as she could. But he just kept on following her relentlessly. By the trash heap next to the truckers' lodge, Lucy stopped running when she found the same food source that was keeping Nelson well nourished since his arrival in Kalispell. She gulped down a half-eaten omelet loaded with cheddar cheese and ground beef, and filled herself up on some curly cheese fries.

By the time she had finished eating, Nelson had successfully mounted her. Lucy, too, was a virgin, and it was only because of her desperate focus on food that she had given Nelson any gap to get what he wanted so much. When Lucy's hunger finally subsided, Nelson's little paws were grasped around her, and he was pushing inside her. It was quite painful, and she could smell a little of her own blood. But for some reason she didn't quite understand, she let him continue pumping in and out of her. She inhaled his scent once again, and this time it was even more pleasing. He was a beautiful dog.

From the window of the kitchen, Marta watched the two little dogs mating. Part of her was happy at the thought of the little puppies she thought might be found close by two months from now. She would feed them, and perhaps let them stay in the kitchen at night. But she was sad, too, because she knew where most of the pups from an unwanted mutt litter would land—dead on the street.

She did not know that Nelson had in fact been fixed, and that although Lucy was fertile, there was no chance of him impregnating her. To Nelson and Lucy themselves, they had no idea at all that sex generally led to young puppies. To them, the act of sex was merely an exciting new activity filled with life and a beautiful rainbow of scents in which they floated with great happiness. As their bodies connected and he felt her warmth and fur rub against him, Nelson felt both fulfilled and as if his entire body was vibrating ecstatically. When his orgasm came, the young dog felt like he was going to explode with joy. Although Lucy's feelings were less intense, she could feel Nelson's joy erupting inside of her, and although totally unexpected, she also felt happy, above all.

Yet, she was a strong young dog, and not apt to give anyone, especially another dog, anything that was not on her terms. At the first sign of Nelson relaxing, she pulled away from him and ran for her life. So, the day ensued. They made love many times that day—perhaps ten or fifteen times. Had Nelson been fertile, Lucy probably would have been pregnant many times over. Their day was an ebb and flow between the two dogs, Nelson enjoying the upper hand as he entered her, but shortly afterward Lucy would run from him on her short little legs, all around the town and into the woods surrounding it. By the fourth or fifth time it was no longer painful for Lucy, and she began enjoying the lovemaking as much as Nelson.

Late in the day, hunger struck them both again, and they enjoyed the remains of some fried chicken from the trash heap. They were dogs, and there was no verbal bond between them, no agreement that they were now together. Nelson wandered off to his sleeping spot near the heating vent outlets, and for lack of anything better to do, Lucy collapsed next to him. The passion of the sex they had enjoyed together gave way to pure practicality at the end of their day. The night was colder than the previous ones, and by lying snuggled up next to one another they helped fight off the cold breezes that the night brought in.

In the months to come even the warmth of each other's bodies, and the hot air from the heating vent, would not be enough to keep them warm overnight. They would awake shivering in the mornings. If they had been sleeping alone in such circumstances, both Nelson and Lucy probably would have died. Together, they escaped such a fate even if they were unbearably cold at times.

Lucy's mating period lasted a few days, and their crazy lovemaking continued. By the end of the few days, the dogs' scents had become very comfortable to one another, and both sensed that the other's temperament was complementary with their own. The nature of love between dogs was not comparable to the Great Love a dog might feel for its master. It was practical matters that kept Nelson and Lucy together. It was warmth, and occasional sex, and the feelings of strength and rootedness that came from being members of a pack. But somewhere in their doggy hearts, it was also love.

Nelson and Lucy

Puppy love! Scan here to listen to "Nelson and Lucy," or go to www.youtube.com/watch?v=XYjn9oiUp30.

16

Herbert Jones did not consider himself an unlucky man. He had lived a long and reasonably happy life with his wife and three children. He had worked as a supervisor in a sawmill for most of that life, earning a steady living. He liked the people of his town, and was considered by most a fair and friendly boss or colleague. Herbert found his job quite rewarding, and on weekends when he had the time he also derived pleasure from the small woodcarvings of birds and squirrels he liked to make from leftover pieces of wood from the sawmill. When he retired at sixty-five this became his predominant activity, and he sold his little wooden animals for a living to souvenir shops in a fifty-mile radius.

At eighty years old, Herbert Jones could be considered unlucky in one way, though. Most men's wives outlived them. In any old-age home, this was self-evident. In his mind, Herbert had never much considered the possibility of losing his wife. After fifty years of marriage, their lives had become so intertwined that it had become almost impossible to separate them. Almost every detail of their daily existence had been fashioned by years of compromise, marked by flashes of conflict, always quelled by enduring love. Like any couple that had spent so many years together they were like a well-worn piece of clothing to one another. There might have been some holes that needed darning, and some missing buttons, but overall the garment was so comfortable and so familiar that it would never ever be traded, and indeed its age and the minor repairs needed were part of what made it so perfect.

When Herbert was seventy-two, his sixty-nine-year-old wife contracted pancreatic cancer and died shortly afterward. His wife had always seemed a little stronger than he did, always took care of the details of their life in such a way that it seemed inconceivable she would leave the earth first. She herself had aided and abetted his belief she would outlive him, reassuring him that after he died she would take care of packing up the house and making sure all of his remaining wooden animals found good homes. She would plan how their small estate would be divided among their three children and four grandchildren, all now living far away from Kalispell.

At first, Herbert engaged in healthy denial after her death. For many hours of the day, he was convinced his wife was still with him. Her ghost would sit and watch as he cooked his own breakfast, giving him advice. He would wait for the bubbles to burst on top of the pancakes before flipping them because his wife told him they'd be best this way. He would remember to add fabric softener to a load of laundry only because his wife's ghost stood over him, gently teasing him about his lack of household skills. Late at night he would reach for her pillows and hug them as he moved in and out of sleep, convinced they were in fact his wife.

But eventually, after about a year, his wife's ghost also left the house, and Herbert Jones was left alone by himself. He was sad, terribly sad, for years it must have been. Herbert worked hard at curing his sadness with routine. He knew how his wife and her routines had made him so happy and so comfortable through the years, the way in which, without much speaking, they would help each other through the day. When she was still alive, in the morning, there would be a cup of steaming coffee with two sugars and a bowl of oatmeal with a few raisins and hot milk waiting for him. At night, he grew to look forward to rubbing her feet as she so enjoyed, even when they were a little smelly from a busy day.

Previously, his wife had bought all the groceries, and she would generally complete one large shopping weekly, arriving home a little hot and bothered with three or four bags. In constructing his daily routine when she was gone, he came to realize that if he didn't spend some time out of the house every day, the sadness would become overwhelming. And, of course, as his own grandmother had told him, exercise was a key part of a healthy mind. So, he took to walking the few hundred yards from their small house, on the outskirts of a pine forest, into Kalispell Main Street, every day. He would walk slowly around the tight and curvy road into the town. He would stop at the convenience store for a cup of coffee and a hot dog or a chicken pie. He would purchase whatever other groceries he needed at the store, or sometimes he would go down to the supermarket if the convenience store lacked something he needed. He resisted buying anything in bulk, as it would make his daily trips seem pointless.

After his time in the town he would trudge home carrying his groceries. The people in the town all knew him, and many came to measure their own lunchtimes by his appearance on the street. When he arrived on Main Street it was around 12:30, and time for lunch.

For three years Herbert had been completing this daily journey. It was generally enjoyable, the endorphins created by the exercise enough to chase away the blues. Only the loud noise and bad fumes of some of the trucks and the occasional crazy biker zooming up the road intruded on the pleasantness of Herbert's daily walk.

Although he still thought of his lovely wife every day, several times in fact, he had somehow become happy again. He enjoyed fashioning his little wooden animals, and the town of Kalispell continued to enchant him with its sweet air, trees, and distant mountains.

On his daily trip to the town, he noticed two small dogs several times. He saw them hanging around in the sandy outcropping just near the curve in the road that took you into the center of the town. One of the dogs was short-legged and reminded him of a dog his family had owned when he was growing up in Arizona. But it was the other dog that grabbed his attention. It had interesting coloring, particularly on its face. When the dog looked at you, it seemed to look right into your soul with a questioning but friendly glance. When the dog's bushy tail wagged, it was a little like a shimmering halo above its unique face. At first, Herbert merely observed the dogs. But one day, he took some scraps from his breakfast, a few slices of pancake, and put them in a small plastic bag when he departed for town. He fed the scraps to the two dogs on his daily walk. They ate them happily, although they were not ravenously hungry, as he had expected.

This became an almost daily ritual. Herbert took his walk every day except Sundays, and the dogs were there or close by almost every day. Soon, the two waited patiently at the same spot, and enjoyed their daily snack. When he'd given them the food he would walk on, and at first the two little dogs made an effort to follow him, particularly the one with the unusual coloring.

Herbert loved dogs when he was a boy. When he got married, before he and his wife had children, Herbert thought a dog would be an excellent addition to the incipient clan he was creating with his wife. But she was highly allergic to both cats and dogs. Just walking into a house where one had been present set her off sneezing and made her eyes water. The arrival of Claritin many years later helped a little, but not much.

So, of course her allergies precluded them ever having any pets. Herbert never regretted this greatly, as his wife's love was more than enough compensation. He was only reminded of the pleasures of a pet years later, when his sons and daughter complained about the lack of a canine in their household.

Now that his wife was gone, Herbert could have housed a dog or two. Sometimes the thought crossed his mind that he should take home the two dogs that he fed everyday. At times they looked in need of a good bath. But Herbert always stopped short of pursuing this idea. Somehow it seemed disrespectful to his wife.

So when the two small dogs chased him after their snack, he shooed them away. After a few days they stopped trying to follow him. He wasn't sure but he thought he saw in Nelson's eyes an understanding that it just wouldn't be right to take the dogs home given Herbert's wife's allergies. She might be gone now, but her wishes should still be respected.

17

Nelson and Lucy were happy together. They were two stray dogs, and so their existence in the world was not easy. The nights were cold, and sometimes in their time together the dogs were sick, coughing and sneezing relentlessly. At such times, one dog could smell the other's weariness and fatigue and sadness. Had they been alone, this may have been enough to kill them. But each dog gave the other extra warmth at night, and they played with each other when they were sick, so their hearts were lifted up enough to keep them alive. When good health returned, the playfulness increased. And so, despite their adverse conditions, the dogs were happy together.

They played endlessly, chasing one another, barking at one another, biting each other gently. Their play was not unlike that of the baby and adolescent wolves that lived in the woods just five or ten miles away from them. But a dog's play became not just a stage in their life, but the defining characteristic of being a dog. It was deep in their souls. Nelson and Lucy's similar size made them perfect playmates. Neither one nor the other could truly attain dominance in their endless escapades and attempts to be the alpha dog in their small pack. Nelson would be the boss for a short time, but never for long. Something in Lucy's canine heart would erupt into action, and she would reassert her dominance over her partner. Only during Lucy's bimonthly heats would Nelson gain any sort of real dominance, and never for long.

Over time, the smell of Lucy became reassuring to Nelson in the same way Katey's and Thatcher's had been. Even without a real home, Nelson and Lucy built a sort of daily routine between them. They would sleep in the same place and eat in the same place every day. They took to spending much of their day around a sandy outcropping just near the entrance to the town, on a curvy bend that led into Main Street. It was generally quiet here, and they were less likely to encounter well-meaning humans who wanted to catch them and take them to the pound. Most important it was warm here. Its position meant it received sun for most of the day, and because it was sandy, the warmth did not evaporate as it might from grassy soil. Because it was sand, Nelson and Lucy could dig, as the female dog particularly loved, building up a secret store of bones they found in the restaurant trash heap, from leftover prime ribs or chicken. Sometimes after a particularly cold night, the two dogs would burrow themselves into the warm sand, allowing it to warm up their frozen bones. Slowly, energy would return, and they would emerge, fur ruffled, and play with one another until the sun began to set and they would head to the town and the restaurants' heating vents for the night.

The old man who gave them food every day also became part of their routine. As his scent wafted up the street from his house when he opened his front door every day, the two dogs looked forward to the daily lunch that he provided. He had a warm and unthreatening scent, although Nelson could also smell something else on the old man. It was a strange odor, of decay and age, of a slow sickness growing inside the man. Nelson did not like the smell very much, and he did not yet know what it would mean.

Nelson and Lucy spent a great amount of time just inhaling and observing the sweet Kalispell air. The ancient mountains and forest and lakes that surrounded the town for hundreds of miles provided an ever-changing and kaleidoscopic story of the region. Just like the story told by the grass of Albany, the air of Kalispell told a long and beautiful tale of the rise and fall of mountains and rivers, and the plants and creatures that had grown and passed away in this beautiful land.

Nelson was not sure what to make of the smell of wolves that he experienced often in the Kalispell air. At first he thought he was smelling some other dogs. But although the smell drew him as a canine scent would, there was something vaguely threatening about the smell of wolf. There was a dark inner core to the smell that confused Nelson. The smell entered his dreams at night on several occasions. Nelson did not know its meaning, or why it kept on returning to him.

Nelson and Lucy also smelled coyote on the light winds of Montana, several times. Where the smell of wolf was distant, and musky like an old book, the freshness of the scent of coyote assaulted Nelson and Lucy's noses. Coyote smelled very similar to the scent of other dogs. In Nelson's brain, coyote was just a variation of dog. But it was a dog of the type Nelson would instantly run from because its aggression defined it. The scent conjured up images of fangs, and blood, and sweat, and squeals in the night.

There were at least ten coyotes living in the vicinity of the town of Kalispell. Like Nelson and Lucy, the coyotes were to at least some extent dependent on the human beings that lived in the town. The remains of their food were essential sources of nutrition to the coyotes. But whereas Nelson and Lucy remained fond of human contact, and filled their dreams at night with scenes of life in human homes, the coyotes were decidedly wild. They instinctually disliked human beings, and would have killed them given half a chance.

At night the coyotes often wandered quietly and surreptitiously through Kalispell looking for food. At times a human being might sight one of them, but more often than not they would ascribe their sighting to imagination, as coyotes were exceptionally skilled at disappearing innocuously off into the night, like dark wraiths.

Coyotes ate many types of human refuse, and small birds, rats, and squirrels. Unlike dogs, it was common for them to kill small animals in order to eat. At times coyotes might decide to breed with a dog their size, and hybrid pups would be born. But coyotes felt little kinship with the smaller breeds of dogs. They might recognize some similarity in their scents to their own species. But this did not provoke fraternal emotion in the coyote. A small animal could easily be killed and ingested. Those human families who were aware that coyotes liked small dogs as food protected their pets at night, and kept them behind strong fences during the day.

18

Nelson was having a nightmare. He was running, sprinting through a dark forest. In the distance somewhere, Lucy was whimpering and crying, but he could not find her, could not reach her. There was the smell of death in the air, the smell of the old man that fed them every day. The forest was thick, but the smells of nature were not there. Nelson puffed and panted as he raced through the forest searching for Lucy. The pungent odor that overcame him as he ran was the stench of coyote.

Sometimes, the content of human dreams might connect with sounds in the real world as a human being awoke. The sound of an alarm clock or creak of a broken window in the room might become fixtures in our dreams, but with a different meaning. The stench of a coyote in Nelson's dream was not connected visually to a coyote.

But as Nelson bolted awake, his heart accelerated as he looked across the street from the sidewalk where he and Lucy lay sleeping, and saw the slim angular shape of a coyote staring right back at him with cold blue eyes. For a flash, the coyote seemed like a ghost, just an apparition in the foggy night. As Nelson adjusted to being awake, the coyote was just some evil dog spirit from the bowels of Nelson's consciousness come to scare him. The short instant that Nelson and the coyote stared at one another seemed much longer than the very short time it actually was. Nelson did not quite know if the moment was just part of his nightmare. But when the coyote bounded toward Nelson and Lucy, there was no doubt the creature was more than real.

It is said that three out of four human dreams are bad dreams, although only a small percentage of those could be termed nightmares. In dogs, the percentages are similar. As the coyote bounded toward Nelson, Lucy, who was lying next to him sleeping, was in fact having a good dream, not a bad one. Her nose twitched, but somehow her brain obviated the smell of coyote. She dreamed she was inside a beautiful kitchen surrounded by the family of her Great Love and the scents of gourmet cooking.

What awoke her was not the smell of coyote, but the odor of Nelson's adrenaline. She had never smelled adrenaline on him in such toxic quantities. She was still half asleep when she smelled the coyote just a few feet from her. The coyote bolted into Nelson, who tumbled against the wall. The coyote pounced on him, but missed. It was a freezing cold foggy night, and the dogs could not see further than six or seven feet in front of them. But both ran as fast as they could.

The coyote was used to moving through all the textures of night, and poor visibility did not daunt him. His sense of smell was finely attuned, and the smell of the two dogs shone a bright light at him through the fog. In fact he knew the smell of the two small dogs intimately. For months, he had tracked them in the breezes of the town at night. His mouth watered when their smell entered his nostrils now.

As Nelson and Lucy ran, their adrenaline gave them a strength they had not been aware of before. Even in the panic of the moment, they whiffed each other's adrenaline, and this also gave them added strength, some innate power in a pack united by fear. So, they managed to avoid the vicious force just behind them for a few hundred feet as they twisted around street corners and over deserted roads. But the coyote was experienced in the art of pinning his prey, and had developed a powerful ability to foresee the moves of his opponents. After chasing the two dogs around the town in a frenzy for some ten minutes, he sensed his moment to pounce, and he leaped through the air, landing on top of Lucy. Her small body was nailed to the hard concrete sidewalk. Nelson, his senses overloaded with the panic of the moment, reacted swiftly and lunged into the coyote, defending Lucy. Nelson sank his teeth into the beast's hind leg. But the coyote was excited at the taste of prey in his mouth, and hardly felt Nelson's bite. The coyote bit into the back of Lucy's neck. She let out a loud heart-wrenching squeal. Nelson manically leaped at the coyote's face, stalling him for a moment. In the same instant, a man in a nearby house turned on his lights, and opened up the window, yelling.

The man was not an immediate threat to the coyote, but the coyote had learned that vanishing quickly was the best strategy for dealing with humans. Sometimes, when confronted with human children, he might be tempted to treat them as a piece of meat, but older humans were a threat to him with their guns and lights and pitchforks. For a moment the coyote wavered. It looked at Lucy, the blood seeping slowly from the small wound he had made on her back. The coyote's heart was beating at the thought of eating her young flesh. He considered picking her up in his jaws and running with her, away from the humans. But the other small dog was still snapping at him, barking loudly, and would no doubt prevent a silent escape into the misty night. The coyote loved hunting for food. He lived for the final moments of a kill, and the first taste of a fresh one. But he also knew that sometimes those moments could be elusive. His own survival was always paramount. So, the coyote disappeared into the night, alone.

Nelson licked Lucy, panting with worry. She merely whimpered mournfully, sounding almost like a small puppy that had lost its mother. The man in the house could almost make out the small shapes of the dogs on the sidewalk, and could hear Lucy's mournful crying. But his warm bed beckoned him. He did not feel like burdening himself with two stray dogs. At least that horrible yelping noise was gone. Must have been a coyote. Or a wolf. But it was gone. His children were safe. He closed the window, turned off the lights, and went back to sleep. Humans living in the cities and towns of America were often unaware how coyotes roamed through their dwelling places at night, quiet aggressors passing close to them as they slept. It was easier for humans not to think about it.

Nelson stood over Lucy's warm body, and smelled her blood leak onto the sidewalk. He tried to stop the bleeding by licking her wound as fast as he could. When young wolves accidentally bit each other, as was often the case, their mother would lick their wounds. The saliva of wolves was designed in fact to be a natural salve on wounds, stopping the bleeding and killing bacteria. And so, Nelson kept Lucy alive. He licked her wound for hours, then for days, and stopped her from bleeding to death.

19

Lucy managed to hang on to life in the days after the coyote attacked her. Nelson's warmth kept her alive at night, and he would drop pieces of food nearby her in the days following the attack, when she found it difficult to move. She had summoned the strength to limp back to their sleeping place near the heating air vents the morning after the attack, leaving a trail of drops of blood. But that night, as Nelson stood guard while Lucy slept, he smelled the coyote close by, and heard its growls through the fog. He woke Lucy and herded her around the back of the restaurant near the garbage cans. It seemed safer there, more confined, although Nelson still stayed awake most of the night, anxious.

The following day they moved to a small mini-mall some blocks away, where Nelson found the air-expulsion ducts of a laundromat provided some warmth in a quiet back alley. Although the place seemed more secure, Nelson was still awakened constantly by the coyote's odor, whether real or illusory. Sometimes Lucy would smell the coyote, too, and her body would shake with anxiety. Nelson would sit quietly, scanning the landscape around them with his nose, his eyes, and his ears, while quietly licking Lucy to reassure her. In truth, the coyote had not forgotten the taste of Lucy's blood and craved more.

Lucy was dependent on Nelson for her food. He would make several trips back and forth from the trash area near the restaurant, making a new game out of getting her to eat. He would drop a piece of half-eaten chicken or steak a foot or so away from her and growl quietly, pretending he was protecting it, teasing her to try and take it away. He'd put up little defense when she responded and grabbed it from him.

Nelson's thoughts were comprised of smells and emotions strung together in a unique language in his canine brain. So, he never articulated, as a human might, the sense of loss he felt at the change in Lucy. But as the memory of the coyote attack lingered, he was left with a different companion. Their play was less intense, the energy and feistiness of the other dog just a remnant of what it had previously been. Her sadness affected Nelson. He felt haunted by a quiet unease.

Often at night, he would experience intense dreams of Katey. Rich in the smells of her and her house and her piano, he would experience a sort of ecstasy in his sleeping life sometimes, as if his Great Love had summoned him. He would play endless games with her and his ugly toy rat, her distinct fragrance rich in his senses. He could see her face right in front of him, her brown eyes sparkling, her smile vivid. But the toy rat would become a real rat writhing in his mouth. He was unable to hold it firmly in his small jaws. When it was free, it would bite Katey. Nelson would lurch forward to protect her, but suddenly his limbs would become paralyzed. The rat would transform into a huge and powerful coyote. It would lunge toward Katey, pushing her to the ground. Nelson would awake, shaken. His Great Love was far away somewhere, unreachable, no matter how deep his longing for her. A hole formed in his canine heart, a deep black hole. It fought for dominance over his curious, playful, and noble nature. It became part of his life, a new and permanent feature of his existence.

Nelson and Lucy would not make love to one another again. She was in heat a few months after the coyote attack, and Nelson was eager for sex. But when he tried to enter her, she snapped at him viciously. Her body just did not feel right for sex after the shock of the coyote bite. It was virtually impossible for Nelson to stay off her during those days, as her scent remained intoxicating, but she simply would not let him.

During the few weeks after Lucy's attack, the two dogs stopped their daily visit to the warm sandy outcropping outside the town. Herbert Jones missed them. The first day they failed to show up he had the remains of some pancakes with maple syrup for them to snack on, carried in a small plastic bag. He stopped and waited for half an hour, expecting them to appear. Everyone in the town who was dependent on Herbert's arrival in the town to signal their lunch break had their timing thrown off. Eventually he went into town, sad that the dogs had disappeared. He brought them snacks for a week after that, hoping they would show. When they did not, he began to fear for the worst. He thought they may have been run over, or perhaps worse. Herbert knew of the coyotes in the woods around, and he knew they could eat small animals on occasion. He prayed that the two dogs had escaped their clutches. The two dogs were really just a small part of Herbert's life, animals he saw for a few minutes every day. But losing his wife had made him sensitive to any loss, and he found himself lying awake at night worrying about the two little animals. Perhaps he should have taken them in, let them live with him. His wife would have wanted him to, perhaps.

A couple of months later he was delighted when suddenly the dogs reappeared, just as mysteriously as they had vanished. He knew right away when he saw the two dogs lying in the warm sand that there was something different about them. The light in their eyes was somehow dampened. A thick brown scab had formed and fallen off where Lucy had been bitten and new hair had grown, covering the damaged skin. So Herbert couldn't figure out specifically what had happened to them, but he knew there must be some sad reason for their disappearance and re-appearance. He returned to his house, took a big pile of left-over potato mash and gravy from his fridge, warmed it up, and brought it back to the dogs in two little bowls. They ate it slowly, then licked his hands asking for more when they were done. Herbert was happy to have them back.

So, things returned to a certain state of normalcy for both Herbert and the two dogs. Herbert did in fact try and coax them back to his house on several occasions, having decided that he should make them a formal fixture in his life. They would benefit from a decent home, he thought, and he would like them to sleep on the end of his bed at night, like his dogs had when he was a kid. Living with him, they would be safe from coyotes, he thought. But this time it was the dogs that resisted. He sensed they were fearful. They accepted food from him every day and sat with him quietly as he patted them, licking his fingers. But whenever he tried to get them to follow him home, they edged away. The dog with the questioning eyes stared right at him, quizzing him, it seemed.

There was something in Nelson's heart that told him not to become too attached to the man. There was that smell about him that made Nelson wary. But he appreciated the daily lunch the man provided to them. So, a certain loyalty to him grew. Loyalty, when it took root in Nelson, was always a very powerful thing.

The sickness growing in the man was not the same as that which killed his wife. It was not really a disease as such. It was just a certain thickening of the blood that happened to people when they got old. Blood had pumped through Herbert's veins for eighty-five years, a long time. But his heart was pumping more weakly as the years went by.

One day, as he fed lunch to Nelson and Lucy, some of the blood in Herbert's brain coalesced, forming a small clot, and the circulation to the rest of his brain went awry. He was patting the two dogs when the stroke occurred. At first Nelson did not quite know what was occurring. Herbert's body issued panic odors, and he crumpled to the ground. The soft warm sand shielded his fall, and he lay there quietly, his eyes open, staring up at the forest and Montana sky he so loved. Lucy and Nelson barked at him, jumped on him, licked him to try and revive him, but he just lay there, helpless. Nelson knew he was facing an emergency. His brain told him, his nose told him. He needed to get help, human help.

Nelson and Lucy had learned to steer clear of the roads, except when absolutely necessary. Those big obnoxious creatures, cars, were to be avoided. But right now Nelson needed to summon one to help the old man. While Lucy waited next to the old man, trying to revive him, Nelson stood proud and tall in the middle of the road into town and barked loudly, trying to draw attention.

A few cars passed, ignoring the dog, and barely missing him with their vehicles. Normally he would have run if a car had come that close to him. But the adrenaline was pumping through his veins, the smell of the old man dying in the air, and Nelson barked louder and louder.

Finally, a car with some young people slowed down when it saw the small dog barking loudly in the middle of the road, and drew to a halt next to him. Nelson barked even louder at them as they pulled down their windows. He backed away toward the old man, and the young man and woman in the car saw the old man lying there, barely breathing.

But as Nelson backed away he failed to see three motorbikes approaching from the other direction. The bikers were driving at high speed around the curvy bend into town, too fast to see the small dog that was standing in the middle of the road. One of the bikers slammed on his brakes when he saw he was about to hit the small dog. But it was too late. He veered to the side, but the heavy motorbike still slammed into the side of Nelson's body. Nelson was taken by surprise, as he had been so focused on trying to save Herbert. Before he knew what was happening, his body took over, and did what was best for him. Nelson disappeared deep down into the dark hole inside of him, into blackness.

Lucy was bewildered by what was happening. At first she barked loudly. But as ambulances and police began to arrive, she scampered off into the woods. She could not get close to Nelson without risking interaction with all of the humans that had suddenly converged on their small sandy resting place. But she smelled coyotes everywhere in the fir trees on the outskirts of town, and so she carefully made her way back down the alleys around Main Street, sleeping by the laundromat as she and Nelson always did. It was cold without Nelson lying next to her. She kept on waking up expecting to find him there. The next day she searched all around the town for him, whimpering whenever she thought she had smelled him, but discovered it was just an old scent. The sandy outcropping where they spent many of their days was quiet, and Herbert was nowhere to be seen. Again she slept by the laundromat without Nelson. Early the following morning she was certain she could hear the coyote snarling in the distance. It was time to leave this place, the voices in her head told her, in some wordless canine language. When the sun came up, she disappeared from the town, and she never saw Nelson again.

The remnants of her wound bothered her for the rest of her life, aching sometimes at night, and particularly when it was cold. Her strong spirit never entirely recovered from the coyote attack. Sometimes, as she wandered through Montana later in her life, she would whiff the stench of coyote in the air, and it would trigger the memory of her near-death experience.

sometimes terribly mistreated by their human masters. After some five years, he had grown very weary of the city, and wanted to live in an environment more similar to that where he had grown up. He was a frugal man and had saved a sizeable amount over the years. He found a small animal emergency hospital for purchase in Montana, on which he made a down payment.

In the twenty years he had lived there, Dougal had built a successful practice. Many animals passed through the doors of his small hospital, and many were made healthy. His work was rewarding, but also painful. He knew he could not save some of the animals that came in to be treated. But more heartbreaking for Dougal were those animals he knew he could save, but he knew did not have a home to return to when he had cured them. His heart always dropped when some well-meaning person brought a stray in. Where would they go when he was done with them? Yes, there were animal shelters in the town. A few lucky ones might find a home. But more than often not, after a week without any takers, the strays would quietly be taken to the pound and given an injection to put them to sleep.

In every case of a stray dog that passed through his hospital, Dr. Evans was sorely tempted to take the animal home with him. Early on in his career, this had happened several times. But his wife had started complaining. Three dogs, five cats, and four birds were more than enough pets for them to look after. So, he had to find it in his heart to resist when a stray dog was well enough to leave his little establishment and head for the animal shelter. When saying good-bye to a stray, Dougal would pat him or her a little longer than he would his other animal patients, and although he was not a very religious man, he would quietly pray that the animal would find a home.

Part Three

Loss

20

When Nelson came to the emergency animal hospital after the accident, he was seen by a vet who was a humble man. Dougal Evans had grown up on a farm in Illinois, and had inherited his love of animals from his father. They raised cattle, but all around their farmhouse were other species—chickens and goats, sheep and pigs, a rat-catching cat, and dogs, several of them, borde collies. From a young age, Dougal was present at the birth of t various animals' children, and he nursed many a young pup and piglet into adulthood. He fed many of the animals d and sometimes slept in the same bed as them at night. Whe finished high school and it came time to choose his career, was absolutely no question what he wanted to do. He s at a top veterinary college in California, UC Davis, and excellent student.

After he graduated, he worked the overnight sh emergency animal hospital in Los Angeles. He saw th animals' existence, particularly that of dogs both b

Dougal saw beauty in almost every animal he treated. But he was fonder of dogs than other animals, awed by their deep affinity for humans. He felt an equal affection for the quiet dogs, the lovable dogs, the vicious dogs, and the crazy dogs. The core of all of them was unique and beautiful. So, his affection for Nelson was not out of the ordinary for Dougal. Nonetheless, it became very strong in the time Nelson spent in Dougal's facility.

Some vets might have suggested putting Nelson to sleep when he was brought in by the two young people after the accident. Dougal did think seriously of this option when he saw the dog. But the young man and woman told him how Nelson had saved an old man's life. It was only because of Nelson barking in the middle of the road that they had stopped and called 911, and an ambulance had arrived to pick up the old man. They knew the old man was in intensive care now, but he had survived. How could they let this dog die, when he had saved a human life?

Nelson was still unconscious when the doctor began examining him. The young man and woman had wrapped him in an old blanket they had in the trunk of their car. The impact of the motorbike had been strong, but it had in fact only touched him on his rear left leg. Most of his body had been spared. The damage on his leg was extensive though. The bones were shattered and crushed and the muscles torn apart on the small limb. Dougal looked carefully at the leg, examining it as the young man and woman watched him anxiously. His X-ray machine was down, but he could tell right away from looking at the dog what would have to be done. He told them that he thought the dog's life could be saved, but he would have to amputate the leg.

21

Nelson awoke in a rush of pain. He was bewildered. He was bewildered by the strange vet and the young couple standing over him. He was bewildered by this place he had never smelled before, although the whiff of chemicals brought back distant memories of other veterinary hospitals he had been in many years earlier. But his bewilderment did not last long, as the intense pain of his injury assaulted his nervous system. He lunged at the vet, trying to bite him. Dougal was taken by surprise when the dog awoke, but managed to move his arm out of the way of the young dog's mouth. He reached for a syringe, and injected anesthetic into the dog's rump. Nelson fell down into sleep again.

The young man and woman discussed waiting until after Nelson's operation, but decided they must be on their way for their brother's wedding in Wisconsin three days later. They would call after their arrival in Madison to find out that Nelson had survived his operation.

Dougal completed the operation on Nelson with his two assistants in a short period of time. Forty-five minutes after entering the operating room, Nelson was taken out. His leg had been removed, and he was fully cleaned and bandaged up.

The small dog did not notice his missing limb as the effects of the anesthetic slowly wore off, and consciousness first returned to him. He was heavily sedated and did not want to stand up anyway. He sniffed the air. Where was Lucy? Her scent was nowhere around. There were three other dogs and a cat in the room, all in comfortable cages. All were sleeping. He could smell the disinfectant that defined all animal hospitals. Nearby, a nurse was working at a table. Nelson let out a quiet whimper, and the nurse, a young man named Juan, recently arrived from Mexico, looked up. He walked over, opened the cage, and gently patted the little dog. Limply, Nelson licked his hands. The nurse brought over a small plate of water, and offered it to Nelson, who managed a few sips. He left a small bowl of soft dog food in Nelson's cage. Nelson sniffed it, and it didn't smell at all good compared to the food he was used to from the truck stop restaurant. Later that day he was so hungry he forced it down when the nurse fed it to him by hand.

The day was a blur. Nelson slept most of the time. Occasionally a door would open, and he would awaken, hoping that Lucy had just entered the room. He let out a weak bark when it was only the nurse. Perhaps if he barked, Lucy would know where he was. But he did not have enough energy to bark again. He had still not registered his missing leg, and was surprised when a warm puddle of his own urine spread throughout his cage underneath him. The nurse swiftly cleaned it up.

When Nelson woke up the next morning, he whimpered with intense pain. Where his leg had once been, there was a dull but jagged feeling. The day nurse, a young woman who was Juan's cousin, Suzi, rushed over to him and gave him some pain-killers. Nelson was hungry, too, and he wolfed down the food she gave him, and drank all the water.

Nelson grew to like both Juan and Suzi greatly. Dougal Evans worked hard to find real animal lovers to work at his small establishment, and he prided himself on a high level of care for his animal patients. But on the day after his operation, Nelson spent most of his time longing for Lucy. He kept on looking over to the other animal cages, half expecting to see her waiting in one of them. But as he inhaled, he knew she was nowhere close. His life during the past few years had become so intertwined with hers, that not having her there was at first more noticeable to him than the fact he had lost a limb.

As the shock of the accident and the remnants of the anesthetic wore off, and Nelson began to heal, he sensed something was missing. The first time he tried to stand up and shake himself as he always did, he collapsed in a heap. It was an altogether strange feeling, not having one of his four legs. Juan sat watching the little dog trying to rise, and falling down. He brought him outside of the cage and sat playing with him, trying to prop him up so that the dog could stand up.

Nelson kept falling down. When Juan held him up artificially, he looked up at Juan with his questioning eyes, and his tail rose in the air, and he wagged it weakly. Juan could only smile. But then Nelson fell down again.

*   *   *

The loss of Katey, the loss of Thatcher, and the loss of Lucy were all things that Nelson never forgot. Their scents lingered eternally in his mind, wafting over him at unexpected moments, sometimes prompted by other smells and emotions. When he imagined them in his mind, he often felt sadness that the real source of their scents was nowhere to be found. But life would take him out of his scented daydreams, and he would forget his loss for a time. At first, when their loss was fresh, their scents would return to him often. But as the years went by, the accuracy of their imagined scents grew less and less, duller and duller, and after some time there was just the idea of their scent, more than their scent itself, that Nelson remembered.

The loss of his leg was a very different matter. It so constrained all his action that it sucked up every single moment of his daily life, in the first month he spent at the animal hospital of Dougal Evans. At first, the dog was so bewildered by the events of the previous few days that his life did not feel entirely real to him. But as the effects of the anesthetic wore off and the vet tried to bring down the levels of the other medications, the dull throbbing pain where his leg had been hardened into a more intense feeling that he carried with him constantly. The dog was aware of his lost limb every waking hour of his day.

Nelson had looked after himself for many years, and prior to that, in his years with Katey, he had always been an active dog, eager to engage with all around him. Suddenly not being able to walk, not being able to move freely, was an assault on the essence of the small dog's existence. A dark depressed feeling descended on him at first. He became meek, submissive, lying around for much of the day, eating small pieces of food and drinking little, just enough to keep himself alive. It was the thought of Lucy that distracted him and kept him from total depression. Juan was aware how Nelson looked up whenever a door opened nearby, his ears pricking up as if he was waiting for somebody specifically. Juan wondered who Nelson's owners had once been.

Every day for an hour, the vet, assisted by whatever nurse was on duty, took Nelson out of his cage and spent time with him, trying to assist him to walk again, to at least balance on his remaining legs. Dougal was a busy man, and he knew no one would be paying him for his time with this patient. But as long as his small clinic was earning a decent enough living to support him and his family, each animal that entered its walls would be given the best possible treatment, hopefully to emerge healed. The vet knew that in the end it would be the dog that decided whether he would function or not function with the loss of a limb. He had seen weakened animals before, and no matter what he did as a doctor, there was a fierce will to survive in certain animals, and others who at a certain point just lost the will to live. In the first few days after the accident, the vet was not sure which of these animals Nelson was.

As the vet and nurses tried hard to rehabilitate Nelson, his frustration at not being able to walk grew. Despite the darkness that overwhelmed him sometimes, the reason for Nelson's desire to walk was quite simple. If he could walk, he could possibly find Lucy. She needed to be looked after. She needed to be protected from the coyote. It was only if he could walk that he could one day find the Great Love. In his canine heart, the will to move freely again on his three legs hardened into a firm and unshakable resolve.

Soon, something seemed to amplify the flickering light that the vet saw glowing in the little animal's eyes. Time after time, Nelson fell down, sometimes whimpering, when the vet and the nurse tried to hold him up so he could balance. But his beautiful tail occasionally started to wag, and the vet thought perhaps this indicated the dog was starting to feel a certain confidence in standing on three legs. Then Dougal noticed an interesting thing. The dog was starting to hold its tail slightly off to one side, in the opposite direction of the missing leg. The dog was trying to balance himself with his tail.

One beautiful day, about three weeks after the accident, Nelson stood upright by himself. His grand fluffy tail stood slightly to one side and balanced him, his body holding him upright. Dougal and Juan cheered, and Nelson could sense their happiness at what he had just achieved. He just stood there for a moment, feeling this new bodily sensation. There was still a dull pain where his leg had been, but his heart was beating fast.

Often he still fell to the floor, but soon Nelson felt quite comfortable standing in his new characteristic pose. His body was slightly skewed to one side, and his tail hovered slightly off to the other side. It was about another two weeks before he was able to take small and lumbering steps forward. At first they were little more than random hops, but after a few days Nelson healed quite rapidly. Dougal, Juan, and Suzi were all amazed at the dog's progress. It was not long before he was moving about freely on three legs, all the time wagging his tail in his unique way to balance himself. His tail truly became a fourth leg. Whereas his front legs moved quite normally, he sort of hopped along on his remaining rear leg, and his large fluffy tail twitched in the air constantly wagging to keep him balanced. Nelson did not remember the vet many years before who had saved his tail from Emil. Indeed, his walking may have been far more difficult without it.

Nelson's desire to walk normally again grew ever fiercer. Each morning when he awoke he stood up immediately and spent his time in his cage watching the nurse carefully to get a sense of when he would be let out to play, when he would be taken for a walk so he could practice his new walking technique. Juan and Suzi tried to take the dog out for short walks several times a day. He was a unique-looking animal with his commanding tail, three legs, and handsome eyes. His characteristic gait was at once unwieldy and yet possessed of some unique dignity and grace. Sometimes he fell, and often he felt uncomfortable. He drew glances from all around him, some amazed and some jeering. But it was good to smell the grass on the sidewalks again, and whiff the pine trees and mountains in the distance. He searched for Lucy's scent endlessly on the passing breezes.

Juan and Suzi were cousins. They talked between themselves about whether they could find a home for the three-legged dog among their family members in the area. Both of them had thought about taking the dog home themselves, but they realized it was not feasible. Juan lived in a studio apartment with his wife and two young children. Suzi lived with her aging grandmother in a similar situation. It would have been difficult looking after a dog.

They asked some of their family members about taking in the dog, but they all laughed when they heard it had only three legs. Why would one want a three-legged dog? How would it catch burglars? Juan got angry with his one uncle, a perpetual mimic, who imitated a three-legged dog walking as his family laughed raucously. It seemed like only Dougal, Juan, and Suzi saw the beauty in Nelson. They knew their feelings were not only from the experience of having rehabilitated the dog so that it could walk again. There was something in the little dog's heart that elevated them.

Nelson's bodily functions changed as well. He would have to learn to pee like a female dog, crouching down, and he missed marking his territory, leg up, as he had always done. At first peeing was uncomfortable, and he felt the warm liquid edge onto his paws a few times. But soon Nelson didn't think twice about it.

At night, his dreams were still deeply unsettled. He dreamed constantly of Lucy and Katey, imagining them in precarious situations. He needed to save them, from the coyote, from Don, from the men with guns at the garbage heap. Sometimes he was able, and sometimes he was not. In his dream he was unconstrained by his three legs. He was fast and powerful, even against enemies he could not eventually beat. But the anxiety of Lucy and Katey's perpetual danger stayed with him even during the day. It was constantly at the back of his mind, and it made him feel helpless and anxious at times. Sometimes

Dougal watched the dog as he slept, sniffing the air in anxious blasts, and wondered what his story was. He could sense it was a complex one.

After some three months, it became evident that the young dog had healed as much as he was likely to. He was able to move around freely, maybe not as fast as he once had, but the loss of his limb was not disabling. Nelson had become accustomed to his routine in the veterinary hospital—the daily feeding and walks. Though he had not quite come to accept Dougal, Juan, and Suzi as family, because he still thought so much of Katey and Lucy and Thatcher, he was fond of them, and they had certainly become part of his routine.

Dougal did not speak much with Juan and Suzi about the impending decision that faced him. He knew that it was he who would make the choice as to when Nelson was fit to leave his small animal hospital. He avoided the issue for some time, reassuring himself that Nelson was still improving, even when it was evident he had reached a sort of plateau of recovery. Often Juan and Suzi would say something when they believed another animal was well enough to leave the hospital, but he noticed they did not say anything about Nelson. They did not want to have to face him leaving.

Dougal entertained the idea of just keeping the dog there with them at the hospital as a permanent guest. He was somehow reassuring to have around. The wag of his tail, the look in his eyes, his unusual gait—Dougal felt happy when he encountered Nelson every morning when he arrived at work.

But Dougal also knew it was unfair to keep him there forever. The purpose of his hospital was to heal animals, not to be a home for them. Other animals would benefit from the extra space created when Nelson left. There was little time in all of their days, and the minutes spent tending Nelson, taking him for a walk, feeding him, were minutes and energy that could be spent on needier animals.

Late one night, lying in bed wide awake, Dougal realized he would need to discharge the three-legged dog and send him to the animal shelter for adoption.

22

Nelson sensed change was about to come. In the six years of his life, he had become acutely aware of the signs of change. It was about small and at first imperceptible adjustments in the behavior of those around him. Often these were accompanied by changes in their scent. He knew all too well the smells of soft anger and simmering anxiety and quiet sadness, little smells that broke through the surface of a routine existence and signaled that much bigger changes might soon erupt from below the surface. He had smelled the discontent on Don's breath, which led him one day to forget to close the gate to his and Katey's house in Albany. He had smelled the sadness of Thatcher's tears at night, which had led him to a bar brawl that would change his and Nelson's life. He had smelled the slow growing death in Herbert Jones' body, which would lead to the loss of Nelson's leg.

Now, the hair on the small three-legged dog's back would prickle when he smelled the first little ruptures of coming change in the breezes that permeated Dougal's animal hospital.

There was a vaguely anxious air emanating from Dougal, Juan, and Suzi. They were more overtly affectionate than usual toward him, spending long minutes patting him and stroking him and cuddling him. But there was more than affection in their pores. There was anxiety. About what, the dog did not yet know.

One night after work, Juan took Nelson home with him to his small apartment. It was cluttered, but an inviting aroma of food on the stove made Nelson feel at home. He played quietly with Juan's two young children, a boy and girl. Juan had brought a couple of small doggie toys from the hospital. The children enjoyed playing with Nelson and the toys. He was not nearly as agile as he had been before the accident, but he still enjoyed pulling the toys from the hands of the kids and running to catch them as they threw them across the small apartment floor.

Juan and his wife began to argue. She had not shown any affection to Nelson in his time at the apartment, and Nelson sensed somehow he was connected with the argument. He quietly went and sat down in the corner, shivering, his tail between his legs. Quietly, Juan picked him up a little while later and took him back to the hospital, spending half an hour patting him and playing with him before leaving him alone in his cage for the night.

Three days later, Dougal and Juan took Nelson to the animal shelter. Suzi was the nurse on duty that day, but Juan came in anyway, wearing a normal set of clothes, jeans and a T-shirt and a sweater. The three spent some time feeding Nelson a special meal of cut-up chicken and rice, and they played with the dog for an hour or so. Nelson enjoyed the attention and affection, but he was also wise enough to know that this was the way humans liked to say good-bye. As Juan drove Nelson over to the animal shelter in his pickup truck, Nelson lay quietly on Suzi's lap as she scratched his head just like Katey used to. He trusted Juan and Suzi, but he could smell he was about to say good-bye to them.

There were two animal shelters in Kalispell. The facility in the center of town was a no-kill shelter, run by a warm and caring staff. It was the preferred destination for strays who spent time at Dougal's veterinary hospital. But it was also overflowing with animal guests, and underfunded, and Dougal was dismayed to learn there was simply not space for Nelson to be there, despite several calls back and forth. Dougal knew they would have to just hope for the best. The other animal shelter in Kalispell was a small gray building on the outskirts of the town. Juan carried Nelson in, stroking him gently on his forehead. The fat lady at reception recognized Juan, and together they filled out some paperwork. Nelson was sniffing the air, apprehensive. The over-whelming smell was of dog. He could isolate ten, no, fifteen other dogs in the nearby vicinity. His ears confirmed it too, as a mixed cacophony of barks filled the air. Some of them were big dogs, and they scared him. He shivered. But there was another odor in the air as well. It was dark and smothering, and unlike Nelson had ever encountered before. It smelled something like dog, but with nasty undertones and menacing intensity.

Nelson tried to reassure Dougal and Juan as they said good-bye to him. He could sense their leaving was not something they wanted to do. He licked the tears on their faces, as they hugged him and patted him a final time.

The fat lady, Cecilia, was one of two humans Nelson would see a lot of in the next week. Cecilia took care of paperwork and some of the less menial chores in maintaining the animal shelter and pound. Another man, Eddie, cleaned the shelter and pound daily and gave the dogs food. As Nelson smelled Cecilia for the first time, there was little evidence of emotion, either positive or negative. She neither liked nor disliked dogs. Eddie carried some unknown pain with him, and did not connect much with any of the dogs in the pound. In Nelson's time at the pound, there was none of the human connection he had enjoyed at Dougal's animal hospital. The shelter was a gray, sad place.

Nelson shivered with fear as Cecilia entered the main shelter area where six large cages held fourteen dogs. At least half of the dogs were pit bulls. Too often, humans purchased pit bulls, obsessed with their strength, but soon they learned they were difficult to handle and handed them over to the shelter. The dogs growled and barked as Cecilia entered carrying the new arrival. Nelson whimpered meekly. The pit bulls and a German shepherd mix snarled, watching Nelson with fierce eyes. Although Eddie was meant to take each of the animals outside for some time each day, he often shirked his duties. The strong dogs' pent-up energy often emerged as aggression.

Cecilia opened the door to a cage at the back for the smaller dogs. She put Nelson down on the floor, and he fell over, unbalanced for a moment. Dougal and the nurses put Nelson down with care after picking him up, but Cecilia had not handled a three-legged dog before. She did not help him up as he flailed, but locked the gate and disappeared. She did not expect to be seeing the dog for much longer.

The two other dogs in Nelson's cage growled loudly at him. One was a medium-size black-and-white mutt with sad eyes and patchy fur. Nelson smelled several old wounds on his creaky body. The other was a corgi mix, a young dog with a lot of energy, which would be adopted two days later. Nelson instinctually backed away from both of them and retreated into a corner on top of an old ragged blanket. He lay there quietly while the pit bulls simmered down. He sniffed the air, trying to work out what the dark stench in the background was.

There was some light in the room from windows on the high side of the walls. Later that day, Eddie entered and placed bowls of dog food inside each of the cages, and new bowls of water. Nelson was ravenously hungry despite his tasty breakfast, but as he edged toward the food bowl, the two other dogs growled at him, the corgi mix jumping to stand between him and the food, snarling. Only later when the other dogs were sleeping was Nelson able to eat the small amount of remaining kibble. He lapped at the water, and then went to sleep. The room was kept warm at night at least. A few times when Nelson awoke he was surprised to find himself in the strange room, rather than the then-familiar surroundings of the veterinary hospital. But his fear had made him tired, and he slept through most of the night.

Nelson did not remember his time as a puppy at Emil's pet shop. Had he, he might have felt similar feelings at times, as there were commonalities between his experience, caged in the shelter, and as a young boisterous puppy in a small cage in the pet shop. At several points during the day, humans would enter the main pound area, guided by Cecilia or Eddie. They would look through the cages, searching for a pet to take home with them. Some would leave, repulsed by the sad, depressing environment. Some would point out a certain dog. Cecilia or Eddie would get a leash, put it on the dog, and the humans would take the dog outside to get a better sense of them. Nelson never experienced what that was like. Either the humans looked over the three-legged dog entirely, or laughed at him. In the low light of the pound, no one took the time to look at his beautiful eyes or vibrant tail. All they saw was a three-legged dog, and who would want to take one of those home with them?

Nelson watched as the little corgi mix in his cage was taken out several times. Eventually, a little girl and her mother took the dog home with them. Nelson and the old black-and-white mutt were left alone in the cage. The old mutt still growled at Nelson come meal time, but one day Nelson barked at him loudly, and after that they shared the food without issue.

While the corgi mix was still there, no one took out the black-and-white mutt to play. The day after the corgi was gone, a sad middle-aged man pointed at the black-and-white mutt; Cecilia put a leash on him, and he lumbered outside with the man, returning some ten minutes later. Cecilia put him back in the cage, and took off the leash. The man left five minutes later, without taking a dog with him.

Nelson watched all of the comings and goings carefully. He had spent many beautiful times with human beings, and he so wanted to leap up and play with these people, lick the salt on their skins, and nuzzle them. But something held him back, and he just lay there quietly. The wound where his leg had been began to ache again. Eddie took the black-and-white mutt outside once for a walk, but did not even bother to leash up the three-legged dog and take him outside. Although Nelson stood up at times and stretched, he did not get the daily exercise he needed to keep strength in his body.

After Nelson had been in the pound for five days, the black-and-white mutt was leashed up by Eddie, and walked out of the room. He did not return. Nelson was alone in the cage, and he sniffed the air wondering where the black-and-white dog was. Later that night he smelled the dog's body heavy in the air, mixed in with the dark stench he could not identify. He had smelled the black-and-white mutt alive, but Nelson did not at first know he was smelling him dead, burned to ashes in the small animal crematorium on the other side of the building. When Nelson sensed the meaning of the dark smell for the first time, his whole body shook, and he shivered uncontrollably. He spent much of the night awake, terrified. While the pit bulls slept, Nelson stalked the edge of his cage, his body shaking with adrenaline. Ritualistically he would stop and furiously try to dig a hole in the cold stone floor. Soon, he would slide down in a heap, but he would jump up again, and the desire to dig was overwhelming. The pit bulls would wake up occasionally from the noise and stare over at Nelson, but would return to sleep immediately. They knew the cages were secure, and it was impossible to escape from them.

23

|||||||||||||||||||||||||||||||||||||||||||||||||||||||||||||||||||||||||||||||||||||||||||||||||||||||||||||||||||||||||||||||||

Eddie had taken the lives of thousands of dogs in his seventeen years working at the pound. He had started the job when he was twenty-nine years old, recently married, and very much in love with his wife. They had a baby on the way, and he had seen the job at the shelter as a filler, something to pay the bills until something better came along. He had dreams of owning his own business, an auto repair shop or something similar, and he had hoped to be out of the pound in just a couple of years.

His baby arrived, and it was clear from the start he was a sickly child. There was constant crying and constant trips to the hospital. Eddie continued his job at the shelter, and also took a second night job working at a convenience store so that he could pay all the bills. The arrival of the child also took its toll on Eddie's marriage. In the little time they spent alone together, Eddie and his wife were more often than not arguing. Two years after their baby arrived, Eddie arrived home unexpectedly in the middle of the day and found his wife cheating with another man, while their baby screamed. She insisted that it was only the second time that this had happened, and he did believe her. But twice was enough, and Eddie never quite recovered. They tried saving their marriage, but six months later Eddie filed for divorce.

So, he kept going in to his job at the animal shelter, and before he knew it six years, seven years, and eight years had gone by. Gray hair decked his temples, and his hairline was receding. Other job offers did not come his way. At night, he was too tired to even contemplate starting his own business. His life was taken up with finding the funds to bring up his son with the things he needed. Try as he might, an emotional connection with his son eluded him. The boy's mother spent many a dinner telling the child how his father had failed her, and how he was a loser. Young minds are impressionable and the boy believed her.

When he was young and in love and not yet hurt, Eddie felt awful when every Friday he was required to exterminate the dogs in the pound who had spent more than a week there and had not been adopted. When he started his job he had read literature from many animal organizations that explained why this was the most humane thing to do given the resources at the disposal of animal shelters across the United States. Left to their own devices, stray dogs lived terrible lives out on the streets of America, cold and hungry. They spread disease and could often be a threat to human life. It was not feasible to keep the animals at pounds for longer than a week or whatever the period local resources determined would be. Sadly, taking the lives of these animals was the most humane thing to do given the circumstances.

At first Eddie dreaded his Friday task. On Thursday afternoon, he was given a list of the dogs that needed to be put down. Initially, this list came from a fresh-faced girl named Holly, who was a genuine animal lover and hated the task. But she got married and moved to California. Eddie never liked her replacement, Cecilia. But even though she was not a personable woman, Eddie knew Cecilia did an excellent job at administering the pound. Never in his years there with her was there a single mistake made in paperwork. Her Thursday afternoon list was always accurate. He grew to respect her, and she left him to his own devices, alone in his gloom.

Generally there were three or four dogs put down every Friday, sometimes more, sometimes less. At first, Eddie tried to perform the act with some love and dignity for the animals. He would give a final meal to the animal, and pat it, before administering an injection of sodium pentothal. As the years went by, he felt that any love shown for the animal was just pointless. If they were to connect with God in some animal afterlife, they would receive enough love then. So, after walking them from their cage to the crematorium area next door to the main shelter, he would inject them quickly. As each dog passed away, he wrapped the body in a standard-issue gray bag, which came in three sizes. The big dogs were sometimes difficult to lift.

After performing all the exterminations, Eddie would stop for half an hour, eat a sandwich, and drink a cup of instant coffee with two teaspoons of sugar. He had established this routine early on in his tenure at the pound, and at first it had been a reaction to the act of exterminating the animals. At first, he would pray a little while he ate and drank, and run through the rationalizations in his own mind as to why the acts he was performing were quite humane. But as his marriage fell apart, he became inured to the death of the animals around him, and found himself thinking about his wife and child more often than not while he ate his sandwich and drank his coffee. By the time Nelson was resident at the shelter, Eddie felt virtually nothing for the animals that he killed. It was just part of his job.

After his break, he would load the bodies into the small crematorium oven. There was a switch and dial at the back of the oven he would turn on, and within fifteen minutes, the animals' bodies were ash. Eddie would return to the central pound area for an hour or two to clean the animals' cages. When the ash in the ovens was no longer warm, he would return to the crematorium and load up the ash in trash bags. He still hated the smell after seventeen years, and he had taken to wearing nose plugs for this part of the process. He completed it as quickly as he could, dumping the trash bags of ash in the large trash containers at the back of pound. Early in his time at the pound, he had even written a letter to officials suggesting that the ash from the animals be used as fertilizer, but had never received a response. The thousands of animals exterminated at the pound eventually became landfill somewhere in America.

24

||||||||||||||||||||||||||||||||||||||||||||||||||||||||||||||||||||||||||||||||||||||||||||||||||||||||||||||||||||||||||||||||||||||||||||||||||||||

When Cecilia handed her Thursday list to Eddie that week, it was raining outside. Nelson watched them carefully. He did not know that his name was on the list to be exterminated the following day. But the smell of the black-and-white mutt after his cremation was still fresh in Nelson's nose from the week before. The three-legged dog had hardly slept during the past six days, as he knew that some unspeakable horror was happening at this place. The wound from Nelson's accident was hurting again, but the dark stench overwhelmed this and everything else. There were moments when Nelson felt crushed. As the fear descended on him, all seemed hopeless. It seemed inevitable that the dark stench of death would engulf him too. But the night before he was due to die, Nelson finally slept from pure exhaustion, and had a dream. He dreamed he was in a garden. It was a huge garden, filled with magnificent trees and flowers, some from Mrs. Anderson's garden. His Great Love, Katey, floated around above him, her scent pervading everything. The smell of her piano's

wood wafted in and out of a rich perfume, the deep and dis-
tilled essence of the tuberose flowers on the most fragrant of
nights. The scents around Nelson were intense and calming. He
floated, happy and delirious. He awoke in the dank pound, but
still the dream stuck with him. He lay awake, his nose bristling,
his dreamscape still vivid. His whole body felt enlivened.

The next morning Eddie came in to feed the dogs breakfast.
He performed this routine every morning, even on the day of
extermination. Nelson was alert, watching his every move.

Eddie was always careful when opening the doors of the
bigger dogs, as often one of them would try and dart out.
Sometimes one would try and lunge at him. But he knew the
three-legged mutt as a passive dog who would just sit quietly
when Eddie opened the cage to give him food. He was totally
taken by surprise that morning when he opened the cage, and
before he could respond, the three-legged dog rose to his feet
and with an extraordinary nimbleness rushed through the open
gate, under Eddie's legs, and ran for the door to the front office of the pound. Eddie cursed at the three-legged dog, and the
other dogs in the pound started barking loudly.

When Nelson ran out of the cage that day, there was no fear
in his heart, only a burning desire to get out of that terrible
place. The adrenaline pumped through his body, animating his
three legs, as he ran for his life. He ran out of the main shelter
area and into the administrative office in front of the building.
Cecilia's desk faced the door to the back area, and she yelled
for Eddie when she saw the scrappy animal running into the
room. The front door was closed, and Nelson searched for somewhere to escape. Cecilia stood up and grabbed a broom. Eddie
entered from the pound area, breathless. The two faced Nelson,

completely surprised by the sudden and intense feistiness of the little animal. As they moved closer toward him, the three-legged dog growled at them, then barked loudly. Eddie was utterly confused, as he had known this dog to be a completely docile animal. As Nelson snarled at them, they suddenly became scared. There had been diseased animals before, and once one had bitten Cecilia. Cecilia and Eddie backed off. Eddie disappeared into the back area to get a dart gun, which could administer sedatives to the animal. Cecilia watched fearfully as Nelson sat near the front door, growling, observing everything carefully.

At that moment, before Eddie could return, Cecilia's sister arrived, with coffee and doughnuts for her sister. Nelson heard the front door open, and before Cecilia could warn her sister, the three-legged dog bolted through the door, and under her legs.

Eddie and Cecilia did not even try to chase the dog. It was raining hard, and what was the point anyway? They had other work to do. Nelson sprinted for his life into the pelting rain.

25

||||||||||||||||||||||||||||||||||||||||||||||||||||||||||||||||||||||||||||||||||||||||||||||||||||||||||

Nelson ran, shivering, through the waterlogged day. He had no destination in his mind. It was fear that drove him, an instinct to run as far as he could from the place of death in which he had just spent the last week. There were few humans around. As the rain came down, most had sequestered themselves in their warm houses or places of business, comforting themselves with coffee and doughnuts, a few grumbling at the leaks in their roofs. Few saw the three-legged dog as he galloped as fast as he could through the rain, and those that did may as well have seen a wraith.

The adrenaline pumped through the little dog's veins. His body shivered from the cold, but inside he felt no pain. His senses were flooded, his nose whiffing the air uncontrollably. Was the stench of death still there? Was the scent of the garden from his dream the night before real? He continued searching for both smells, all the while running, running, hard into the cold gray day.

Night fell. The dog was in some strange suburb of a Montana

town. The rain had washed most of the scents away. Nelson suddenly felt exhausted. As he slowed to a walk, the biting cold hit him for the first time, and his body ached as if a pile of stones was on his back. He looked into the coming night and whiffed the air for clues. Nearby, a small convenience store was the only source of light. Nelson hung around by the back door.

The owner, of foreign descent, was taking out the trash, and saw the small three-legged animal look up at him with questioning eyes. The man did not object as Nelson slunk into the back room of the store and huddled shivering in a corner, backing away whenever the man came close to him. The man had dogs of his own, and he threw an old blanket next to Nelson, who rubbed himself dry. The man had seen many three-legged dogs during his childhood in a faraway land, and he felt compassion for the animal. There were two hot dogs left inside the warmer in the store, and the man knew they would not be good the following day. So he cut them into small pieces and placed them down in a small paper tray near to the small dog, who wolfed them down as soon as the man backed away. The man was scared he would return the following day to find his back room ruined with piss and shit, but he could not bring himself to toss the little stray out into the night, and so he locked him in the back room when he left for the evening, leaving a small lamp on in one corner.

Even after the food, Nelson was still shivering. But his exhaustion plunged him into a long deep sleep. He was still asleep when the man returned at six the following morning to open his store. Nelson bolted awake when the door opened. His body was still sore all over, but he was no longer cold. The two hot dogs and the blanket had revived him somewhat.

As he awoke that morning, there was something in the dog

that wanted to run from all human beings. This was a new feeling for Nelson. He had always treasured the company of humans. But the events of the previous weeks had left the dog with a deep confusion about humanity. He had saved a man, but lost his leg as a result. Then, the humans had healed him. But after that, they had sent him to die. None of it made sense, especially to a canine brain. Humans could not be trusted. He must get as far away from them as he could. He did not know where to go, or how he would find his way. But part of him wanted to escape human towns and settlements forever, and find another way to live, separate from them.

So, he could have waited that morning and hoped the man at the convenience store would look after him as some other humans had. But Nelson did not wait. As soon as the door opened, and he awoke, his body propelled him out of there, like he had run from the pound the day before. The man almost tripped as the three-legged dog scurried under his legs and disappeared. The man had work to do, and soon thought no more of the animal.

There were still gray clouds in the sky, but the rain had abated, and specks of sun illuminated the trees nearby. A human could see for miles in either direction, as the rain had cleaned the air, and visibility was excellent. So, too, Nelson could smell for many miles around. The air was fresh and bright, and scent pathways were clearly visible to the dog's nose.

Nelson was near the outskirts of a town, and the smell of forests and mountains hovered in the distance. In his years of life, Nelson had always felt at home in human settlements. As the small, beautiful dog sat on the cold earth that morning, and surveyed the world with his powerful nose, something had shifted in him. He felt ambivalent and torn about the scent of humans and their world. Once he had felt safe there, but now those smells felt in many ways threatening to him.

Beyond the world of humans, the ancient rocky, musty scents of the mountains beckoned to him, peaceful. Far outside the town, there were rivers that flowed, with fresh water and salmon. There were endless green forests where the smell of humans did not dominate or control. There was deep mud and rich soils, which Nelson's nose told him had been there for eons. There was grass, rich and beautiful, that beguiled Nelson.

He smelled insects, too, ants and their settlements, and he smelled lizards and snakes that slithered in the wild land before him. His nose on this clear day was his binoculars. Even more complex than the animals whose scents entered his neural pathways were the endless plants and flowers that dotted the landscape beyond.

But nearby there were humans, and their houses, cars, and shops. There was their food, which had always pulled Nelson closer before. As much as he felt pulled toward the scents of the wilderness, the dog had lived his life in human settlements, and the smell of food in trashcans kept him on the outskirts of the human town, on the border between human life and the wilderness, on that verdant line where the wilderness began to encroach. It was a strange feeling for the dog, being pulled in opposite directions. The trauma of his time at the shelter had left a confused animal, unsure of his place in the world, of where he truly felt at home. In the days that passed after he escaped the pound, Nelson lived in an unsettling interregnum, cast from the human world he loved, yet fearful of embracing the wilderness beyond.

Once or twice he smelled the whiff of coyote in the morning breezes. When he did, it also impelled him to run back toward the safety of human settlement. But then fear of the pound kept him from venturing too far back inside the homes and roads and processed woods of the town.

There was one smell in the breezes that he recognized. He had sniffed it many times as it wafted through the long winds into Kalispell. It was a smell that had once scared him, that had seemed alien and threatening. But now it drew him as much as it repelled him. It felt strangely comforting. It was rich and mysterious, and not completely different from his own smell. It was wild and ancient. It was the smell of wolf.

26

The wolf mother was sad. The sadness came in waves, but at times it overcame her. She had not known the two dead wolf cubs very well, as they were gone within three days of her giving birth. So, perhaps the loss was not as intense as it might be when another member of the pack died. When an elder of the pack got that certain odor, that odor that said soon they would lie down and no longer hunt, and kill, and eat with their pack, the wolf mother felt deep sadness. The sadness at losing her pups was different, and perhaps softened by the immediate necessities of caring for the three remaining cubs. They were demanding, sucking at her constantly. Her body was creating huge amounts of milk for her new pups, and she herself was ravenous, craving red bloody meat constantly, her nose prickling at any mention on the breeze of a young animal nearby she could kill easily, and then consume. In general, the wolves liked to hunt at night, but the wolf mother found herself roaming during the day sometimes, her cubs close by, in the hope she might find an additional small meal to sate her ever-brewing appetite.

The wolf father helped her, making the hunt as easy on her as he could. The family of five lay warm in their den at night. As the wolf mother inhaled the smell of the wolf father and her three puppies clogging the air, she felt a deep sense of contentment and happiness. But then the memory of the lost cubs would return, and sadness would descend.

Nearby the den, the four other fully grown members of the wolf pack guarded the area, three females and a male. Sometimes the wolf mother heard their howls at night, and as her babies voraciously sucked on her, she felt glad they were safe and secure, protected by their pack. Sometimes the whiff of bear or coyote would enter her nose, and she would bark in low tones to let the whole pack know they must be on guard. The wolf father would quickly survey the nearby area, sometimes snapping at the other wolves to let them know the safety of his children was at stake, and there were to be no intruders permitted. The other wolves crouched down sometimes when the wolf father was close. He had bitten them all on occasion, and then healed them with his saliva, licking their wounds. He punished and loved, both with great passion. They knew he loved them all, but they had also learned never to question his authority or that of the wolf mother.

The wolf mother and father had ruled their pack for four and a half years, and in that time they had bred exclusively with each other. Their territory was a little closer to the human towns than the wolf mother or father would have preferred, but as they had roamed from the lands of their own parents, this was where they had eventually settled without threat from other wolf clans. The scent of one another was the most powerful force in their small universe. When the wolf mother was in heat, the wolf father could barely restrain his powerful desires, and together they had parented about thirty cubs. Of those, at least half had not survived through cold or the fangs of bears or coyotes, or resisted the microbes of strange diseases that lingered in the wolves' fur. But the other cubs had grown into handsome young gray wolves.

The wolf father and mother loved their children intently, and when they were cubs they were the focus of their lives. But when they were fully grown, there always came that time when they must leave, just as the wolf mother and father had left their own parents' clans. No wolf in their pack should ever grow powerful enough to challenge the authority of their parents. The wolf father always sensed it first, that moment when a cub had grown into a young wolf powerful enough to perhaps challenge him. He would begin snapping at the young wolf then, with his powerful jaws. The wolf mother's bond with her children was powerful, and at first she would ignore the wolf father's behavior. But soon she, too, joined him in hurting their children with violence. It was their way of loving their children, to chase them away, into the wilderness, so they could form families of their own. Yes, the wolf mother felt loss when her children, their light wounds still fresh from their father's bite, slinked off into the wild, never to be seen again. But she would always awake happy the next day. She had been a good mother to raise children that had grown tall and strong, ready to survive by themselves.

The wolf mother always felt safest in the first few weeks of raising her children. Most of their time would be spent in their den, and milk was all they would need. But the wolf pups would grow rapidly, and soon they would need more than just milk. By ancient instinct, they would begin to lick her mouth, and begin sticking their little tongues inside. She knew what this meant. After two to three weeks, she would begin regurgitating many of her meals, in addition to producing milk. Her cubs would feast on the regurgitated food, not unlike half-cooked human food, which would begin training their young stomachs for the fresh raw meat that would eventually be their diet.

Along with this change in their diets, the young wolves opened their eyes, and their rapidly growing bodies started to feel confined in the small underground den the wolf father and mother had dug. The wolf father and mother carefully escorted their children outside every day. There, they played on top of the small hill at the center of the wolves' territory. The wolf mother and father watched carefully as the rambunctious pups scuffled with each other and the other wolves in the pack. Sometimes during the day, the hungry wolf mother would roam from their territory, at a slow pace, her cubs close at hand, hoping to find an additional small morsel.

On a nightly basis, the pack hunted, and during that period she was left alone to look after the three little cubs as they waited an hour, sometimes two, sometimes three, for the wolf father and the rest of the pack to return with food. The cubs were too young to know the potential danger they were in. In times past, a little cub wandering just a few feet beyond the perimeter of his mother's watchful eye had been picked off by a coyote as an easy dinner. So, the wolf mother always felt exposed during these nightly hunts.

She would feel relief when the pack returned, carrying a young deer or large rabbit in their jaws, and place it down in front of her. She and the wolf father would always eat first. The entrails of an animal were the tastiest part. The wolf father and mother relished the kidneys and liver of an animal, finding them with their precise scents, and gorging themselves on the prize meat. The other wolves in the pack would stand back as they ate these at their own pace, before allowing the other wolves to join in feasting on the rest of the kill.

The cubs would scamper around the kill, but they did not yet have the taste for raw red meat. When their mother had finished eating they would crowd around her, licking her lips and sometimes sucking on her to drain the last of her fading milk supply. An hour or so later, when her stomach juices had sufficiently dissolved the raw red meat she had just eaten, her body would lurch, and she would throw up much of her meal. Her cubs would eat every last morsel of it. Just like her pregnancy had made her tired, and producing milk had made her tired, the endless cycle of regurgitation also weakened her. But she loved her cubs, and loved watching them grow every day, and she was determined to keep them safe.

She did not know why her other two cubs had mysteriously died in their first week of life. When they stopped breathing, the wolf father picked them up in his mouth and took them outside the den. Other wolves in the small pack ate them when the wolf mother and father were not around. So, now they were just memories in the mind of the wolf mother. But the sadness endured.

The sadness was with her as she roamed one fine sunny morning. She had awoken hungry and exhausted from looking after her children. She sat gnawing quietly on a remaining bone from a kill the wolf father and other wolves had pulled in two nights before. The night before their hunting effort had not been successful, as was often the case. Despite her failure to eat the night before, her cubs relentlessly buzzed around her, determined to find milk or regurgitated food. Hunting was the last thing she felt like doing, as her body was weak and tired from the constant feeding of her children. But eventually she rose to her feet and slowly walked from the center of the wolves' territory in the hope she might find some food. Her three cubs cavorted around her.

The wolf mother generally avoided humans. She had had few encounters with them over the years. Once, two hunters with a gun had walked unwittingly into the wolves' territory. She had pounced toward them, snarling, and their big gun had been fired. No bullet had hit her as she and the wolf father ran away. She heard another shot go off, and then the scuffling of feet as the hunters themselves ran, fearful of the wolves. The incident had remained with her.

As Nelson himself was kept in the ambit of human settlement by their food, it was in fact the smell of food that lured the wolf mother toward the human town that day. The particular direction of the breezes that morning had sent a scent of meat from a barbecue into the wolf mother's precise nose. It was many miles away, but nonetheless she was so hungry that morning, that she raised herself up and walked slowly but surely toward the source of the smell. Her cubs followed behind her, snapping lovingly at her heels.

As she inched within a mile of the human town, she did not know quite what to make of the animal that lay quietly in the sun, twenty feet away from the road nearby. Had the rest of the pack been there at the time, it is unlikely Nelson would have survived his encounter with the wolf mother and her cubs. In their desire to protect their cubs, the wolf father, or one of the younger wolves would have instantly killed the dog, and probably eaten him. Nelson would have been easily crushed in the powerful jaws of a wild wolf.

When the wolf mother saw Nelson for the first time, killing him was her first instinct. He was not a member of the pack. He had no right to be there. She lurched forward, landing just a few feet in front of him, ready to pounce and eliminate him. She snarled as she stared Nelson in the eyes. Her huge incisors hovered in the air in front of him, as her enormous jaws clapped. She prepared to pounce again and kill the small animal in front of her.

But the cubs had not yet learned to kill, and their instant response to Nelson was to view him as a playmate. Before their mother could pounce on the dog, the cubs rammed him and nuzzled him, as they would their own. The wolf mother held back for a moment, her senses already somewhat dulled from her exhaustion.

The smell of wolf had been thick in the air for the last hour or two. Something about it intrigued Nelson. But when the huge gray wolf mother first stood before him, he felt fear like he had never known. The animal was huge and beautiful, but he knew she was ready to murder him. Nelson recognized the strength and power of the wolf in front of him. He was paralyzed for a moment as she leaped in front of him. But then the cubs nuzzled him, and gave him a moment to react. Terrified of the wolf mother, he rolled over onto his back, exposing his neck to her, whimpering.

As he lay there on the ground before her, the cubs took his

submission as yet another signal to play. They rolled into Nelson, and he took their invitation. The three little wolf cubs and the three-legged dog rolled in the sand, play-biting, pushing, and jumping.

The wolf mother walked up to the dog and smelled him, smelled the fear on his pores, smelled the wound where he had lost his leg. She growled quietly. Like Nelson and others of his species, the wolf was a deeply emotional animal, and the sadness of losing her pups felt present once again. She sniffed him quietly, and although he was not wolf, he was not unlike wolf, and she retreated. Her attention was also taken by a half-eaten chicken carcass that Nelson had dragged from a trashcan the day before. The wolf mother grabbed it and retreated under a bush, consuming the chicken. She closed her eyes and took a nap, happy to rest from her pups' endless demands for a few minutes.

The three pups continued their intense play with Nelson. He was about the same size as them, and he had played just like them for seven years with human beings and other dogs. He was an expert at playing, like wolf cubs loved to do. As they nuzzled each other, and rough and tumbled together, their smell rubbed all over Nelson's skin.

Twenty minutes later the wolf mother rose and began walking the miles back to the center of her territory. The little cubs followed her. Nelson felt an affinity for the creatures, and without thinking much about it, he followed too. The cubs tumbled along with him, their new playmate.

When they returned to the den an hour later, the pack noted the arrival of the three-legged dog, but already it smelled like one of them, one of the cubs. One of the younger pack members, a large wolf with an unusual diagonal white stripe along its side, snarled at Nelson, but the wolf mother quickly jumped forward and nipped the white-striped wolf on his thigh. He retreated, whimpering. As the wolf mother lay down, and her cubs crowded around her, she licked Nelson's stomach just like she licked her own offspring. The message to the whole pack was clear. Nelson was one of the cubs. Do not harm him.

The Wolf Mother and the Three-legged Dog

"The Wolf Mother and the Three-legged Dog" brings to life the curious interaction of Nelson and the wolf pack. Scan here to listen, or go to www.youtube.com/watch?v=4F4FEqtTYls.

27

||||||||||||||||||||||||||||||||||||||||||||||||||||||||||||||||||||||||||||||||||||||||||||||||||||||||||||||||||||||||||||||||||||||||||||||||||

At first Nelson ate little of the regurgitated raw meat the wolf mother gave to him and her cubs. It felt natural to lick the magnificent creature around her mouth as her cubs did, to stick his tongue inside her huge jaw. He had not associated this instinct with food before, although he had licked all his human companions, and Lucy, in the same way. When the wolf mother first heaved and a mush of warm, saliva-filled chunks of half-chewed meat came out of her throat, Nelson was taken by surprise. He shook himself off, as the three cubs ate furiously. He tasted a little, and it was not to his liking at first.

But as the hours wore on and his hunger grew, he was soon eating the primeval mixture voraciously. It was a little like half-cooked human food. It was food designed to nourish a young body, filled with natural juices that might appear repulsive to a human, but in fact would build bones, fur, eyes, and nose in a young wolf. Nelson's species shared much in common with these wolves. They had once been one and the same, many mil-

lennia earlier. So, the food from the wolf mother soon tasted
and smelled delicious to him. It strengthened him and healed
his wounds. His fur developed a glow about it. His tail shone
in the morning sun. His eyes sparkled. His nose imbibed all
the exquisite detail of the hills and forests and wolf territory
around him.

Nelson was in fact older than both the wolf mother and father. His seven years was a ripe old age for a wolf in the wild. But
he would never be more than a cub to the wolf pack. To play was
a vital part of Nelson's nature, and he felt a natural affinity with
the cubs. But the adult wolves had long abandoned play. Their
life was about survival, protecting their pack, and finding food
to make it through each day.

Nelson never dared threaten one of the larger wolves.
Whenever there was the slightest hint of aggression from one
of the adults, a snarl, a look, a questioning sniff, Nelson would
retreat, buckling his body, or lying on his back, whimpering,
submissive. Often, the young white-striped male would stare
at Nelson intently, and clap his jaws in an attempt to assert
his station in the hierarchy of the pack. But the three-legged
dog's smell was now that of the pack, and so the lesser wolf
knew to accept him or risk the wrath of the wolf mother and
father. On his first night with the pack, Nelson followed the
other cubs into the den where they lay each night with the
wolf mother and father. The wolf mother and father did not
stop him. They lay close. The wolf mother licked his stomach.
Edging her way down, she spent a long time licking the scar
where his fourth leg had once been, making sure her saliva
entered his skin.

Nelson was warm for the first time in months, as the heat

of the wolf family infused his bones. He lay awake for some time as the wolves around him slept. Outside he could hear the murmurings of night, the occasional scuffling of the other adult wolves, the rustle of a night breeze, the distant cries of animals proclaiming their territory. But the gentle heaving of the wolf mother and father as they slept reassured him they were perfectly safe.

Nelson mapped his memories largely through smells, and there was no linear path, no rational explanations, no real analysis of the complex links between Katey and her piano and Thatcher and Lucy and the stench of death in the pound. He did not think about what had impelled him here, to live with the wolves. But he felt secure on that night and knew he would not roam the following day. He would live here for some time. The dog closed his eyes and drifted off into richly scented dreams. The wolf mother and father dominated his dreams that night, protecting him, nurturing him, loving him as one of their own.

Within just a few days, Nelson felt at home in the wolf clan. The wolves did not live in the secure grounds of a house like the Great Love had lived. Cold breezes sometimes permeated the den at night. Nelson smelled the constant bristles on the back of the wolf mother and father as they surveyed the wilderness air for potential threats to their cubs. But at the same time, he knew the pack would die to defend him and the other cubs. To the cubs Nelson was one of them, perhaps a weaker version of themselves, one who fell to the ground easier than they did, and tired sooner. But he played just as they did. He put their little limbs in his jaws and bit them gently. He pulled at their tails. He jumped on them. They responded with the same playfulness. It was in their nature as it was in his nature. Nelson did not know that their endless play, guided by the wolf mother, was in fact training for the day they would kill other animals.

Often in the early evening, the wolf father and the other adult wolves would head off into the approaching night. The wolf mother would growl quietly at her cubs, and they soon learned to play a little closer to her, as she watched them with a careful eye. One night, Nelson ran whimpering to her side when the strong stench of a coyote erupted in his nostrils. The wolf mother had smelled it, too. She surveyed the undergrowth with her cold steel eyes. A loud howl erupted from her insides and pierced the night. The young cubs imitated her. But this did not stop the nearby coyote. It was hungry. A wolf cub would be a delicious dinner. Nelson shivered behind the huge gray hulk of the wolf mother as the ruffled and dirty coyote emerged from the undergrowth nearby. He was a cousin of the one that had tried to kill Lucy.

The two wild canines stared at one another. The wolf mother did not wait to see the coyote's approach. She leaped into the air and landed eight feet closer to the hungry coyote. Nelson was scared when he saw this angry, wild creature that lived inside the wolf mother for the first time. She snarled viciously, and her huge jaws clapped in the air. The coyote, undaunted, snarled back at her and moved forward a step. The wolf mother did not hesitate, leaping into the air and making contact with the coyote's neck. Whimpering, the coyote disappeared off into the bush. The wolf mother howled again, and the cubs joined her. Minutes later the wolf father and the other adults returned. Together, the wild clan howled into the night. Like singers in some primeval choir, the different wolves took different pitches as they howled, forming ancient and passionate chords that reverberated into the wilderness. Nelson was not even aware of it when he spontaneously joined the wolves' chorus, but his ancient kinship to these creatures compelled him to do so. The message was clear to the coyote as he scampered away from the wolves, their howling erupting in his ears. No animal entered the territory of the wolf with aggressive intention and was given a polite response.

After that incident, Nelson was always a little wary when the other wolves went off to hunt. He knew the stakes the wolf mother understood in her canine brain. Her children could be eaten and gone forever in the blink of an eye. The cubs did not yet understand the meaning of fear and continued to play endlessly, carefree. Nelson played along with them, but he had smelled enough of the horrors of the world to be a little scared at all times. He felt grateful to the wolf mother for her protection.

The wolf father and other adults would return home about half the nights with food. Sometimes there was just a mountain rabbit or small beaver in their jaws. Sometimes all the wolves dragged a goat or a young or sickly elk or deer. The wolf father and mother would feast first on the entrails. As the weeks went by, the wolf father and mother began encouraging the cubs to try the raw meat before the other adults were allowed to join in the feast. The cubs treated the dead animals that were their food with the same playfulness as each other. They would tug at the carcass and bloody meat as if they were just playthings. After a time the wolf mother and father would growl, and the other wolves would take over from the cubs. But slowly but surely, the cubs' stomachs adjusted, and they began to savor the smell of bloody red meat over the regurgitated meals their mother began to give them less and less often.

Nelson picked at the red meat on the carcasses the wolves brought to their den, but he never really developed a taste for it. At seven years, he was a mature dog, perhaps even starting to get a little old. For seven years he had eaten mainly cooked human food, and his stomach had adjusted to it. He threw up the first day after eating raw meat. The cubs ate his vomit. He ate little pieces of raw meat after that, but preferred the warm regurgitations of the wolf mother.

Nelson soon got used to the smell of blood. It was everywhere. It was on the carcasses the wolves dragged into their dwelling place. It was on the jaws and teeth of the adult wolves. Often it stained their fur. Nelson could whiff the excitement on the wolves when fresh blood dominated the air around them. He did not quite understand the rapture it created for them, but he accepted it. Blood's scent was full of life to him. The blood of every creature was different and vital. It was a smell he had not encountered much in his life in human settlements.

Sometimes Nelson could sense the anger in the air as the other adult wolves watched as the cubs were given eating preference over them. The white-striped adult wolf lunged at Nelson one day as he stepped forward to eat, ahead of the adults. The wolf was swiftly met by a snap from the jaws of the wolf father. The hierarchy in the pack was strict and ordered. They were a strongly functioning unit, and any wolf that dared break the hierarchy would be dealt with. The wolf mother and father were huge, magnificent animals to the small dog, and he always deferred to them. He knew he would enjoy the protection they offered to their cubs only while he acted like a cub. He observed his place in the pack, and he felt secure as a result.

But when the wolf mother and father were not close by Nelson, more often than not he caught the steely glare of the white-striped wolf staring at him, his nose eagerly sniffing. Nelson would crinkle his back, or sometimes lay down with a quiet whimper to let the wolf know he, too, was Nelson's master.

28

As the weeks and months passed, the young cubs grew rapidly. Nelson did not want them to grow. He wanted them to remain his size forever, to be his playmates forever, so that he could stay here with them in what felt safe to him. Sometimes at night, he still awoke with nightmares of the dark stench of the pound. He awoke to the whimpering of the old black-and-white dog that had died in the furnaces of that awful place. He often yearned for the Great Love, and for Lucy, but as the negative odors and images of the shelter rattled round his dreams at night, he remained determined to stay as far from human life as possible. His survival seemed to be at stake.

As the cubs grew, their constant play began to tire Nelson. They were becoming too strong for him. Their constant biting, once harmless, began to pierce his skin. The wolf mother licked the blood off his wounds, and they seemed to heal rapidly, but a certain sense of helplessness set in. He could not stop the cubs' growth. Soon they were double his size.

*   *   *

Nelson had become accustomed to the daily routine in the pack. He knew that every evening, the adults would go for a few hours and often return with food, and the wolf mother would guard him and her cubs. But he sensed a growing restlessness in the wolf mother as she watched them each evening. One night she disappeared with the rest of the adults. Nelson and the cubs were left alone. The young cubs whimpered, and hovered anxiously around their den. Nelson was much older than the cubs, and he felt an urge to protect them even though he was much smaller than they were. He stood guard, until the wolf mother returned with the other adults shortly afterward. She dragged a small spotted deer into the middle of their enclave. Its blood had spattered on her coat. Nelson could still smell the adrenaline pulsing through the wolf mother's veins, the excitement. She feasted on the young animal's entrails with a particular viciousness.

The following few nights she did not go out with the adults, but exhibited a mild aggressiveness toward her cubs. A few nights later when the adults were ready to go out hunting, she growled aggressively at the cubs. As the other adults wandered off, she followed them slowly, growling quietly at her cubs as she left. The little cubs were unsure what to make of it at first. One, the strongest, followed her off into the night. The other two scampered into the den, and Nelson followed them. They lay together writhing playfully, but Nelson did not know what to make of the changes in their daily routine.

A few hours later Nelson and the two remaining cubs heard howling outside, and they scampered outside, where the adults were tearing at a small elk doe. The cub that had ventured out with the pack stood with the adults tearing at the raw bloody meat in front of them. Nelson and the other cubs moved to the kill as they always did, accustomed to the protection of the wolf mother and father as they ate. But this time, the wolf mother snarled at them as they moved forward to eat. Quickly, the white-striped wolf leaped forward and snarled at Nelson. The wolf mother did not defend the dog. Nelson retreated, whimpering, as the white-striped wolf lunged into the kill, gorging himself. The other two cubs tried to eat again, but again were warned by their mother not to. The other wolves tore at the meat eating their full. Finally, when they retreated from the carcass, bloated, and with bloodstained teeth, the remains of the carcass were left to Nelson and the other cubs. They ate quietly. The white-striped wolf stood up for a moment and edged toward Nelson as he ate. The wolf mother lay nearby watching them, and a quiet growl erupted in her throat. The white-striped wolf backed off and lay down again.

Something had changed in the pack. As the next few days passed, the message of the changes became clear to Nelson. If you wanted to eat, then you participated in the hunting. One of the other cubs now joined the pack as they went out to hunt. Only the smallest cub and Nelson remained behind. They shivered in the cold night, waiting for their pack to return.

Nelson and the small cub howled together, and Nelson caught the whiff of a coyote in the wind. Two days later, when the pack went out to hunt again, Nelson and the remaining cub initially remained behind. But as the pack slinked off into the wilderness, the white-striped wolf waited with the three-legged dog and the wolf cub. He bared his fangs at Nelson, and for a moment it seemed like he might pounce. But the wolf mother was still close by, and she swiftly returned, barking loudly at the white-striped wolf, to defend Nelson and her cub. But as she moved off again to join the hunt, there was no alternative for Nelson and the cub but to join her and the pack.

29

||||||||||||||||||||||||||||||||||||||||||||||||||||||||||||||||||||||||||||||||||||||||||||||||||||||||||||||||||||||||||||||||||

The pack of gray wolves moved like a shadow in the night. Occasionally their cold eyes caught a glint of moonlight, and the grass rustled as they passed. But only a trained eye would have seen them.

The young cubs moved behind the pack. The playful, lovable animals Nelson played with were gone. They were quiet and serious, already aware of what was to come. When the weakest cub whimpered, the wolf mother quickly turned and growled quietly, but with a deadly seriousness. None of the cubs uttered a sound after that. The strongest cub stayed as close to the adults as he could. Already, hunting was becoming second nature to him. In just a few months he would abandon play completely when he became an adult wolf. Play had been just a preparation for hunting. The real thing would satisfy his deeper nature.

For some time the pack drifted over miles of the surrounding countryside. Nelson struggled to keep up, his three little legs working hard. Should he separate from the pack, he would be an easy target for the white-striped wolf. Nelson had become accustomed to moving little outside the area around the wolves' den. He was a curious creature, but this was not the way he liked to explore. He was rushing to keep up with the other animals, and there was something ominous in the wind. He knew the pack as a bonded, loving, and protective family, but tonight their pores emitted something quite different.

Suddenly the pack slowed, and they crouched low in the bushes. Nelson's senses were well developed, and he quickly smelled the wilderness hare nearby. He looked through the undergrowth and could see the animal eating grass. The wolf father was poised to pounce when the small animal must have caught a whiff of wolf in the night air. The hare bolted. For a moment the wolf father looked like he might follow, but then he just quietly growled and walked slowly on. The pack followed. There was no sense of disappointment. The hare would not have been enough to feed all of them anyway.

Twenty minutes later Nelson was the first to whiff the family of deer on the nocturnal breezes. He growled quietly, a reflex meant to protect the pack. But it was not the pack that needed protecting. When Nelson growled, the rest of the pack quickly turned and stared at him. The white-striped wolf growled, as if to warn Nelson not to disturb their hunting ritual. But the wolf father sniffed the same animals on the breeze that Nelson had smelled and quickly jumped in the direction of the animals. The pack slinked slowly forward behind him.

The two adult deer grazed quietly in the moonlight. Their dappled coats shone in the silvery light. If a pack of wolves hadn't been nearby, it would have been a pretty picture. The two adults were both female. The male with whom one had mated some seven months earlier was grazing a hundred feet away. He was a magnificent tall creature, with dramatic antlers and persistent eyes.

But it was not the two adult deer that intrigued the wolf father. It was the young baby deer that grazed quietly in their shadow. The doe was just a few months old. She had only recently begun to eat grass, before that surviving on her mother's milk.

The wolf father moved quickly in leading the pack in the hunt. A moment's delay, and an opportunity could easily be lost. The two deer had smelled wolf and coyote many times in their years in the wilderness. Many times before they had avoided the powerful jaws of the wild dogs. When the powerful odor of wolf hit the deer's nose, their very first instinct was to run, run for their lives. One of the deer disappeared quickly into the undergrowth. But it was the instinct of the mother deer to protect her young doe. She quickly nudged the doe forward, trying to provoke her to run in the direction away from the wolves.

But the doe was not yet aware of the dangers of the world, and she stubbornly refused to move. By then it was too late. The wolves leaped forward. Three of them, aided by the strongest cub, snapped at the legs of the adult deer, the white-striped wolf biting into her skin, so that blood spurted out. The mother deer howled in pain. The wolf mother and father pounced on the young deer, pulling her to the ground. She struggled, but was ill equipped to deal with the powerful jaws and heavy bodies of the two huge wolves.

The two other cubs ran forward instinctually, and Nelson followed. But he held back a few feet away from the kill that was beginning. He knew instinctually the doe was a young animal. To him a young animal was something to be played with, to be frivolous with. He watched, bewildered, as the wolf mother bit into the throat of the young doe. It yelped with excruciating pain. The doe's mother watched for a moment, her animal heart breaking, but she disappeared off into the night, protective of her own life now. She knew her baby had but moments to live. A few hundred feet away, the father of the doe heard its crying, but knew what had happened. He would not try and stop the pack of wolves.

As the mother deer ran into the night, the remaining adult wolves piled around the young doe, as the wolf mother sucked the fresh blood from its veins. The other adults snapped at its heels as the life drained from the young animal, and she fell limp to the ground.

The whole pack was there. There was no need to drag the animal back to their den, now that the mother and cubs were not there. They would eat the animal fresh. The wolf father and mother quickly ravaged their way to its entrails and gorged themselves. The adult wolves and the young cubs followed, tearing at the fresh, young meat. The smell of fresh blood painted the air.

Nelson just watched, bewildered. He could sense that as the wolves ate their kill something deep in their nature was being expressed. But it was not his nature. He had felt a deep kinship to these animals, particularly their cubs, in his time living with them at the den. He had felt like he was one of them. But in the moments of the kill the dog felt something different. He felt alien and alone. It was simply not in his nature to kill like a wolf did. It was not his purpose. Had he encountered the young doe alone, she might have been his playmate.

Dogs had evolved from wolves. Millennia before, humans had picked up little wolf cubs left alone in the wild after their parents had been killed by bears or other predators. They had fed them around their campfires, and the cubs, with their instinctual sense of hierarchy, had made their place in human tribes. They had become an integral part of human society. Humans were good at domesticating animals, and over time, the particular characteristics of individual wolves that were suitable to the humans had been enhanced. As wolves evolved into dogs through their special interaction with humans, they had kept much of their wolf past inside them. But they were fed on human scraps, on human food. There was no longer any need for them to hunt. So, they had lost the powerful desire to kill that defined wolves. Dogs never truly progressed beyond the playfulness of wolf cubs into real hunting. They would remain permanently adolescent wolves, joyful and loving and defined by their play.

So, Nelson stood bewildered before the wolves that night as they killed and ate the baby deer. In that moment, as he stood before them, for the first time he felt an instinct to leave these creatures. The cubs he loved were becoming something other now, something he himself could never become. As the white-striped wolf stared back at Nelson, his eyes steel daggers in the night, his jaws stained with fresh blood, the dog felt a deep chill ripple through his entrails.

30

When any creature senses that change is in the air, their first response is always to deny its existence, to continue living in the same way as they have before. Nelson had lived through so many changes in his short life. But his body was beginning to tire of them. He had learned to live nimbly with his three remaining legs, but still the accident had taken years from his life. In his first months with the wolves, the dog had felt settled and secure. But the night they returned from the hunt for the first time, the wolf mother and father pushed the young cubs and Nelson out of the den for the first time. Nelson did not resist, but he felt sad. He did not know that this was the first in a series of rejections for the cubs that would eventually lead to the wolf mother and father chasing their children from the pack when they began to threaten their dominance. The cubs would eventually begin packs of their own, if they survived out in the wilderness. This was the way of the wolf. In the complex life of dogs and their human masters, leaving each other was

never part of the ordained plan. A dog never lost its desire to remain with its human master. When the Great Love was sealed,
it never died.

Nelson could not sleep much that night, even though the
warmth of the cubs was reassuring to him. He was smaller than
them now by quite an amount. The three surrounded him like
a warm blanket. He cried a little in the middle of the night,
caught in some strange dream, and the other cubs licked him
quietly, nuzzling him. But he did not fall asleep again. The other
adults were close by.

The wolf mother had raised Nelson as one of her own for
those few months. She did not know why he looked different
and at first smelled a little different from her own cubs. But she
was not an animal who questioned these things. Something in
her brain had registered him as a cub the day they had met, and
her maternal instincts had taken over. She had raised him just
like the others, fed him, kept him warm at night, and protected
him from predators.

But now more and more, she was sensing the difference in
him from her other cubs. They were evolving from soft and playful creatures into strong adult wolves. They were learning to hunt
and learning to kill. She was sensing the day would soon come
when they needed to be exiled from the home of her and the
wolf father. But she did not know what to make of Nelson. He
was not changing as she was used to her cubs changing. There
was a part of the wolf mother that loved Nelson as she loved her
own cubs. But she was not a loving creature in the same way
that a dog was, or that humans could be. The pack, the safety of
the pack, and the dominance of her and the wolf father over the
pack; these were the things that were her overriding concerns.

Nelson could sense the growing antipathy of the wolf mother and father. He did not move close to them as he had before, spending his time playing with the cubs as best he could. As the cubs grew stronger and stronger it became more and more difficult to play with them as he had before. More often than not, he would lie on his back and whimper, signifying his submission to them. Their play had become more aggressive since they had been joining the hunt, as it was now a metaphor for hunting and killing. He had seen them bite each other so that blood flowed. By continually submitting, he avoided wounds.

The night after Nelson went on the hunt with the wolves, the wolves grouped together again to head off into the night. Nelson was scared to stay alone at the den, but he did not want to go out hunting with the wolves that night. He sat down and did not move. The wolf mother looked back at him as they crept off into the cold evening and growled. The desire to kill the three-legged dog entered her brain. As the pack moved off into the night, she walked slowly back toward Nelson, and stared at him with her intense eyes. She snarled. He was upsetting the order of the pack. He was disrupting the nature of things. The three-legged dog rolled over onto his back, submitting, hoping the wolf mother would leave him alone. But she stalked ever closer to him, her mouth abruptly opening, revealing her sharp teeth. The hair on Nelson's back rose. The wolf mother's jaws tensed as she prepared to pounce.

In the distance, the wolf father barked loudly. He wanted the wolf mother with him on the hunt. In the pack, only the wolf father's power was greater than her own, and so the wolf mother slowly turned and ran off into the night. Nelson turned over, his entire body shaking with terror.

Had Nelson stayed that night, he would have been killed by the wolves. He never knew that. After the wolves had left on the hunt, he just sat there for a while, whiffing the evening breeze. He was cold, and so he crept inside the wolves' den for a while, trying to keep himself warm. It was cold there, too, without the other animals' body heat to warm him up. So, he sniffed around the area outside the den. He dug up a bone from a deer that one of the wolves had buried, and chewed on it for a while, sucking out the marrow. It satisfied his hunger for a couple of hours.

Dogs do not think like humans, and so Nelson never consciously made a decision to leave the wolves' den. But the fear in his heart after the wolf mother almost killed him did not subside. Everywhere around him there was also the intense scent of the white-striped wolf that was stalking him. The fear kept on growing even though Nelson was all alone at that moment. He walked slowly away from the wolves' den at first, in the opposite direction to the path the wolves had taken that night. But after just a few minutes, he was running for his life.

When the wolves returned that night, Nelson was gone. They still smelled him around their den. The wolf mother briefly sniffed his path away from the den, and she considered following him. But she was bloated from the meal they had just enjoyed, and had drunk gallons of water from the river, and she wanted to sleep. Already in her mind, Nelson was no longer one of them. So, she went to the den and slept. She dreamed of blood.

The white-striped wolf too noticed the dog had gone, and a

belligerent feeling of triumph leaped up inside of him. He had proved his dominance over the smaller animal. The cubs felt a certain sadness at the loss of their brother. The weakest of the three felt the loss most keenly. She was now the one who would feast last, and be forced into constant submission by the rest of the pack. But this was a blessing in disguise for her. Her two stronger siblings were chased from the pack two months later by their father and mother. The strongest of the cubs had growled one night at his mother as she began to feed before him. The next day he was bitten by his father, and hobbled away into the wilderness. The middle cub was also chased away a few days later. These cubs did not withstand the ravages of the wild and died some months later, without finding another pack to lead. But the weakest cub lived out her long nine-year life with the pack even when her mother and father eventually grew old and were replaced by one of the other adults.

The wolf mother and wolf father were omnipotent that night, as they lay in their den. But a few years later, a cold winter would weaken them, and they would sneak away from the pack, to lie under a tall tree and die.

31

Nelson was running. He had first walked slowly away from the wolf den, with no particular purpose. But before he knew it, he was far away from his home for the previous four months, and he whiffed bear and coyote in the wind. He ran without purpose into the night, stumbling under bushes and trees, sometimes near the dens of creatures great and small.

An outside observer would have seen a wretched creature. He was a scrawny three-legged dog, with long matted air, dirty beyond measure, and with a repugnant odor. No one in the whole wide world would have known had Nelson lain down under a tree that night and died. The leaves of autumn would have blown over him and small animals and worms would have slowly removed him from the world. There would have been no hearts broken. Katey and Thatcher and Lucy and all the others who had been touched by Nelson in his short life would never have known that this was the night he left the sweet earth forever.

Nelson was confused and cold and hungry. He did not know

where to go. The smell of wolves was unsafe for him, but so was the smell of human settlement. It was his curious nature that had led him to roam many years earlier, and by now his nose had surveyed and cataloged vast swathes of the world. It was a deep reservoir of knowledge, scents and odors and emotions and hopes and fears all intertwined. It was the strongest part of his consciousness, his crumbling map in a harsh world. But he trusted it somehow, and he wanted in some deep pocket of his canine brain to live, to survive. Lying down to die that night, under an icy moon, was never something he slowed to consider. He would follow his nose to a better place.

32

Rick Doyle was not a typical dogcatcher. He had loved history since he was eight years old and grew fascinated with the American Civil War. His passion for the subject had grown year by year, inspired by great teachers and the pile of history books his grandfather had left to him. There was no debate as to what his major would be in college. But when he finished the degree, the world hit him like a ton of bricks falling. His student loan bills were mounting up, and his passion for history was not enough to pay his rent. He saw an ad placed by Animal Services in the town of Chico, California, which was around four hundred miles from Los Angeles, where he had completed his undergraduate degree. Chico was the "City of Roses," a pleasant historical town with beautiful parks and a university at its heart.

Rick had always liked dogs, and cats, too, for that matter. He did not love them with the same passion he had for history. But he was fond of them, enough that the job looked vaguely appealing until he could find the wherewithal to complete a master's degree, and maybe get a teaching position. The hours were good, too, and he would be pretty much his own boss, not forced into a stifling office environment of the sort he needed to avoid at all costs. There would be plenty of time to think about history while he drove around apprehending strays. Within a few months, that time in the animal services truck thinking about his passion led to the beginnings of a book, and soon writing that book became his favored nighttime activity. He stopped thinking about further studies as his book about the lives of unknown soldiers during the Civil War would take at least a few years to finish.

Rick was a highly intelligent man, and thought about the consequences of his new job as a dogcatcher. At first he wondered if the animals he caught would be better off left running wild in the streets, rather than picked up and possibly destroyed, even though he knew stray animals were health hazards to the human community. But then, shortly after he began his job, he spent a day at the animal shelter and saw how some of the animals he picked up, when cleaned up, found their way into human hearts and homes. In the moments when a human family picked up a dog from the shelter, there was incipient love in the eyes of both the family and the dog in question. Chico was a small town, and sometimes he would see some of these families playing or walking around the town with their new pet some weeks later.

Cats, too, often found happy homes with humans, although he remained divided as to whether picking up feral cats was best for them. Feral cats had escaped from human homes, or had never lived in them, and had returned to the wild in every sense, fending for themselves as wild cats did, hunting and killing for food. They ate small rodents and birds, and took pleasure in killing them. They were not dependent on human food sources. More often than not, Rick found stray dogs congregating around rubbish heaps, or trash cans in back alleys searching for human food. They could not survive without it, and were lousy hunters themselves. But cats were different.

Rick picked up a variety of stray dogs, big and small. Some had roamed for just days, some for weeks, and a few for years. Sometimes he looked into a stray dog's eyes and wished the dog could tell him its story, tell him where it had traveled, what it had seen, how it had survived. Some of the dogs he had to bring in were aggressive, but most were passive, many scared more than anything. Sometimes stray dogs moved together in packs. It was rare Rick could pick up more than one dog at once. If he caught one, the others in a pack of strays would quickly vanish into the surrounding area. Sometimes he would see them again a few days afterward.

Rick could fit about six animals in his small truck, which was equipped with six built-in kennels in the back. Rick would patrol for three-hour stretches looking for strays and would generally return to the animal shelter with his truck full by the end of that stretch. Often he would help cleaning and inoculating the animals, which was the first thing to occur on their arrival at the animal shelter. This was not strictly part of his job description, but he had become friendly with Angie, the woman who took care of this every day, and she let him help her. It was always satisfying to see a dirty dog that had been on the streets for months transpose into something closer to a household pet. Often the dogs' moods would visibly improve just from interacting with human beings again. They would play with the water and gulp down their first meal at the shelter. Rick would generally leave happy, his heart elated. That night he would happily work on his history book for three or four hours. He could smell the dog on his clothes, and often he would pick up the slight repugnance of women he brought home to the smell of dog everywhere in his apartment. The smell never bothered him.

Rick knew that a small percentage of the dogs he brought into the shelter never found a human family to take them home. He had not visited the pound, where unwanted animals were exterminated. This was in a separate facility from the animal shelter, in the town of Chico. Angie had told him it was very depressing, and he could not face going to see it. Sometimes late at night he questioned whether by bringing in stray animals, he was a murderer, because some of the dogs he brought in would die in the pound. He knew this was a ridiculous thought, as many of the animals he brought in found wonderful homes with human beings. But what of those few that did not? Would they be better roaming the streets of human towns, alive at least, even if they didn't have a human family?

Sometimes, when he saw a particularly sad-looking dog, an old dog, a sick dog, an injured dog, or a very aggressive or sub-missive dog, out on the streets, he would consider just leaving it there. He knew the chances of the dog being adopted were minimal. A few times he actually let a dog go because he knew it had such a slim chance of being adopted. When he did this, it plagued him, and he eventually confessed to Angie what he had done. She was furious with him. She had worked at the shelter for twenty years, and she said she was sometimes very surprised by the animals that were adopted. Dogs that she thought were

goners were often taken home by sympathetic people. She ac-
cused Rick of playing God in deciding which animals to bring
in to the shelter. He was quite deeply affected by their argument, but the week afterward they went out for dinner and had
a quieter, rational discussion about the matter. Rick decided he
would never purposely leave a stray out on the streets again.

When Rick found a small three-legged dog wandering the streets
one cold winter's day, he did think for a moment as to whether
there was any point in bringing the dog into the shelter. He was
convinced no one would adopt this animal. It had three scrawny
legs, and it walked slowly along. Rick was not sure what breed it
was, but its hair had grown long and messy, and it was covered
in dirt, grass, and bugs. He could literally see the fleas walking
across the animal's fur as the dog stopped and scratched. He had
no idea how the animal had survived. In the end, it was pure
sympathy that made Rick decide he would bring the little dog
into the shelter. He was convinced no one would adopt the dog,
but at least at the shelter it would be cleaned up, eat a few good
meals, and stay warm until the day would come when it would
be sent off to the pound. This was surely better than dying out
on the streets, in the winter cold.

    When Rick got out of his truck and walked up to the small
dog, it looked back at him through its messy hair with questioning sad eyes, but it did not run away. The two just stared at each
other for a moment. But when Rick moved forward to trap the
dog in his large net, the little dog barked at him with some force.
Rick sat down on his haunches and calmly tried to edge forward
toward the dog. But the dog simply barked loudly once again,

and then ran off down the road. Rick followed. Despite the dog's three legs it could still move very quickly, and Rick was quite out of breath when he finally cornered the animal in a cul-de-sac, up against a brick wall. The dog growled at him, staring him right in the face. Rick lunged forward with his net, and the little animal was trapped. He barked furiously at Rick. Rick managed to jab him with one of the small sedative syringes he carried with him, and in minutes Nelson was lying sleepy on the ground.

Rick carried him back to the truck and put him inside. Half awake, Nelson looked up at Rick with mournful eyes. Rick would never know Nelson's story. Nelson himself remembered little of his last year roaming through America, since he had left the wolves. But he had survived, and would have continued to survive out on the road had Rick not picked him up that day. He knew enough to find the food to keep him alive. He followed his nose, still curious when he was not cold or hungry.

When Nelson arrived at the shelter the sedative had worn off, and he panicked. He remembered the smell of the last shelter, and although he did not whiff the stench of death at the Chico shelter, he remembered it all too well.

33

Nelson's nose was his compass. It was not a scientific instrument, and it was not guaranteed to always be accurate. However, it was an instrument of deep mystery and ancient wisdom, and could sometimes produce extraordinary results.

It was his nose that led him to California. He had roamed for thousands of miles since he left the wolves. It was not a straight path, but a zigzag route through the roads and towns, mountains and forests of America. He was often cold and often hungry, but the small dog had a strong will to survive. For those without a nose like Nelson's, it was difficult to describe what had slowly but surely drawn him to California. It was something about the odors emitted by the dry California soils that signified sunshine and warmth. It was the scents of fruits on the wind that traveled for thousands of miles. It was the distant smell of the sea and salt. Nelson did not know what this faint salty texture on the breezes was, but it was intriguing to him. Somewhere deep in his smell memory, he associated it with the smell of the sea in the Boston air that filled the pet store where Katey had first found him.

Nelson did not reflect on the fact that his nose had led him to yet another animal shelter. Had he had the wiring in his brain to connect these things, he might have lamented his nose and its failure to lead him to a better place. But he never doubted his nose.

Nonetheless, he panicked when he entered the animal shelter. In the route he had navigated since he left the wolves he had always avoided any odors that reminded him of the shelter back in Montana. The shelter in Chico was a warmer and lighter place than the one in Montana. It was bigger, too, and there were at least six full-time staff members. He smelled the friendliness on their skins. Yes, the stench of death was absent, but there was enough in the shelter to let Nelson know in exactly what type of place he was.

Rick carried Nelson into the shelter in a cage, as Angie had her hands full that day and could not clean him immediately. Nelson responded by howling uncontrollably with a high-pitched and intense noise that emanated from some strange place deep in his small body. His howling made everyone in the shelter crazy, except the dogs. For the most part the dogs listened, although some responded, as their ancient wolf instinct compelled them to do, and also howled. The mysterious chorus was heard beyond the shelter, too. People in the street stopped to listen.

Rick set the cage down and tried to calm the dog by patting him and stroking him. Nelson had forgotten what the touch of a human could be like. At first he resisted Rick and just continued howling, but after a few minutes Rick's big warm hands and the quiet tones of his voice calmed the dog, and Nelson lay down on the floor, submitting. Rick tried to leave, but Nelson started howling again, so Rick stayed until Angie was ready to clean him. He opened the door of the cage, and Nelson slowly crept out. He watched Rick closely.

Nelson had lived away from humans for a long time. Angie was experienced with dogs and approached him with a quiet confidence. A part of Nelson had become wild, though, and a part of him was scared by her. Nelson snapped at her, grazing her hand. She stepped away for a moment, just watching him, while she disinfected her hand. Then, with Rick watching, she lay down on the floor and slowly edged up to Nelson, talking quietly while she did so. She just lay there for about five minutes with Nelson watching her closely. Finally, she put out her hand for him to sniff her, which he did. Nelson quivered with emotion. In the moment he smelled Angie, fully inhaled her, he was reminded of his Great Love. It was a powerful scent, and somehow it broke down the doors his time in the wild had built in Nelson's heart.

Gently he licked her. Angie let him do this for a while. Within fifteen minutes she had picked up the dog, and he let her bathe him in warm water. He had not experienced this for so many years, and it was calming. After all that time in the wild, his bones felt cold all the time. The warmth of the water slowly seeped into him, and Angie quietly massaged him at the same time. She replaced the water three times as she cleaned him with various shampoos. Both she and Rick were astonished at the dirt that came from the dog. Finally, on the third bath, Angie felt the little dog was getting clean. She put him back in the cage after towel-drying him. His hair was long and matted and would need to be cut, but she would wait for him to be entirely dry before doing so.

Nelson lay there quietly. Rick had left, he noticed, but he felt comfortable with Angie nearby. He inhaled the fresh scent of his hair, and fell asleep. Angie woke him a little while later, and he briefly began to howl again. She calmed him down and placed him on her grooming table. Slowly, she shaved the vast swathes of matted thick hair off the dog. She gulped when she finally got down to his skin. She had seen many scrawny dogs in her life, but this one was truly skin and bones. She could also make out the contours of the wound where his leg had once been. Slowly she stroked him, wondering what his story was.

The three-legged dog looked up at her, and they stared into each other's eyes. Angie loved dogs, of course. But it was rare that she would shed a tear for any of the hundreds of animals that passed through her small grooming room. But there was something in this dog's look that touched her. When she had gently cut away the fur on the dog's face, his eyes looked at her with even more sad intensity. She saw Nelson's unique coloring clearly, for the first time. His eyes were sad, but still they carried with them that intense probing curiosity that Nelson had always conveyed to humans.

She did not cut much of the fur off Nelson's tail. It was not badly matted and was quite clean after three baths. She stroked his head, and he slowly wagged his beautiful big tail back at her. She kissed the little dog on his head. She knew Rick had fed him a bowl of kibble when he arrived, but Angie broke the rules of the shelter and hand-fed Nelson half of her own lunch, which she warmed in the microwave. Nelson gobbled down some pieces of chicken and macaroni and cheese.

He would eat well in his two and a half weeks at the shelter, and put on weight steadily. He ate dog food like the other dogs there, but Angie and some of the other workers at the shelter regularly sneaked him off for snacks on human food. After a few days, Angie was relieved to see that Nelson's ribs no longer poked through his skin.

Once he was cleaned, Nelson was put in the main holding area where dogs were placed for adoption. It was a much bigger room than the one at the pound in Montana. There must have been thirty dogs up for adoption at any given time. Nelson was placed in the cage for small dogs, along with three other strays of his own size. He was not much in the mood for playing, and lay quietly most of the time, occasionally growling at one of the other dogs if they tried to interact with him. He slept a lot. The noise of the other dogs in the large chamber, and the sound of humans passing through continually did not disturb him. His long travels in the wilderness had demanded he be constantly vigilant, and he was constantly searching for food. Now that meals were being provided to him twice daily, he could relax a little. His body had taken a beating in the previous years, and it needed rest to heal. He constantly drifted off into sleep.

His dreams were the richest of his life. His nose had constantly observed new smells since he had escaped from the pound in Montana, but in his desire to survive, Nelson had not really processed all of them in their entirety. As his brain sensed a space to rest and recuperate, it also began to organize the smells and scents in his subconscious, grouping them and drawing connections between them. So, Nelson's dreams were a mélange of smells in unique configurations. Nelson's brain was the result of millions of years of canine evolution, and there was some unique logic in the dreams it spewed forth into Nelson's mind while he was sleeping. They were geared to his survival, toward perfecting his nose, his compass.

There was no stench of death in this pleasant Californian animal shelter. At times, Nelson still felt vigilant because the other characteristics of the shelter in Montana were present—the many dogs placed in cages in one large room, and the human beings who trampled through day after day looking for animals to adopt. It was all too familiar to Nelson, and sometimes he felt a chilling fear. But he needed to rest, and he was just too tired to be scared of what was to come.

A few of the humans who went to the Chico animal shelter for a pet to take home with them noticed Nelson. Some noticed his beautiful coloring, and the powerful curiosity with which he looked at them. Some even thought he was a beautiful small dog. But whenever they noticed he had only three legs, they quickly dispensed with any thoughts of taking Nelson home with them. No one wanted a three-legged dog for a pet.

34

The animal shelter in Montana allowed one week for a dog to remain there before a determination was made they must be eliminated. At the shelter in Chico, an extra week was allowed before they were sent to the pound across town. Some years before, a Hollywood TV actor who had been born in Chico had made a generous donation to the shelter. The money had been well managed, and so the shelter had better resources than most. Two weeks was a good amount of time for many of the dogs that passed through the shelter to be connected with a suitable owner. The procedure was familiar to Nelson. A human or a group of humans would pass through the holding area looking at all the dogs. They would point at one, and one of the shelter workers would take the dog from its cage to a nearby yard, where the owners would play with it. Sometimes this would be repeated with other animals. When a human found an animal they liked, it would be removed from the cage on a leash and handed to the joyful new owner, who would lead it eagerly out to the front office for processing. Nelson would quietly watch as the dogs wagged their tail on their way out.

Nelson was a dog, and so hope was always in his heart. As the humans tramped through the shelter he looked at them with his bright eyes, and quietly wagged his fluffy tail. Sometimes he recognized a smile on their faces, but they would always pass him by. He did not know why. As the days wore on, and his body recuperated from his time as a stray, a quiet anxiety began to grip him.

Angie, like Rick, knew when she saw Nelson it would be extremely difficult to find a human willing to adopt the three-legged dog. She did not discuss this with Rick, as she feared it might open up their old argument about whether it was best to leave some dogs out in the wild. But as she lay in bed at night next to her sleeping husband, the little dog's face passed through her mind a hundred times. Like so many who worked at animal shelters, she was frequently faced with the choice of whether to adopt a particular dog that she knew would probably not find a home. She lived in an apartment, though, which did not allow pets. She quietly began to canvass her relatives in the area as to whether they might consider adopting a rather special pet.

Rick was in a similar situation. He could not adopt Nelson. He lived in an apartment, alone. Who would look after the dog during the day? He could not take the dog with him while he worked. Rick did not have family in the area, but he did ask a couple of friends about adopting Nelson.

Other workers at the pound also developed an affinity for the dog. But as the two-week deadline for Nelson's adoption drew closer, there were no takers. Angie knew this, and so did Rick.

Nelson himself did not know he was just a few days away from having his life taken away from him. Yet he felt a chill inside just the same. Seven long years out in the wild had tuned his senses, so that he knew when a threat was drawing closer. He did not remember his escape from the pound in Montana. All he remembered was the stench of death that permeated the place. At times, there may have been the chance of running quickly from the cage, but the facility was bigger, and there were more staff, and Nelson never saw an opening to escape the Chico shelter.

In Nelson's short and eventful life, there had been much hardship and many adventures, ones he remembered fondly and ones he remembered with pain. There were dogs in the shelter that lay quietly on the floor and had tired of living. They had been beaten one too many times, or been hungry one day too long. Being sent to the pound would be a certain relief for them. Not for Nelson. No matter how much the darkness he had encountered in his life weighed him down, he still felt incurable joy when he smelled grass in the air. Good food still made his heart beat with excitement. Affectionate moments with humans remained a rich pleasure for the three-legged dog. And he remained curious about the world he had not explored. There were moments alone, when Nelson was resting with his eyes closed, when he could feel his breathing, the air inhaling and exhaling into his small body. He did not contemplate the miracle of life as a human might. He did not philosophize or think about God. But nonetheless that experience of breathing was powerful and visceral to the small animal, and it overwhelmed fear. At moments like these, Nelson was sure he would one day find his Great Love again. So, Nelson's desire to live would never ever falter.

*   *   *

On the day before Nelson was scheduled to be sent to the
pound, Angie checked the computer in the front office to make
sure it was the right day. She had accepted that the dog was
to die. She knew they could not hold him indefinitely at the
pound, as there were other dogs who also needed a chance at a
better life. But she wanted to make sure that he would have a
decent good-bye. She had spoken to Rick about this, and they
had agreed they would bathe Nelson in warm water before he
was sent to the pound, as they knew he loved this, and feed him
steak and eggs that Angie would cook the morning of his departure. Rick made the comparison between Nelson's final meal
and that of a man about to be executed. The difference was that
Nelson had committed no crime.

When Angie came and took Nelson out of his cage that
morning, he instantly sensed something was wrong. He knew
she was a gentle woman, but he noticed she was extra careful
and loving with him, stroking him continually on his little
head. In the grooming room, Rick watched Angie quietly as
she gently washed Nelson and blow-dried his hair. Nelson
loved the warmth; it was still a novel sensation to him after
hundreds of cold nights. But he could sense sadness in both
Rick and Angie, and he didn't know why.

After he was bathed, Rick held the little dog in his arms, and
Angie handed him the steak and eggs cut up into small pieces.
The food was very tasty, and Nelson enjoyed it. Rick stroked
him on the head. When he had eaten his meal, Rick and Angie
played quietly with Nelson. He licked their faces and wagged
his tail, and they quietly wrestled with a small stuffed animal

as still sleeping as Rick slowly carried him down
the front office to take care of paperwork. In the
man from the pound filled out the paperwork
move the three dogs. While he did so, Rick and
Nelson, who had woken up and was looking
e sniffing apprehensively. Rick and Angie tried
n.

he was ready to go. Rick quietly handed Nelson
from the pound, and he said he was ready to go.
kissed the little dog good-bye. Nelson was put in
still half asleep. The man from the pound was
ut he did not display any affection toward the
e had learned not to get emotionally attached to
d up from the animal shelters across town.

k kennels in the man's truck, and they were full.
in a kennel with another small spotted mutt,
quietly. Slowly they drove off to the pound. It
utes away.

y arrived, Nelson smelled the stench of death.
began to jump around his cage with all the
howling uncontrollably. The man from the
ehavior like this before. He would not comfort
ng them. He had sedatives in his glove com-
long syringe he jabbed Nelson, and the small
sed in a quiet heap, his eyes barely open. The
ur to Nelson.

as powerful, and although Nelson could still
und him, it had little effect. Nelson and the
oved into the small waiting office in the front
son waited quietly near the crematorium, as

Angie kept in the gr
Rick and Angie's eye

Angie needed to
taken the morning
little dog soon fell
as to why he was re
get it. As he drifte
teristically human
He had once run f
own ancient ances
before he was due
of happiness and
dog. He was inex
dog was to be for
In his small canii
Rick's arms forev

There were th
day. There was a
was a strong mu
age, who was jus
the shelter looki
AM, the man from
the bigger dogs
when it came ti
and at first nob
ter workers ren
grooming area.

The man fr
and knocked o
Quietly, Rick s

The little dog w
the corridor to
front office, the
necessary to ren
Angie stroked
around the offic
to keep him caln

The man said
over to the man
Rick and Angie l
the pound truck
not aggressive, b
dog. Long ago, h
the dogs he picke

There were six
Nelson was put
who whimpered
was only ten min

As soon as the
He panicked. He
strength he had,
pound had seen b
the dogs by patti
partment. Using a
dog quickly collap
world became a bl

The sedative w
smell death all arc
other dogs were m
of the pound. Nel

other dogs around him were removed and taken to their death. He heard the final bark of the sad pit bull and the spirited rustling of the German shepherd–Labrador mix as they were taken away from the world.

Nelson did not register when Rick Doyle entered the small waiting room of the pound, with another man and a young boy. There were some words between Rick and the workers at the pound. Paperwork was exchanged. Nelson hardly knew what was happening as Rick and the man and the boy came up to him and stroked his head.

The little boy picked Nelson up, rather clumsily, and carried him out to freedom. Nelson fell into a deep sleep.

Part Four

Home

35

It was Oliver who saved Nelson's life. His father had been against the idea of adopting the animal. But when the boy entered his father's bedroom at 2:00 AM, unable to sleep and in tears because he could not stop thinking about the three-legged dog, his father finally relented and promised they would visit the shelter the following day and adopt the dog.

Oliver's father, Jake, had been christened Jacob by his parents, immigrants from Mexico who were certain their American-born son should have a biblical name. Jacob was a more unusual choice for the time, but his mother wanted something special for him, that would set him apart. The nickname "Jake" was all he was called by the time he was ten. The love of his life was an American woman, of Irish and German descent, Laurie. They were sweethearts in high school. She had gone away for college, but was as beautiful as ever when she returned four years later. Jake proposed a few weeks after her return, and she accepted without hesitation. Laurie was pregnant within a year, and gave birth to a healthy baby boy soon afterward. He was christened Oliver, after Laurie's grandfather, who had died at Normandy. Laurie stopped working to look after the child, and Jake felt the burden of supporting his new family. His auto shop grew a firm customer base, as he developed a reputation for swift and reasonably priced repairs. His calm demeanor reassured his customers, and the female ones enjoyed his boyish good looks.

Jake was a practical man, but he was at first unable to come up with practical solutions when his wife died at the age of twenty-eight. This was not part of Jake's plan. He enjoyed routine, and had planned a long happy life with a big family. The first signs of change happened when Laurie started complaining of being tired constantly. Jake attributed it to the exhaustion of being a young parent. Suddenly one day she collapsed in a heap on the floor. She called Jake, and he came home immediately and took her to the hospital. The doctors did endless tests, and eventually concluded she had a very rare immune system disease. It was a very strange thing to happen, a genetic aberration. She died a month later.

Jake was bereft. Their little boy, Oliver, was at first confused more than anything. Jake told the child his mom had gone away. Oliver asked when she was coming back. Jake told her that he was so sorry, but she would not ever be coming back. Then he thought about it and decided Oliver deserved the truth. He told him his mom was dead. He realized though that understanding death was something that did not come naturally to children. In fact, it didn't come naturally to adults either. Jake found himself lying awake many a night, in a long state of disbelief about his wife's passing. It was impossible to understand how such a vibrant and beautiful and caring presence in his life had simply disappeared. She literally didn't exist, as she had requested herself that she be cremated. He could not bring himself to delete her cell phone number from his phone. Months afterward, several times a day, he found himself picking up the phone to call her.

Oliver at times seemed to be coping. But he struggled to sleep at night, beset by nightmares. Two years after his mother's death, he would still enter Jake's room in the middle of the night, fearful, after he dreamed of hungry serpents and tigers. Jake's mother, Norma, helped look after him during the days, and Jake cut back his hours at the auto shop as much as possible to spend time with the boy. He did not really know how the boy was being affected inside. He worried about him, wondered if the loss of his mother would damage him somehow. So, he was concerned at the late-night tears the boy said were about the three-legged dog.

The day before was a Sunday, and they had visited some family for a barbecue. Jake and Oliver were eating burgers and chatting with their cousins when Jake noticed Oliver listening to a conversation at a neighboring table. A man was talking about his niece who worked at the animal shelter, and how she had been trying to persuade everyone in her family to adopt a small three-legged dog. The man described how the dog had just a few days before it was to be taken to the pound to be put to sleep. He said, in a joking tone, yes, that was a sad story, but who would want to adopt a three-legged dog? He was a good mimic, and he imitated the movements of the three-legged animal as he imagined them. The people at his table chuckled.

Suddenly Oliver started shouting and yelling at the man, calling him cruel and a nasty person. Jake calmed him down and apologized to the man for his behavior. When the tears had been wiped away, Oliver said he wanted to go and save the three-legged dog, and in order to defuse a conflict Jake said that would be fine, and found out from the man the name of the shelter where his niece worked. In fact, he was not certain they would actually adopt the dog, but he wanted to pacify his son at a public gathering. He had not seen his son as emotional like this before. Oliver had Jake's calm demeanor, and his obsession about the dog took Jake by surprise. Oliver continued to talk about the animal for the rest of the day and spent the night crying about it, and so his father promised him they would pick up the dog from the shelter the following morning.

When they arrived at the animal shelter on the morning Nelson was scheduled to be exterminated, they found out that the dog was no longer there, and Oliver was heartbroken. He cried in a powerful and visceral way, in a way he had never sobbed after his mother died. Oliver kept on yelling that the dog was dead, the dog was dead.

Jake sat down and held the boy in his arms as the staff from the animal shelter looked on. He was concerned with reassuring his son, and barely noticed the phone call one of the shelter staff was making, talking about the three-legged dog. It was with immense relief Jake found out that the dog was still alive, and they could pick it up at the pound.

Home

Scan here to experience the sweet sounds of "Home," or go to www.youtube.com/watch?v=ofgE2QRdyQY.

36

Nelson dreamed of the Great Love. He was a puppy again. Katey fed him, and bathed him, and played with him. He lay under her vast piano, feeling the music flow through her. Soon they would be going for a walk together. The deep, scented memories of his puppyhood flooded back and washed over him, reassuring him. These memories would always be the most powerful of all. Those moments with his first owner had determined who Nelson was at his core. His first owner would remain his Great Love forever. So it was with all dogs.

He awoke groggy, the effects of the sedative still in his system. He was in a warm room full of sunlight, lying on a comfortable bed of old pillows. As his eyes opened, and his nose reentered reality, he became aware of the child sitting nearby. The boy came over and picked him up and hugged him. Children emitted a purer version of adult human smells, and Nelson found it reassuring. The boy called out, and a few moments later another man entered the room, the one who had been with the boy when he had rescued Nelson at the pound. The boy handed the dog to the man, and he held him in his arms stroking Nelson's head.

Nelson did not recall anything that had happened the day before. But he felt entirely at peace in Jake's arms, safe and secure. Jake placed the dog down on the pillows. Nelson was still very drowsy, and he just lay there as the man disappeared from the room and returned with a small bowl of warm milk, with some tortillas cut in pieces and mixed in with it. Nelson stood up and ate quietly from the bowl of warm food. He was ravenous. The little boy stroked him as he ate.

Later that day, Oliver took Nelson outside into their small yard. Some of it was paved and some of it still had grass. It was a scrappy garden in visual terms, but scentwise it was rich. There were some small rose bushes in pots, and Nelson nosed around them happily. Oliver wanted to play with him, and Nelson obligingly went and fetched the ball that Oliver threw around the garden. This was so easy to do compared to the work of surviving the past few years.

Jake was impressed with how agile the dog was on his three feet. He was proud of his son's instincts to save the dog. By the end of the day, Jake could not bear to think of the fact that this little three-legged mutt would have been dead by now if they had not saved him from the pound. Nelson looked up at Jake with his curious bright eyes, and he wagged his big fluffy tail, and both Oliver and Jake knew the dog was a keeper. All of Oliver's panicky sadness had evaporated, and Jake felt grateful to Nelson for this.

Oliver and Jake tried to come up with a name for the dog, and eventually they settled on Jupiter, which was Oliver's favorite planet. Jake had a feeling that the name just didn't quite fit, but he went with it, as his son was enthusiastic about it. Nelson began answering to the name quite soon.

Nelson slept a lot during his first few weeks at Jake and Oliver's house. The recuperation that had begun at the animal shelter continued. He gained weight, and soon began developing a droopy stomach characteristic of more senior dogs. Jake tried feeding him dog food and kibble, but Nelson refused to eat it. One of the advantages of living out on the road all those years was the human food. It had been a terrible struggle to find it sometimes, but his taste buds were now firmly attuned to human leftovers. Dog food smelled and tasted like nothing, and something in Nelson had now decided he would not eat it under any circumstances. Jake was concerned about this at first, as he had some friends who would not give their dogs human scraps, saying it was very bad for their stomachs. But then he had other friends who argued that dog food was a human invention, less than one hundred years old, and that dogs had in fact evolved over millennia eating the scraps from human tables. Jake came to favor the latter argument, but it was not really by choice. Nelson simply would not eat dog food anymore.

Oliver and Jake would feed him scraps of meat and chicken, and rice and tortillas. Jake heard that carrots were good for a dog's eyes, and Nelson loved them. He would crunch on baby carrots endlessly, and pieces of apples, too. Jake reckoned they were bones of sorts. They would feed him leftovers from their own food, although nothing spicy. Jake would always thoroughly heat and boil any leftovers to destroy germs, and Nelson ate them happily. Oliver loved pizza, and he soon discovered that Nelson loved it, too. At first they would feed him leftover cold pizza the day after Jake and Oliver had one, but soon they would share it with him warm when they ordered a pizza on the weekend. Oliver would break a slice into little pieces for Nelson, who would gobble them down.

Oliver and his grandmother, Norma, walked the dog every afternoon, when Oliver returned from school. Norma was in her eighties and had undergone a hip replacement, so she walked slowly. Nelson didn't mind. He took his time to sniff out the neighborhood in great detail. It was somewhere between a working-class and a middle-class suburb, with small houses, a diverse population, and a community atmosphere. There was a wide variety of dogs living in the neighborhood, and Nelson came to know all of their smells. Some sniffed him eagerly as they met on the street. The granny, the boy, and the three-legged dog became a fixture in the neighborhood. Sometimes humans gawked at Nelson with his three legs, but they were impressed by the way he seemed quite unaware of his disability.

Norma developed quite a love for the dog she knew as Jupiter. She was a traditional woman, who had grown up in a small town in Mexico, moving to the United States at the age of seven. Most mornings she would sit quietly with the dog on a small swing in Jake's yard. He would sleep on her lap, occasionally barking at sounds outside or birds flying by. If he woke up and started sniffing around, she might go inside for a while, where she liked to do the dishes and listen to the radio. Norma loved listening to old songs, and she would hum along.

She did not live with Jake, but rather in a small apartment nearby, and on those days her age was getting to her she would not come to the house until it was time for Oliver to return from school. On such days, Nelson would be left alone, out in the garden, behind secure gates, or in the small laundry room at the back of their house on colder days. He had little sense of his own vulnerability, and quickly assumed the mantle of protector of the house while Oliver, Jake, and Norma were gone. He would bark at the mailman in the mornings, or at the other visitors who came to the house when there was no one there—Jehovah's Witnesses, salesmen, or friends. Jake chuckled when his neighbors told him what a great protector of the house the little dog was.

When Oliver or Jake came home, Nelson would jump around eagerly, his tail wagging, his tongue panting. His transition back into a house dog happened quickly. This was the way he had yearned to live again. His brain contained memories and records of thousands and thousands of smells that the average house dog had never enjoyed. They filled his dreams at night, and sometimes he would whiff them distantly on the neighborhood breezes. But he never yearned to return to the wild, to the stray dog's life.

At night, Nelson would sleep on Oliver's bed. Oliver now slept soundly every night, going to bed at around nine and waking up at six-thirty or so. At first, Granny Norma had not been happy with the dog sleeping in the bed, saying it was not clean for the boy to sleep with a dog. But as she grew lovingly attached to Nelson, she soon stopped complaining. Oliver would spend at least half an hour at night playing with Nelson on the bed, after they had let the dog out for a final

ablution. Sometimes Jake would sit on Oliver's bed and join
them. He found a large stuffed rat toy at the nearby Walmart
one Saturday, and this became part of Nelson's nightly routine. He would pounce on the rat and wrestle with it, and
Oliver would pretend to try and take it away. Then Nelson
would growl playfully. Oliver and Jake would laugh endlessly
at the little dog's playfulness, not knowing he had once had a
similar routine many years before. They also did not know he
had once seen wolves kill animals, and choosing to play with
toy ones was an expression of Nelson's loving nature over the
wolves' desire to kill. Jake would hug his boy goodnight, and
Oliver would close his eyes, holding Nelson close by. He found
it comforting to hear his dog snoring steadily when he woke
in the mornings. Oliver asked his dad several times what he
thought dogs dreamed, and Jake told him they dreamed in
smells, unlike humans.

Nelson had nightmares sometimes, but dreamed happy
dreams most of the time after settling in with Oliver and Jake.
But he still dreamed of Katey, the Great Love, continually, and
would often wake up in the middle of the night yearning for
her. He loved Oliver and Jake and Granny Norma, but he was
a dog, with an intensely loyal heart, and even after all these
years, he wanted to be with the Great Love again, to protect
her, to serve her, to make her happy, to love her. The desire
was as powerful as it ever was. He would dream sometimes
that she was in the house with him and Oliver and Jake, but
he could not find her as hard as he looked. He would dream
sometimes that Don was trying to hurt her, and he was the
wolf father protecting her from Don's blows. Sometimes he
dreamed that the stench of death from the pound in Montana

was engulfing her, and he could smell her adrenaline as she tried to escape her death. Nelson would bark loudly in the dream, but he couldn't make the stench of death go away. He would awaken, longing for her. He would sniff Oliver's room, hear the steady breathing of the boy, and smell his breath. He would lick his face with quiet affection. The room would be quiet and warm, and Nelson's anxiety would vanish, and he would drift back to sleep. But the dreams would keep on repeating themselves.

37

Jake encountered grief for the first time when he had lost his father some years before Nelson's arrival. Before that, death had been an abstract thing. When friends or acquaintances lost family members, he would offer his condolences. But it was only after losing his father that he felt like he truly understood the pain and grief others in his situation felt. It felt impossible to describe the sense of loss. One of his friends joked to him that when you lost a parent you became a member of a special club, one whose members had gone through a unique experience that others did not truly understand. Jake thought this was an accurate description. The grief itself was bodily, rather than mental. Yes, the emotions were powerful, but one's physical functions felt stripped and denuded. Uncontrollably, tears would begin to flow at strange times. It was a powerful and raw feeling, which felt primeval on some level.

His wife, Laurie, had stood beside him and comforted him during the time of his father's death. Before losing his father, he had often felt at a loss for the right words to say to someone who had lost a loved one. But when he lost his own father, he realized that a grieving person did not need words. What they needed was one's presence around them to let them know they were not alone in the world. They needed the soft touch of a hand or a gentle hug. Words were pretty useless at times of intense grief.

Loss was loss, and grief was grief, he kept on telling himself when he lost his wife, Laurie. Losing his father and losing Laurie were not quantitatively different experiences, he kept on telling himself. But somehow they felt like they were. With Laurie, added to his grief was the feeling that he had been cheated, cheated of years spent with her, cheated of the other children she would bear, cheated of an old age when he no longer needed to work and could spend all his hours with her and his family. This feeling of being cheated was profound, and mingled in a toxic brew with his grief. The emotions continued unabated for months before settling, and although his mother and family did their best to comfort him, their attempts continually reminded him that Laurie was not there to comfort him, like she had been when he lost his father.

The only thing that kept Jake from falling apart was his son. He was determined to be a strong father for his child every minute he was with him. Without Oliver, Jake might have let himself become totally adrift, but he kept everything firmly together because of the love he had for the child. With the arrival of Nelson, some of the pressure Jake had felt to help his child through the loss of his mother abated. Nelson's love was so abundant, and he could see Oliver was so happy and uplifted by the little three-legged dog.

Jake's mother urged him to start dating again a year or so

after Laurie's death. Jake understood on a rational level it would probably be the right thing to do. He was a handsome man, and there were no shortage of women willing to date him. He tried to go on dates once or twice. Once he even brought a woman home for the night. But he couldn't bring himself to make love to her, and she left. He felt guilty about doing this to the woman, who was pleasant enough. So, he decided not to date at all until he felt entirely ready. This would frustrate Norma, who would have been happy to have more grandchildren around her. But Jake told her that this was the way things were going to be.

Nelson had been with Oliver and Jake for about six months when the second anniversary of Laurie's death came around. It happened to be on a Sunday, and Jake and Oliver put on their best clothes and went to spend time at his father's grave. Laurie's ashes had been scattered by the river, but Jake felt like he needed a specific place to go and sit that day. He bought a huge bunch of colorful flowers and placed them down at the grave. He was sitting, and Nelson hopped into his lap to try and comfort him. Oliver cried a little, but Nelson licked his hands, and he was soon distracted. Nelson and Oliver played quietly while Jake sat at the grave for about an hour.

Nelson did not think much about the loss of his limb. Occasionally a certain smell in the breeze might remind him of a time when he walked with four legs. But now he walked with three, and it felt quite natural to him. Sometimes on cold nights, the wound from his amputation would itch a little, or throb with a dull pain. Jake and Oliver would notice him licking himself at the site of his lost leg, and would give him the pain medication that the vet had provided at their request. As a small dog, Nelson was born likely to have a much longer lifespan than bigger dogs, and have many years of health before he began to suffer from some of the ailments that afflicted bigger dogs at quite young ages. The biggest dogs of all, Great Danes, lived the short lifespan of wolves, six or seven years, even in a loving human home. Jake and Oliver did not know exactly how old Nelson was, although their vet had said he was a mature dog. They did not know when his tenth birthday passed without celebration. But Jake did notice a certain stiffening of his body that occurred around that time. His walking and running became a little more ponderous. Once a month or so he would fall down on the floor, which Jake never saw him do in their first six months with them.

Jake was scared he was seeing the first signs of old age beginning to appear in Nelson. One of the health problems encountered by three-legged dogs, said the vet, was that the arthritis and stiffening of joints that always appeared in older dogs might occur a little quicker, as a lot of extra pressure was placed on their remaining joints and legs. Sometimes at night, Jake would massage Nelson's little body with his hands, and he showed Oliver how to do it. The dog seemed to like it very much.

One morning, Jake was getting ready for work when Oliver yelled from downstairs in a panic. He had been feeding Nelson his breakfast when suddenly Nelson sat down and refused to get up. When both of them tried to push him up to walk, he snarled at them. He seemed to be in a great deal of pain. Oliver seemed upset, but Jake managed to get him off to the school bus, and promised him Nelson would be okay by the time he returned from school that day.

Nelson trusted Jake, and he allowed him to pick him up

carefully and wrap his body in a small blanket. Then Jake carried Nelson to his car and put him on the back seat. The little dog whimpered quietly in pain. Whenever he tried to move his legs, a sharp biting pain occurred in his body. The drive to the vet was short, and Jake carefully carried Nelson inside, stroking his little head.

Jake and Nelson both liked the vet, Dr. Richards. She was a young woman, in her mid-thirties, and emanated both knowledge and real affection for animals. She told Jake she was pretty certain Nelson was suffering from problems with calcification of his joints, but that she would like to do a full set of X-rays to confirm this. This would be covered by the pet health insurance Jake had purchased a few months before. If the problem was what the vet thought it would be, Nelson would be in much better condition after a cortisone injection.

Jake returned to work for a few hours. Nelson watched him go with mournful eyes, and Jake found himself thinking of his wife with more sadness than he had felt in some months. He was relieved to see the vet looking upbeat when she entered the examination room later that day on his return. Even better, Nelson walked with her on a leash, a little slowly perhaps, but he happily wagged his tail when he saw Jake.

The vet told Jake that the X-rays had confirmed that calcification was affecting Nelson's joints, but the cortisone injection should be very effective in removing the pain and allowing Nelson to walk without issue. Apart from his joint issue, Nelson seemed in very good health, the vet said. Nelson looked up at them, as if he knew they were talking about him, and he wagged his tail again. The vet recommended he be kept inside and watched carefully for the next few weeks.

Oliver was so happy Nelson was okay, even though he was a little slow when they played together that afternoon. Norma had also become very attached to the dog, so she was determined to watch him carefully in the weeks to come, as the vet had recommended.

Every morning when she arrived at Jake's house, she would massage the dog all over while they sat in the living room, listening to the radio. She thought it better to be inside in the warmth of the house so that Nelson's joints could improve. Nelson seemed to love this, and Norma hoped she was adding a few years to the dog's life. However, she was quite unprepared for the strange events that occurred just a week after Nelson's joints had frozen up.

38

||||||||||||||||||||||||||||||||||||||||||||||||||||||||||||||||||||||||||||||||||||||||||||||||||||||||||

Norma loved music. When she was a very young girl in Mexico, she had snuck out of the house against her parents' wishes and listened to the mariachis through the walls of the expensive club on the main street of her town. It felt like their music was taking her to a special place in another universe, a world of endless happiness. When her family had moved to America, she had swiftly become fascinated by the enormous selection of American pop music. In many ways it had defined her life. When she listened to her oldies radio station, she could often remember where she had been when she heard a particular song for the first time. She remembered the good times and the difficulties in her life, the many changes the country had lived through. She had noticed at a young age that most songs were about love. It was definitely the most common word to appear in songs, and she reflected often on how this was the thing that people most wanted to sing about.

So, it was not often that a song that was not explicitly about love came up on the radio. She had always liked the Beatles.

Their songs were happy and soulful at the same time, and their lyrics were often unusual and intelligent. So, she was happy to hear one of her favorite Beatles songs, "Here Comes the Sun," play on the radio one beautiful, sunny California morning.

However, Norma did not enjoy the song for long. It was the reaction of the three-legged dog that totally jolted her from her calm morning-radio-listening routine. Inexplicably, he jumped from her lap and started leaping slowly around on the floor in a jagged circle, as if the issue with his joints had never occurred. It was a strange dance. And then, he began to howl. The sound was loud and piercing and completely haunting. It sounded to Norma like the dog was in some extraordinary and intense pain. She called him, but he did not respond, just continued jumping around and howling ever louder. When she turned off the radio, he abruptly stopped. For a moment, he just stood there, as if he was coming out of a trance. Then slowly he walked forward and licked her feet.

That night, Norma told Jake of Nelson's unusual behavior. Although Jake was perturbed, Oliver merely commented that Nelson must have liked the song. After dinner, on a whim, Jake went up into the attic and searched through his old vinyl records collection, which he had built up religiously as a teenager. Many old Beatles records were there, including *Abbey Road*, the LP that featured "Here Comes the Sun." Jake still had his old record player, and had been planning to educate Oliver about analog sound for some years. This was as good a time as any. He carried the record player downstairs, along with the LP.

Nelson hovered around, interested as always in what the family was doing. Jake plugged in the record player and tested it. It was still working, despite seven or eight years up in the attic. He cleaned the LP carefully and placed it on the turntable. "Here Comes the Sun" was the opening track on side two. The familiar opening ukulele strains of the song began to play. Everyone watched Nelson carefully. For a moment, he just stared up at them, not sure what to make of the attention. But then Jake started tapping his feet to the song and clapping along. Oliver joined in. And once again, the memories of Katey singing the song to Nelson as a young dog were unleashed, the particular rhythm and pitch configurations colliding in his canine musical understanding. Just like he had that morning, Nelson felt the deep and overwhelming desire to be with Katey well up inside of him. There was no way to express that feeling but to howl. He needed to let her know where he was, so that perhaps she could find him. He needed to let her know that he had not forgotten her. He needed to proclaim his territory as the wolves had, so that Katey would know where she could find safety and warmth with Nelson.

Like Norma, Jake was immediately struck by the sad and plaintive quality of the dog's howling. He was also very concerned about the pressure Nelson might be putting on his joints with his strange dance. But Oliver thought Nelson's unique three-legged dance with a howling accompaniment was hilarious. He couldn't stop laughing at the dog hopping on the floor, and he danced with him, trying to imitate Nelson's howling. But quickly, Jake lifted the needle off the LP, and the music stopped. Oliver asked him why he had stopped the music, as Jake knelt down and stroked Nelson's little head as he calmed down and looked mournfully up at the family around him. Jake told Oliver the little dog was sad and they shouldn't make him dance any more.

Jake could not sleep that night. He lay awake, mystified by the dog's behavior. He knew dogs responded to music in some ways, but this was a remarkably intense reaction. He had often wondered about the dog's history, and what it had lived through. Had he been abused perhaps? Jake hoped not. The three-legged dog had healed his son, and he would defend him to the death.

The memories of the strange events of that day soon faded. Nelson seemed to recover from his joint stiffness, and life continued. Jake was only reminded of the song's effects on Nelson about three months later. At Norma's insistence, he held a Fourth of July barbecue. She kept on telling him he needed to begin socializing more, and the whole family was asking why he had not seen them. He eventually gave in and invited everybody round. It was actually good to see many of his family members he had not seen since Laurie's funeral. But he was made a little uncomfortable by the several women friends some of his family had brought along, whom were clearly intended dates for Jake. He had to rudely walk away as his irritating cousin Tony, a little drunk and always loud, started interviewing him with a video camera about what he thought of a certain young red-haired friend of his wife's he had brought along to the barbecue.

Jake was outside barbecuing meat when he heard the recording of "Here Comes the Sun" emanate from inside. Sure enough, Nelson's howling began minutes later. Jake quickly took all the meat off the grill, and rushed inside. By the time he reached the living room, five or six family members were stamping their feet and clapping their hands as Nelson hopped around doing his strange performance, howling in the midst of them. Jake realized

Oliver must have put the record on, thinking Nelson performing his dance would be an entertaining party trick to show the family. Somewhat inebriated, everyone was laughing at the dog. Jake was angry with Oliver for a moment, but he knew the boy meant no ill. Quietly, he turned off the LP, and the music stopped. Everyone groaned with disappointment. For a moment, Jake lost his cool and yelled at everyone to leave the dog alone. He knelt down and cradled Nelson in his arms. Aware he had done wrong, Oliver sat down tentatively next to him, watching his father and stroking the dog's head at the same time. Nelson was soon calm, but remained sad and listless for the rest of the day. That night as Jake kissed his son goodnight, the little dog looked up at him with intensely mournful eyes.

39

Seven months later Jake had a strange call from his cousin Tony. He did not speak to Tony very often, and generally the call had something to do with money Tony wanted to borrow for some new business venture. So Jake hesitated when he saw on his cell phone that Tony was calling. But he decided to pick up the call and get it over with. For a while, they exchanged pleasantries. After a few minutes, there was an uncomfortable silence and Jake expected Tony to make the usual request for a loan. Jake braced himself to say he would not be lending him money this time, as too many previous loans had not been repaid.

But it wasn't money Tony asked about. He told Jake he had been receiving endless emails from a woman who wanted to contact Jake, and would it be okay if he passed along her contact details. For a moment, Jake thought this was another scheme set up by Norma to marry him off again, and sharply told Tony he wasn't interested. But then Tony made it clear the woman he was talking about wasn't trying to contact him for romantic reasons. She wanted to contact him because she was claiming Jake's three-legged dog was hers.

Jake inhaled sharply. What on earth was Tony talking about? Tony babbled for a few minutes and only gave Jake the full picture when Jake told him quite bluntly to spill the beans. Tony admitted he had shot some video footage of the dog jumping around and howling to that Beatles song at the barbecue. Jake was furious to hear he had posted the video online. The first thing he asked was if Oliver was in the video, which he was. Jake erupted on his cousin, asking how he could post video of a child out there for everyone to see. Tony babbled on some more about how there were lots of funny animal videos online and he thought the dancing, howling three-legged dog would be a big hit. By then, Jake's thoughts were turning to the woman. Who was she? he asked. Tony said he knew little about her except she lived in Los Angeles. She was desperate to contact Jake and see the dog she claimed was hers.

Jake spent a few days mulling over what to do with the information that Tony had given him. He had no idea who this person claiming to be Nelson's previous owner would turn out to be, and whether she would want the dog returned. In the more than a year he had spent with Nelson he knew the little animal was a special creature. Who would not want such an animal back if they had the chance? He knew that if this happened, Oliver's heart would be broken. Late at night sometimes, Jake would check up on Oliver, and he would see the little boy fast asleep, with a peaceful expression on his face. Sometimes Nelson would be sleeping, but sometimes he would look up at Jake with his curious sweet eyes, as Jake looked in on Oliver. Sometimes Jake would imagine Nelson was speaking, reassuring Jake that Oliver was fine, and would always be fine while he was there.

Jake did not discuss the matter with his mother, as he knew what she would say. He knew she loved the dog, too, but she was a woman of firm principles, raised a strict Catholic. He knew she would tell him the right thing to do was to find out who the woman was, and whether the dog was truly hers. If she wanted the dog back, he should be returned.

Jake's integrity had always benefited him in his business dealings. After wrestling with his conscience for some days, he decided to call the woman. A man's voice was on the answering machine, and Jake left a message explaining the situation.

A woman called back about three minutes later. She was in a state of disbelief. She asked if Jake could describe the dog to her, which he did in detail. He began by describing Nelson's eyes and body and fur, and then told her that the little dog had three legs. He heard the woman wince on the other end of the line. She paused and said it sounded like the dog could be the one she had known, except for the missing leg. She had chanced to come across the video online. The picture was quite blurry and dark, and there was just a few seconds of the dog dancing and howling. But she had a strong feeling the dog had once been hers. Jake's heart dropped, because he knew what he was about to face with Oliver.

The woman asked a little about Jake's family, and how long they had had the dog. He was somewhat reassured to find she seemed sensitive to how difficult the situation was. She asked if she might come and visit them, and see the dog, and then perhaps they could decide what to do. She asked if they were available that weekend, perhaps on Sunday, which was five days away. Jake confirmed they were. It was about a four-hour drive from LA, so she would see them around noon, if that would be okay. Jake confirmed this was fine. She thanked him and hung up.

Nelson could smell the unease on Jake's skin in the days that followed. He showed him plenty of affection in response, in an attempt to calm troubled waters. Oliver, at least, seemed his normal self.

Although Nelson was aware that something was distressing Jake, he was totally unprepared for the events of that Sunday morning. The day before had been marked, Nelson had noticed, by lots of extra attention for him. Jake had bought barbecue for lunch for everyone, and had personally fed Nelson a small plate of the unspiced meat, cut up into little pieces. Jake had told Norma about the special visitor they had coming the following day, and she, too, had responded by giving Nelson an extra dose of affection.

Later in the day, Nelson watched as Jake called Oliver into his bedroom and closed the door behind him. Nelson lay on Norma's lap as he listened carefully. At first there was quiet talking, but soon Oliver was crying and shouting. He emerged from the room with tears in his eyes and ran to his own bedroom. Jake followed. Nelson leaped off Norma's lap and ran into Oliver's bedroom, where Jake was stroking his head as the boy sobbed in his pillows. Nelson climbed onto the bed and licked the boy's face, but Oliver just turned and faced the other way. The three of them just sat there for a half an hour or so.

Then Oliver roused himself quietly, and walked slowly into the living room with a sour face. Jake and Nelson followed him. They all watched a DVD that night. Nelson was confused by Oliver's distance from him that night. In bed that night, Oliver did not cuddle him goodnight as he normally did. Nelson awoke in the middle of the night to hear the boy quietly crying again.

Jake lay awake in his bed. He found himself praying that the woman was not truly the owner of the three-legged dog. He prayed she would arrive the following day, see the dog, and immediately let them know it was not hers. Surely, there must be a good chance it wasn't her dog. It was just a dark and blurry online video she had seen.

Precisely at noon the following day, the doorbell rang. Jake was reading a book on the couch. Norma was napping. Oliver was playing with his toys in his bedroom. Nelson lay there quietly, respecting the boy's decision not to interact with him.

Jake opened the door. He instantly liked the woman who stood on the doorstep. She was in her late thirties, and pretty, but it was her gentle manner that Jake liked. She was respectful from the beginning.

Nelson had heard the front door ring. He did not want to leave Oliver, but he also felt his duty to defend the house from outsiders. So, he hopped down from the bed and scampered out to the front door. Jake was speaking to a woman.

Nelson inhaled the air. The scent that entered his nose was overwhelming and powerful. For a few moments, his brain circuits were jammed. Then he leaped toward the woman. It

was she. It was Katey. It was the Great Love. Somehow, she
had returned.

The little three-legged dog went crazy with excitement. He
jumped all over Katey, erupting with uncontained joy at seeing
her again. He barked uncontrollably as her smell engulfed him
like a deep, sweet perfume. It enveloped his entire being and
his body shook with an intense ecstasy. The soft sound of her
voice as she spoke his name for the first time in nine long years,
washed away all remains of the dark stench of death from his
heart.

Katey lay down next to him, and the little dog flooded
her with kisses all over her face. She had aged a little, but she
smelled just the same. She hugged Nelson in her arms as he
wriggled, unable to control himself. She stroked the place
where he had lost his leg, and Nelson tasted the salt of her
tears for the first time in many years. He furiously licked them
away. For several long minutes, their reunion continued. Katey
scratched his head as she once had many years ago. He stared
deep into her eyes, her face inches from his as he had dreamed
about for years out in the cold. The little dog's curious eyes
watched the reflection of the sun sparkle in the eyes of his
Great Love, and a deep, warm peace filled his soul. Jake looked
on with a bittersweet smile.

Katey, like Nelson, was overwhelmed when she saw him for
the first time in all those years. She had struggled to imagine
Nelson with three legs. But when the little dog emerged from
Jake's house that day and jumped all over her, all she felt was the
love she had known for him all those years before, and such a relief he was safe. He had the same beautiful eyes, and soft fur, and
beautiful tail. His essential nature remained just the same. She

looked into his eyes and wondered where he had been all these years, what he had lived through. How on earth had he traveled all the way from Albany to California? Something terrible must have happened for him to have lost his leg, but he showed no signs of sadness on that Sunday, only uncontrolled delight that she had returned to him. As Nelson kissed her and jumped all over her with exuberant love, she too was lost in happiness.

The loss of Nelson had been very difficult for Katey. For months and months she had scoured the neighborhood for him. She had placed signs everywhere, for miles around. She had lain awake at night, unable to sleep, and furious at Don for leaving the gate open. As the months wore on, she became aware that her chances of finding the dog were lessening. The shelters all told her that if the dog was not found within twenty-four hours, there was a very slim chance that he would ever be found. More than anything, she felt so concerned about Nelson. What was he eating? Where was he sleeping? Was he cold? Was he even alive at all?

She became scared that the dog was lost forever. She spent months angry that she had never chipped him with an electronic chip identifying him, as had become commonplace. After years she would still wake up sometimes and miss Nelson's warm presence next to her stomach. The ugly toy rat she had bought him still lay on the bed with her at night. She would finish her piano practice and spontaneously begin to play "Here Comes the Sun" before she realized Nelson was not there to enjoy it. Soon, she stopped playing the song altogether.

But years later, Nelson on her mind, and the distant flicker of nestling in her father's arms as a child, she browsed around on-line video sites watching renditions of "Here Comes the Sun" by various artists. When she saw a little dog jumping around howl-ing to the song, she could instantly feel the sadness in the terrible sound he emitted. When she looked closer, and saw Nelson's face peering into the camera, she began to sweat profusely. Her body shook when she realized he had only three legs. She felt like her insides were being carved into pieces by a sharp knife. Again and again she watched the short, blurry clip of the dog hopping around in his strange dance, her mind conjuring up endless ter-rible scenarios about how his fourth leg had been lost. What had happened, she wondered. Had he gone through terrible pain? Could he even walk?

After trying to calm down a little, she began trying to con-tact the person who had posted the video. Only his email details were online, and he did not reply for weeks. But she kept on spamming him and eventually he emailed back saying it was not his dog, but he would try and contact the owner letting him know she was looking for him.

As Katey drove from Los Angeles to Chico that Sunday, the stark Californian desert stretched endlessly from horizon to ho-rizon. In centuries past, many a traveler had died crossing this desert, chasing some dream of gold that turned out to be a mere mirage. Katey listened to some Mozart for a while, but turned it off and drove on in silence, deep in thought. There was a long moment when she felt she was being desperately foolish, going off on this jaunt across California to find a long-lost dog. How could the animal in the video possibly be hers? He was three thousand miles away from where he had been lost. He had three legs. He was howling. Nelson had never howled when he had been Katey's pet. Was she just deceiving herself? It was just a blurry, dark online video. Nelson was long gone. She stopped at a rest stop and had a snack. In the bathroom she looked in the mirror and splashed cold water on her face, expecting reason to return. But she knew then she would not turn back to Los Angeles. She still loved Nelson with all of her heart. Even if there was just the slightest chance that the three-legged dog was Nelson, she needed to complete the journey to Chico.

And now, here she was on a front porch in a small California town with the dog that had roamed from her house thousands of miles away, many years before. Finally, she looked up and looked at Jake looking down at her. A little embarrassed, Katey got up off the ground and stood up. On the other side of the room, a little boy stared at her with a sullen face. But he quickly disappeared back into the house.

Nelson would not leave Katey's side, and continually erupted into more expressions of love. Happiness pulsed through every pore of his small body.

Jake prepared some coffee and cookies, and Katey thanked him so much for the hospitality. She shook hands with Norma, who instantly inquired about Katey's marital status. She told Norma that she was in a relationship, and Norma sighed. The three sat quietly sipping their drinks. Jake called Oliver, but he refused to come out from his bedroom. Nelson sat quietly at Katey's feet. Jake fed him a little leftover chicken, and was pleased to find out Katey approved of this.

Jake was interested to find out what Nelson's name was. He had never felt comfortable with Jupiter, and thought that Nelson fitted the dog and his personality much better. Jake told Katey about how they had rescued Nelson from the shelter just before he was about to be put down, and he could see her eyes were wet. She quietly asked about Oliver, and Jake was honest about his attachment to the dog. Jake asked her about Nelson's early life, and she told them how they had bought Nelson at a little pet shop, and what he was like as a puppy. Katey told them how a gate had been accidentally left open one day, and how Nelson had escaped. She told them how sad she had been to lose him.

Both Jake and Katey understood the complexity of the situation, and both hovered around the question of what was to become of Nelson. In his heart, Jake knew that this woman truly loved the animal. He knew he could not deny her the chance to reunite with her pet if that was what she wanted. In her heart, Katey knew that Nelson meant so much to both the little boy and Jake, and that they would be heartbroken to lose him. She knew the pain of losing a pet, and she did not want to inflict it on others. But at the same time, she was so happy to have found Nelson again after all these years. She could sense the power of the love that the little dog still felt for her, and she wondered what Nelson wanted. Would he prefer to come home with her? He would not leave her side, even for a moment. He followed her into the bathroom when she went. When Jake instinctually called Nelson to leave her be while she was in the bathroom, Nelson ignored him. He looked up at her constantly. She wished he could speak, but from his actions it seemed like he wanted to be with her.

In his doggy heart, at that moment, Nelson did want to be with Katey. She was his Great Love, and he had yearned for her all those years. He wanted to be with her forever. He loved Oliver, too, and he loved Jake, but the power of his Great Love for Katey that Sunday overwhelmed everything else.

Katey caught little Oliver peeking at her from the passage again. She asked if she could speak to him. Jake sighed and told her it was probably better if she didn't. It might confuse things. He told her that they would miss Nelson terribly, but he knew the right thing was for her to take Nelson with her. Nelson was her dog, and she was his rightful owner.

Katey was moved by the decency of the man. She knew how painful this decision was for him. She thanked him and promised that they would stay in touch. Jake smiled quietly at her. He asked if he could take Nelson to say good-bye to Oliver. Of course, she said. He picked up the dog and carried him to Oliver's room. Nelson stared back at Katey, scared they might be separated again.

In Oliver's room, Jake spoke quietly to Oliver, who was lying quietly on his bed pretending to sleep. Nelson sensed his sadness and cuddled up next to him, licking his face. Grudgingly, Oliver stroked Nelson's hair as Jake confirmed that he would be taken away today. Oliver hugged Nelson quietly, and the little dog licked his face, unaware that he would soon lose him.

As Katey drove back to LA that day, Nelson sat on the seat next to her, and didn't stop looking at her for the whole journey, imbibing her scent.

Oliver did not cry any more that day. His sadness hardened into a cold, hard feeling in his stomach that would not go away. That night, he wished his mom were there.

40

||||||||||||||||||||||||||||||||||||||||||||||||||||||||||||||||||||||||||||||||||||||||||||||||||||||||||||||||||||||||||||||||||

Katey pulled up at her house in the suburbs of Los Angeles. It was almost nightfall. The sunsets were often spectacular in Los Angeles. Nelson whiffed the pollution in the air that helped create some of the rich colors in the sky. As the car drew to a halt, he explored the neighborhood with his nose. The grass was quite dry, but there were plenty of pleasant trees and flowers in the vicinity. There were dogs everywhere. He smelled them and heard a few barking in the distance. Katey picked up Nelson and kissed him again. She put on his leash and walked him up the short driveway to her house. It was about the same size as the house where he had once lived in Albany. Nelson instantly noticed the richness of the garden, just like the one Katey had tended in her previous home. He was happy to find Katey had planted a large patch of tuberoses next to the front door. Night was just falling, and the fragrant flowers seeped their magic into the air. Nelson inhaled them in deep gulps, and Katey could see he remembered them. For a long moment, the two sniffed the tuberoses together again for the first time in nine years.

As the front door of the house opened, the smell of a man entered Nelson's nose. He barked instinctually. Somewhere in his smell memory bank, the whiff of Don colored his emotions. But it was not Don that walked out the front door. Katey kissed her boyfriend, Evan, in greeting. Nelson looked up at the man, and sniffed him. He was in his forties, slightly overweight, with a kind smile. Nelson could instantly sense Katey felt comfortable with him, and the dog let Evan pat him in greeting. He licked his fingers. Evan was quite gentle with him, and Nelson liked him.

Katey and Evan let the dog sniff around the house. It was a strange sensation for Nelson. He had never been to the place before, but Katey's scent was everywhere. Many of her things from before were in the new home—a couch, cushions, and, of course, her grand piano. Its scent had intensified and richened in the nine years Nelson had been gone. The woods had aged and intermingled, and the California warmth and dry air had brought out deep earthy smells in the piano's layers of woods.

Katey's playing had become richer and more nuanced over the years. After a hearty dinner of rice and ground beef that Katey made for him, Nelson lay underneath the piano for the first time in what seemed like an age and inhaled as she played. On so many nights he had dreamed of lying under her piano again, and the reality of the experience was just as invigorating as in his dreams. He relaxed into a deep calmness as she played some quiet nocturnes. But then she could not resist playing "Here Comes the Sun." Nelson no longer howled when he heard the song. He leaped into her lap, kissing her face again.

Afterward, for the first time in years, Katey carried Nelson upstairs and put him on the bed while she brushed her hair. Then she held him close to her chest, and the little dog closed his eyes, enveloped in Katey's beautiful scent. She scratched his head. He fell straight to sleep, and did not even notice when Evan joined them later.

In the days that followed, he enjoyed reliving many of the other old routines that had defined his life as a young dog. He enjoyed Katey feeding him and bathing him. He enjoyed her taking him for walks round their quiet suburb. He enjoyed time with her on the couch looking into her warm eyes as she played with him. Katey bought him a new toy rat, as the original had been lost in the move to Los Angeles, and he quickly lapsed into his old nighttime routine of playing with Katey. Evan was also kind to Nelson. He fed him bones and scraps, and sometimes took him for walks.

Nelson's happiness at being reunited with Katey was only tempered by the feelings he had for Jake and Oliver. After just a few days, Nelson found himself sniffing around Katey's house looking for them. When the doorbell rang, or there was the sound of someone walking up to the house, Nelson would bark, hoping it was Oliver arriving. At times, Katey would notice a quiet sadness descend on the dog, but she did not know it was Oliver he was thinking about.

Nelson could smell the happiness on Katey's skin during the first few weeks of his return. During his years wandering, his canine brain had never worried, as a human might, that Katey no longer loved him as she once had. But even had he contemplated such thoughts, they would have dissipated quickly on his return to her life. She loved him just as she once had, perhaps more. Truthfully, she had never really spent a day since he had roamed without thinking about him, even if just for a moment.

The loss of Nelson had all occurred in the midst of the breakup of her marriage. After disappearing for two days, Don confessed he had slept with his mistress again. Katey had promised herself that if Don cheated for a second time, their marriage would end, but this was easier said than done. Two months went by before Don left the house. The toxic mix of intense anger and strong residual love was too complicated for either of them to easily resolve. Don explained his infidelity as needing to feel strong and manly again, something he claimed Katey was not helping him do. He still loved her more than anything, he said. She so wanted to believe him as he sat before her with his earnest eyes, the man she'd fallen deeply in love with just a few years earlier. But Katey knew that the man she thought she'd married would have been strong no matter what, and that Don had let himself be cowed by circumstance, despite her love and support. When she finally asked Don to leave, the emptiness without him and Nelson there was excruciating at first.

So, the loss of Nelson and the loss of her marriage became inextricably intertwined. She had loved their house in Albany, but after a year or so, felt she couldn't live there anymore because of the bad memories of Don. At the same time, she felt so scared one day Nelson might wander home and she would not be there if she moved.

At the same time as her marriage had collapsed, Katey's career had boomed. Perhaps they were not separate events really. Often on a lonely night at home, Katey would practice her piano performances for want of anything better to do, and while her piano had always been an outlet for her emotions, it became doubly so during that time. Those who listened noticed, even if they didn't know the source of the passion in her playing. More often than not, her performances took her to California, where a lively cultural scene in San Francisco and Los Angeles welcomed her. When her agent suggested she move to the West Coast, she was firmly against the idea. In the back of her mind, she knew this was because she feared Nelson might suddenly arrive home. But after six months of indecision, and some persuasion by friends, she decided to make the move. She liked the sunshine there, as it lifted her spirits, and so, she summoned up all her energies and relocated.

When she finally made the move, she took well to Los Angeles. She was happier certainly, without the constant memories of a marriage gone wrong all around her. The light on a sunny day in Los Angeles was bright and white, unlike any she had known in the places she'd lived before. Sometimes, driving through the vast city, one could enter a state of semibliss just from the endless sunlight that permeated everything. A rainy day was a rare occasion in Los Angeles. So, everyone who lived there seemed inoculated from many of the actual stresses of life. The initial pain of losing Don and Nelson lifted.

Nelson inhaled Katey's scent perpetually when they first reunited. It was the same as before in many ways. But there was one texture in her complex fragrance that was new. He could not quite ascertain what it was. His nose twitched as this scent from deep within her body rounded out the complex body odors that made up Katey's unique smell. It was a scent he had never smelled on a man before, and certainly Evan did not have the same scent, although he was roughly the same age as Katey.

What Nelson knew from his remarkable nose was not something Katey herself smelled. But it was one and the same as the emotions and thoughts that trickled through her consciousness quite constantly. When she had married Don, she had always assumed that they would have children quite soon, sometime in her early thirties. It was not something she thought too much about at the time as she enjoyed her passionate feelings for her husband and her career grew. But she had thought the day would come when she would love to carry Don's children. His infidelities had ruined all of that. She had thought little of children after he left, but as her thirties slowly went by, and she settled into Los Angeles, she began to notice babies on the street in strollers more than she had before. She would listen to the giggling of children in the park when she went to her weekend outdoor aerobics class. She was aware how many of her friends' lives were changing one by one as a baby arrived. It suddenly became a very conscious feeling for Katey, of wanting a baby, and yet it seemed to come from somewhere deep within her.

She even entertained the idea of raising a child as a single mother, but she worried about who would look after the child when she was away performing. Her memories of a childhood partially without a father decided her against this idea. She dated several men after arriving in Los Angeles, but it took time before she finally met someone that she thought might be right. She had met Evan at the post office one morning. He was waiting behind her to mail a letter, and offered to lend her the change she needed to buy a book of stamps. They began to chat. He was funny and sweet, a screenwriter. Dinner followed. She became quite fond of him over a few months. Finally, they drank a bottle of Pinot one Memorial Day and slept together. Both of them had been celibate for some time, and experiencing the pleasure of two bodies together for the first time in years obscured the fact for both of them that they lacked real sexual chemistry. They liked each other, though, and neither of them wanted to be alone, so they remained lovers, and moved in together three months later.

Katey had been drawn to Don like a magnet when they first met, and their sex had been powerful and strong before things went wrong. As a young pup, Nelson had experienced the eruption of scents from both of them as they made love. As he lay in the bed at night with Katey and Evan, he noticed that the scents both of them emitted were very different. The dog did not ponder the meaning of the different scents, but merely observed them. Katey had felt anger toward Don for years after their breakup, and yet she still remembered the moments of passion they had shared together. After the initial quiet bliss of sharing her bed with Evan, she did think about how different it was from the intense sexual pleasure she had enjoyed with Don in the early days of her marriage. But she convinced herself it was good enough, and that her feelings were merely less because she was a little bit older right now.

They had lived together for eight months when Nelson arrived at their home. Thoughts of babies still filled Katey's mind, yet something held her back from wanting them with Evan. She had pondered this as she flew across the country to concert performances, or tended her garden. Theirs was a calm and loving relationship, and she knew he would be a kind and considerate parent. Why then was it not clearly obvious to her that she should bear his children? She just did not know the answer to this question. She would sit playing with Nelson in her garden and look at him, wishing in her heart that he could answer the question for her. Then she would chide herself—how could a dog provide an answer to a question that was such a matter of the human heart?

Nelson, in fact, did know just the answer to the question that lingered in Katey's heart.

41

Oliver remained sullen after Nelson's departure. Jake had expected the child would take the events that had happened quite badly, but he did not expect the child's emotions to be affected for so long. The boy retreated into himself, spending long periods in his bedroom, often crying. The happy child Jake knew seemed to disappear from their lives. Jake himself missed Nelson, but he was far more concerned for his son's feelings than his own. What made it more difficult was that Oliver spoke little about what he was feeling.

Jake tried everything to cheer his son up. He took him out to movies regularly, played ball with him in the garden, and purchased a video game system he knew Oliver had wanted for some time. He even offered to get another dog for Oliver, but the boy was deadset against the idea of a replacement for Nelson. Nothing seemed to work to make Oliver feel better. After much thought, Jake decided to call Katey, to ask if she wouldn't mind if they came to visit Nelson one weekend, maybe even a few times just so that Oliver could see that the dog was doing fine, and could possibly move on from his sadness.

Evan answered the phone when Jake called, and told Jake that Katey was away for a few days on a concert tour. Jake explained what he was calling about, and Evan said he was sure a visit would be fine, and he would ask Katey to call Jake on her return. She did call Jake back a couple of days later, and she seemed genuinely sad to hear of Oliver's feelings. She suggested they come by and visit that weekend.

When Jake told Oliver they would be going to see Nelson in Los Angeles, Oliver's mood instantly changed. Jake could literally see the excitement bursting forth from the boy, and he felt so relieved. Oliver had only been to Los Angeles once before, and on the four-hour drive to the city, his eyes were wide open looking at the surroundings. Jake reminded himself how everything seemed so much bigger when one was a kid. The two stopped for a hamburger, and Oliver insisted they take a small one for Nelson as well.

They spent about two hours at Katey's house. If Nelson had given Katey a huge welcome on their reunion in Chico, he reserved a similar welcome for Oliver and Jake. As the front door opened and Nelson saw them standing there, he leaped up and down with excitement, panting and barking. As Oliver sat down and hugged him, the little dog splashed kisses all over the boy's face. Jake's heart warmed as he saw the smile on his son's face. It took several minutes for the dog to calm down. He cavorted back and forth between Katey and Jake and Oliver, showing all of them the love he felt for them.

Katey laid out lemonade with chocolate chip cookies, which Oliver loved. They sat out in the garden. Evan came to say hi briefly, and he shook hands with Jake. He apologized and said he had a work deadline for the following day. He disappeared off to his study.

Oliver was lost in play with Nelson, as before. Katey and Jake watched Oliver. He thanked Katey for letting them come to visit. She thought for a moment, and then said they were welcome to come as often as they liked. She could see Nelson loved them both dearly, and she was happy for this to occur.

In the months that followed, Jake and Oliver did visit quite regularly. There was never more than three weeks without a meeting. Jake felt a little uncomfortable about imposing at first, but he could see Katey was sincere about letting them visit, and he truly appreciated the hospitality. It was really Oliver who made sure they visited as regularly as they did. He would remind his dad within a few days of a visit to set a date for another one, and Jake obliged. The drive from Chico to Los Angeles was quite long, but Jake didn't mind as he could see it was keeping his son happy.

Sometimes Evan and Katey would both sit with Jake and Oliver. Once, Katey was away on a concert tour when they came, and Jake sat quietly by himself as Oliver played with the dog and Evan worked upstairs. More often than not, though, Katey sat alone with Jake and Oliver and Nelson. As Oliver got used to her, he invited her to play with him and Nelson, and the four of them would toss a ball around the garden. Katey could see the joy on the boy's face, and it would stay with her at night when they had gone home. As she hugged Nelson close to her breast, she also felt for the little boy whose parent had been taken from him, and then his dog. She had experienced both things.

*   *   *

Jake was taken aback by the call he received from Katey just a few months later. Would Jake and Oliver mind looking after Nelson for a week while she was away? She sounded quite stressed, and Jake did not ask why Evan was unable to look after Nelson, as Jake knew he normally did when Katey was away. By chance, Jake had to go to Los Angeles to pick up a consignment of parts he needed for his shop, and so he offered to pick up the dog the next morning, before Katey flew to New York the following night. He noticed Katey was a little sad when he arrived at the house, and Evan was nowhere to be seen. Jake did not ask questions, though, and Katey was very thankful Nelson would be in good hands while she was away.

Katey reflected on the events of her past few days on the plane to New York. Evan had sat her down two nights before and delivered surprising news. He had been in contact with an ex-girlfriend from years before. She could see it was difficult for him to tell her the news, but he had decided he wanted to try again with her. He told her that the woman was the one he considered the love of his life, and he would be moving out in a few days. He felt terrible about hurting Katey, he said, but it felt like the best thing to do in the long term. Katey was very upset at first. But strangely, on the plane to New York, she felt relieved. She had enjoyed her time with Evan, but something had never been quite right about the relationship. She knew in her heart she wouldn't miss him. She did wish his timing had been a little better, and felt relieved Nelson would be well cared for while she was away.

Oliver was ecstatic to have Nelson back at their house for a full week. Each day revolved around the dog. Granny Norma had not seen the animal for months and was also delighted to have him back. Nelson ran around the house and yard, sniffing, happy to be back in his own territory. He lay cuddled up with

Oliver at night, just like before. Jake noticed how the dog sniffed the air hopefully each time someone arrived at the front door, and so he knew Nelson was missing Katey.

Katey came to pick him up a week later. Her tour had gone well, but she was happy to be home. She could see Oliver was sad to give the dog up again, but they made plans for a visit to Los Angeles two weeks later. She hugged the boy and reassured him he'd be seeing Nelson again soon. As they hugged, Katey held Nelson in her arms, and he licked both of their faces happily. Jake smiled to himself.

The visits to Los Angeles continued every two weeks or so, sometimes more often than that. As the months went by, Katey grew to look forward to their visits. It marked her weekends. She did not miss Evan much, but she was lonely sometimes, and Oliver's smiling face and Jake's warm presence were a pleasure to have in her home.

She had noticed Jake was a handsome man the very first time she met him. But she was involved with Evan and was an intensely loyal person. So, she did not allow herself to feel more for Jake at the time. As she found herself looking forward to their weekend visits, she also found herself looking forward to Jake's warm face close by, and his dark eyes. As the months passed, they talked about many things on Jake and Oliver's weekend visits. Jake opened up about the loss of his wife and how difficult it had been. She was impressed by how committed a single father he was. He was not an overly talkative man, but she could tell he was thoughtful and highly intelligent, and possessed of a great decency. Sometimes as they played in the garden with the dog, his hand would touch hers for a moment, and she would feel a thrill race up her arm.

One Saturday, they were so engrossed in conversation that time was completely forgotten, and the sun was setting when Jake realized they should head back to Chico. Katey offered for them to spend the night. She had a comfortable guest room that they would be welcome to use. Jake was taken aback, but Katey insisted. They got pizza and watched an old Coen Brothers movie on cable. The boy fell asleep on the couch while Jake and Katey chatted some.

Katey was just a little surprised when Jake leaned forward slowly and kissed her. They embraced, and Katey's heart leaped as Jake's warm body and lips enveloped her. It was a kiss to build a dream on.

Down at their feet, a little three-legged dog looked up and whiffed the air. Both Katey's and Jake's passion filled his nose. He knew what was about to come, and he knew it was time for him to let the humans go about their strange business of making love. As Nelson drifted off to sleep that night, he felt a deep happiness in his heart. He had no ego, but had he reflected on his accomplishments that night as a human might, he may have felt great pride at the immense magical powers of dogs.

The Immense Magical Powers of Dogs

Who but a dog can bring a family together?
Scan here to hear "The Immense Magical Powers of Dogs," or go
to www.youtube.com/watch?v=U5tSiruxQpM.

42

It was not unusual for the sun to shine brightly in California on Christmas Day. The little three-legged dog lay on Jake's warm back porch, enjoying the scents of the holiday, and the hustle and bustle of the family as they prepared for a celebration. Nelson whiffed the fresh pine aroma of the large tree he had been rather surprised to see Jake haul into the living room a few days before. At first Nelson was reminded of his time living with the wolves, but Oliver's excitement was contagious, and soon Nelson was intrigued with the many boxes the family placed under the tree, including one he knew was especially for him. He had noticed Katey look at him with a smile as she placed the box under the tree the day before. He knew that inside there was a large and meaty bone for him to enjoy. If he was younger he may have ripped apart the box immediately to reach its contents, but Nelson had learned the value of patience, and he was biding his time until Katey gave him the go-ahead to enjoy his gift. Besides, he was content to savor the golden aroma of the special Christmas cookies Granny Norma was baking in the kitchen, a delicious concoction of butter, sugar, roasted nuts, and fruit. There was Katey's apple cider brewing on the stove, and from throughout the neighborhood bold and meaty aromas drifted in on the breezes as families all around prepared their favorite holiday dishes. Nelson imbibed them all.

There was also the smell of the grass in the garden, the rich, deep, mysterious grass that Nelson had first smelled when he was just a little puppy. It still intrigued him like nothing else. In his years roaming, he had learned much about the world and about the many scents that were wrapped up in the soil that lay beneath that rich, beautiful grass. Yet his curious nature endured, and he could still smell grass for hours, intrigued, wondering what its deepest and most enduring layers of smell were truly about.

Curious as he was, Nelson now felt no great desire to roam. Katey and Jake were responsible owners and would never have left a gate open. But even had they, Nelson would not have been tempted to leave the house. The world outside continued to intrigue him, but the dog also felt a deep happiness at remaining just where he was, here with Katey, Jake, and Oliver, his family. It was just a few months after Katey and Jake's first kiss that Katey had moved in with Jake and Oliver. They had discussed which town should be their home base, and in the end had settled on Chico. Jake's business was there, and as much of Katey's work involved traveling, it did not really matter where she was based.

Now, there was such joy in Nelson's daily routines, in the breakfasts his family would share, the walks they would enjoy together, the long deep sleeps they would have at night, lying right next to one another. Once rejected by all the humans that encountered him, the three-legged dog was surrounded by all the love that he deserved. As he lay in the sunlight sniffing the perfumed air, he felt profoundly happy. He knew the world could be a harsh and uncaring place. He knew human beings could break your heart sometimes. But he also knew in the deepest recesses of his heart that he was born to live and love with human beings, and that overall the world was a most beautiful and wonderful place. From time to time he remembered the scents of those he had met on his journey. Thatcher and Lucy and the vet Dougal, and Juan and Suzi, and the wolves—a part of him wished they would return to his life. But Katey, Jake, and Oliver were there in his life, every day for the rest of his life, and he loved them dearly.

Nelson was an old dog at eleven years old. His time out in the wild had shaved some years from his life, and the pressure imposed on his joints by his missing leg had also taken some years away from him. But Nelson would continue to play and wag his tail and lick the face of his owners for many more years than either Katey or Jake ever expected.

Finally at the ripe old age of sixteen years, Nelson would not wake up one morning. Katey, Jake, and Oliver would spread his ashes among the rosebushes, and say a quiet prayer, and sob for the rest of the day. Oliver would take Nelson's death badly, but he would move on and grow into a strong young man.

They would remember Nelson when he was long gone, and they were old, looking back on their lives. Katey would squeeze

Jake's hand with a particular softness, and he would know just what was on her mind. Nelson was just a small dog, but he walked around their memories on his three legs for as they long as they lived.

But Nelson knew nothing of that on the Christmas morning he lay on the porch. The little dog inhaled the rich scent of newly baked cookies, and went to sleep in the warm sun.

Acknowledgments

I would like to especially thank my terrific editor, Sarah Durand, and my extraordinary agent, Henry Dunow.

Thanks also to Elena Evangelo, Maria Greenshields-Ziman, Bill Jacobson, Jori Krulder, Gillian Lazar, John Lazar, Tiiu Leek Jacobson, Christine Luethje, Larry Maddox, Sean McGinly, Susan Rosenberg, and Irene Turner.

This novel was largely inspired by three dogs—Chicky, Milan, and the real Nelson.

Thank you to the Lazar family, the Schwartz family, and the Ruiz family, and in particular, my mother, Claire, and my father, Stan, who loved dogs.

The Smell of Grass

ALAN LAZAR

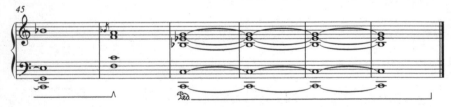

The Great Love

ALAN LAZAR

Gentle Waltz ♩ = 120

a tempo, poco rubato

Journeys with Thatcher

ALAN LAZAR

Nelson and Lucy

ALAN LAZAR

The Wolf Mother and the Three-legged Dog

ALAN LAZAR

Home

ALAN LAZAR

Gentle ♩ = 60

The Immense Magical Powers of Dogs

Reprise of "The Great Love"

ALAN LAZAR

Gentle Waltz ♩ = 120

Notes and Resources

||||||||||||||||||||||||||||||||||||||||||||||||||||||||||||||||||||||||||||||||||||||||||||||||||||||||||||||||||||||||||||||||||||||||||||

Every year approximately five million dogs and cats are killed in shelters in the United States, which is about 56 percent of the animals entering (The Humane Society). In six years, one unspayed female and her offspring can reproduce 67,000 dogs, many of which will die in shelters. To help change this very sad situation, please be sure to adopt a dog or cat from a shelter the next time you're looking for a pet. Also, please make sure that your animal is spayed/neutered. Speak to your vet about implanting a microchip in your dog or cat to make sure they return home safely if they get lost. You can also donate to some of the following organizations:

- The Millan Foundation—www.millanfoundation.org
- The Humane Society of the United States— www.humanesociety.org
- The American Society for the Prevention of Cruelty to Animals (ASPCA)—www.aspca.org